I0825799

A Science Fiction Novel

by John T. Cullen

YA Teenage Author Age 19

Summer Planets

Clocktower Books
Exciting Reading for Avid Readers—On the Web Since 1996
P. O. Box 600973
Grantville Station 92160
San Diego, California 92160-0973

E-Mail Contact: editorial@clocktowerbooks.com

Full history of this novela available upon request from Editorial at Clocktower Books.

Look for other exciting fiction and nonfiction at the website of Clocktower Books: www.clocktowerbooks.com/.

Contents

PROLOG 7

PART I: MERCURY 11

1. Summer Planet 12
2. Menkent Express 21
3. Dawn Plot 28
4. Memory 31
5. City 35
6. Exalted 37
7. Stella Grateful 42
8. Father Mercury 43
9. Lyxa 46
10. Death 56
11. Ankhfire 59
12. Year Of The Bread Ships (5000 CE) 61
13. Dreams Gone 62
14. On The Run 65
15. Olympia House 68
16. Starbath 70
17. Dust 72
18. Betrayal 74
19. Raskia 76
20. Underworld 77
21. Sun King 80
22. Surrender of Procyon 83
23. Underworld 84
24. Arena 92
25. Attack 94
26. Dawn 100
27. Winter 103

PART II: ARCTURUS 107

28. Sun 109
29. Battle Of Suns 111
30. Rainbow 112
31. Arco 114
32. Cantamucho 117
33. Mala 123
34. Star Mate 128
35. Samba 130
36. Apartment 132
37. Conspiracy Again 136
38. Sun Flare 140
39. Hurried 145
40. Flight 148

PART III: LETHE 149

41. Lethe 153
42. Rain Looking 159
43. Bel Air 163
44. Gypsy Jug 167
45. Pol 168
46. The Legend Of Valdo Rey 174
47. Vardis 176
48. Vengeance 178
49. She Came In A Blaze Of Stars 180
50. Star Bath 183
51. New Stars 185
52. Hunters 188
53. Ministering Stars 191
54. Three Angels 192
55. Star Mate 195

EPILOG: VELLALLO 197

About Clocktower Books 200
Clocktower Books Museum Site 200
Author's Special Note 201
BRY-2019 201

Prolog

VELLALLO

Myths of the Sleepy Ages

Enigma: countless tiny twinkles of light spattered the black canvas of space.

On a planet in a system in a galaxy in another universe, Larth Atuuinl lay beside his sleeping mate Ramtha, gazing up at eternity and infinity in a black sky filled with stars.

The two Vellallan bipeds, male and female, had finished their evening love rites. Larth, exhausted and still glowing from their passions, wondered if anyone was up there in those frozen whirlpools of light.

Here on Vellallo, under that endless night, stretched a flat plain of wind-rippled grass in a fragrant wind, on which Larth and Ramtha lay together—she, blissfully satisfied from love making and asleep with a smile on her sweet features; he, with one arm around her waist, and the other propping up his head as he gazed at the heavens.

Nearby, in a valley shaded by night and sleep, was his world's new space launch facility. Tomorrow, at dawn, he would become the first of his race to ride into the heavens atop a flaming rocket booster at exactly the velocity needed to put him into orbit, to make several rotations around the globe, and if all went well, to land back here in a parachute-assisted descent. If anything went wrong, he and his ship would become yet another short-lived, flaming golden meteor in the sky. He didn't want to think about it, if only because a sad vision rose in his imagination. He imagined Ramtha's tear-filled eyes and grieving face as she looked upward hoping for something else to happen—but that would be it, the end, his final signature scrawled across the stars. She and his people might build a monument with his name on it, and the age of exploration would continue, but in a melancholy alternate reality where he would never know it, and she would be alone.

Don't even think about it. Be positive. Everything will go well...

So he thought, shaking his fears and worries away. He looked at her as she slept. Ramtha, love of his life, continued smiling in her innocent sleep, dreaming of how they would be reunited when he returned from his great adventure as the first of their race to touch the stars.

But what is this?

Something was wrong, but what? A new feeling filled him, as if a ghost ship from far away among the stars were rushing across the world, enveloping him in a fantastic vision. It was the inside of a space vessel whose cockpit was peopled by alien beings. Their feelings of passion and joy filled him as if they were his own. He glimpsed the interior, with its myriad rippling indicator lights, and a gloved finger reaching for some control switch or other, while joy and wonder radiated out to capture Larth's senses in its glowing aura.

He rose, holding his head with both hands, and almost hollered at the overwhelming terror and beauty of this vision—not to mention melancholy, because the pilots of that vessel from far away were all dead…

Ghosts in a ghost ship, streaking through time and space…

From the author's original manuscript:

"Go to, let us build us a city and a tower, whose top may reach unto heaven: and let us make a name for ourselves lest we be scattered abroad upon the face of the whole earth."

—Genesis II:4

Part I: Mercury

Part I

MERCURY

Fall

1. Summer Planet

Jared Fallon, a young star fleet officer on vacation, found the beaches of Alda Meina III crowded as always, despite rumors of war. The millennium year, 5000 OC, was about to break.

You could stand in your surfing shorts and enjoy warm sunlight on a crowded beach, where little sugar curls of surf rolled up under palm trees and the sand curved out forever to the horizon and the sea.

You could lie on a mat and watch beautiful young people from a hundred nearby worlds strolling past, and if you made a girlfriend, you'd share drinks and conversation at a cabana, or rent a room for an hour of raging brief passion. You were on vacation, and could forget so much chaos and distress at home.

Jared had come to the so-called Summer Planet for ten days to get away—alone except for his beautiful assistant Stella—a Platonic relationship, because she was a construct, neural salvage, most commonly called *djia* (for diaphanous, or see-through). *Djia* felt solid, but were visible mostly as an electron cloud inside their clothes and veils, with vague facial features that were constantly re-sketching like pencil cartoons as you looked at them. Stella was a gift from the beautiful, selfish young Princess Lyxa, who had made Jared into one of her personal staff pets, derailing his career. His entire life, though he made the best of being a handsome young play toy with limitless credit, was one gigantic 2BD (2-B-Determined). He sometimes wondered if he wasn't part *djia* himself, and longed to escape.

An Olympian runner just a few years ago, he still had a trim, hard physique to show for it. Slightly above average height, he kept exercising the hard muscle cords in his arms and legs and on his abs. His short dark hair curled slightly at the edges over smoothly tanned skin with an underlying beard shadow like fine coffee dust that wouldn't go away, no matter how he tried with razors, lotions, and depils.

He had piercing dark blue eyes, a strong jaw, and a finely chiseled nose and lips. His features had always drawn the attention, desire, and envy of women. He'd learned to avoid all those attentions because they almost always led to unforeseeable consequences. At the same time, he picked the women who interested them and spent hours, days, weeks, until the realities set in and he was adrift again until the next fling. Whatever his next young woman's realities that caused her to move on, his reality bore the name Lyxa. He was a kept man, which was both good and bad. His mistress, who was just about his own age, twenty-something not much, was a young princess, the heir apparent to the extinct House of Mercury. When Lyxa had seen him run the Victory Arch with his torch in hand, she'd pointed to him and told her courtiers: "I want him."

Lyxa had burned herself out, as she always did with men and her other interests. Then she'd begun to lose interest, before Jared had time to register that the love of his life, the reward for his hard work and Victory run, was an ephemera. The princess was a public media queen, and privately the manipulator of fortunes and power. She let him down, set him down, but never let him go. So now at the beach on Alda Meina III, Jared sat looking stony behind his sunshades. As always, he was contemplating escape. Call it running away, yes. It was complicated. He'd lose a lot, and it might cost him his life, which was why he stuck with his current existence—always for the moment, he thought. It was always for the moment.

The capital city and world were a brief journey across the Aldeb System (Old Aldebaran). For the moment, he'd managed to escape his duties as a staff officer in the capital, and was making a temporary escape here to the vacation world.

The beaches were crowded, but he was staying in a first-class hotel on the government tab, and he wasn't complaining. Yet he felt a deep discontentment, because he had so much, but he wanted to little, and his dreams had been stolen from him by a selfish though beautiful and sexy princess back in Mercury City—Lyxa (Li Sha, Elizabeth).

"Pardon us," a man's voice said.

Jared lifted his sun shades and gave a dark-blue look. An elderly man, obviously wealthy and dignified, with short white hair and a too-festive summer shirt in red and yellow geometry, stood holding the handle of a beach chair with one hand, and the hand of his companion. The other must be his wife, Jared thought, because she seemed too matronly to be a mistress. The lady favored Jared with the sort of interested eyes and flick of the tongue wetting her lips that he was accustomed to. Ignoring her sort of appetizer stare, he rose to his feet and bowed slightly. "You can have my chair if you need it."

"That's very gallant of you," she said. She looked stately in a frilly lavender bathing dress that hid more than it revealed. Underneath, as the fashion dictated nowadays, would be a one-piece bathing suit of some modest shade, unlike her husband's loud attire.

"Thank you; we'll just grab these two," said the man. "Please, stay relaxed." He pulled a beach chair close for his wife, and held it while she swung into it. "I'm Franjek Hordibay and this is my wife Iada."

"Pleased to meet you. I'm Jared Fallon, lieutenant first class in the Mercury star fleet."

Ohh, they both said admiringly with raised eyebrows. She said: "You seem so young for such an advanced rank."

Little do you know, Jared thought. Savvy woman. *Hit it right on the head.*

"Very impressive," said Hordibay. "Academy?"

"Yessir." It was true. He'd come from a poor family on a farming planet, excelled in his studies, and had been accepted into the top military academy on his athletic strength.

Hordibay, a slender man with bluish veins beginning to show in thinning arms, ordered drinks for himself and Iada. The waiter, a pale man who looked more like a boy with his short blond hair and a slight harelip in a baby face, wore a white suit with gold braid and the hotel's livery (all first class). The waiter, holding a tray, bowed and hurried away through the throng of tanned or tanning bodies of all ages and configurations.

"You look familiar," Hordibay said, folding his hands over his sunken stomach in that bright shirt.

"I carried the torch a few years ago."

"No," Iada said with open mouth and shocked eyes. "How sublime."

"I do remember now. Jared Farland."

"Fallon."

"That's right. You were in the news with… er…"

"Princess Lyxa."

Hordibay brightened. "Ah, yes—Li Sha. You two were the envy of civilization."

Iada added with a scholarly smile: "Princess Elizabeth. We thought you were quite an item."

Jared smiled acidly. "Fame is short-lived."

"What have you been doing since? Protecting us all, Lieutenant?" He meant it kindly.

"After a fashion," Jared said.

Running the victory lap had been the crowning moment of his life. He'd carried the famous Olympic torch over the great arch in Mercury Free Port City, capital of the free worlds. At the time, he'd bathed in the cheers and adulation of a thousand worlds. The run had been a victory lap for Mercury FPC, which had taken more honors than any of her allies or opponents in the United Galaxy Organization or UGO. After running strenuous *klikz* in the actual competition, the run had been an easy ramble that had not cost him any breath. As he ran, he'd assumed he would qualify for an assignment of his choice, which was to be with a first order battle fleet on the frontiers. The academy had prepared him to eventually reach flag or star rank. He could have been an admiral or a general. All of that had been derailed by the selfishness and power of one spoiled young woman. Lyxa was beautiful, fabulously wealthy, highly educated, and poised. Her task in life was to be the star guest at important public events, accept flower bouquets from knicksering school children, give short scripted speeches (always the same; she'd memorized the text) praising local statues and fat mayors and wealthy donors; and reward herself with sex, opium, and dazzling young men (throw in a few dazzling young women as the occasion proffered). That would have been the concise reply to Franjek Hordibay's question.

"I am a civilian supply manager with the armed forces," Hordibay said blandly. Jared was sure Hordibay must be highly placed to merit luxury like this vacation world.

"We love watching the Olympic games and we're always so proud when Mercury takes the torch," said Iada still brimming about his achievement, while eyeballing his lean, muscular frame with obvious appetite, which her husband ignored.

The three of them together sat so their chairs pointed toward a common point, with crowds roiling around them. They sat by the pool on a concrete deck at the hotel, and the waiter arrived with a laden try. Soon, they were sipping the famous local Sea Tea.

"Oh this is good," said Iada, sipping gingerly but eagerly.

"Careful," Jared said, "two or three of those, and you could be carried back to your room for the night."

"What is this stuff? It's divine," Hordibay commented as he looked at his tall, frosty glass full of amber liquid with a decorative baby frond of a local micropalm standing up in it.

"Lucky for you I've been here for ten days and I've learned what needs to be learned. That is Sea Tea, as they call it here in the colonies. It contains equal amounts of a peppery, cinnamony spice, plus a dollop of raw brown sugar, and a potent but smooth white alcohol that's sort of like wood varnish with the edge removed. The spice makes it velvety, and two or three of these could be more than you want to tackle."

"Sort of sneaks up on you," Hordibay commented. "Love it. Iada, you can carry me to the room. I'm having another."

"So am I," Iada giggled. Her rouged features and quivering neck already looked a bit flushed and redder.

At that moment, Iada rolled her eyes with delight, as a diaphanon walked up. He was like Jared's own pet, only male. The diaphanon, so-called because he was partly invisible, was what someone important had once called the ultimate evolution of personal electronic and digital assistants. "Thank you, Edzar dear," Iada gushed, as the *djia* leaned over her in a slight bow and presented her with a big, perfect dark red rose.

"Come sit down," Hordibay said patting the edge of his deck chair. The *djia*, who moved like a shadow in water, complied as if he (or it; that was a great debate) were a pet. He was about the same height as his master and mistress, perfectly apportioned like an ideal young man. He moved in smooth, articulated motions whose angular moments were normalized by wetware algorithms. He was a creature of electrons, a memory of someone's nervous system, and clothed in the illusion of skin to make him not look like a complex spider web of underwater rillfeed. Some *djia* were like that—graceful, smooth, beautiful to look at for what you could see—while others were stocky and some could have passed for beasts of various types. The ideal *djia* for a wealthy couple, in any case, was a walking pen and ink sketch of perfection.

At that moment, Jared's own *djia* chose to return from her assignment which had been to gather some contact information for him from the hotel's register cloud in the lobby. He'd seen her fine shape, apparently dressed in the illusion of a white short gown, as she stood before a high desk in the rotunda lobby under glass ceilings and alien skies floating with wine-colored fire.

"Well," Hordibay said gruffly as Stella's jazzy shape drifted close. One saw the white curvature of a luxurious dress, the poetic motions of fine legs on high heels, the swinging motions of silvery wrist bracelets in the air, the phantom movements of her beautiful arms, her long neck and finely apportioned face, the suggestion of a hanging fall of glowing blonde hair. Her eye color, in that ink sketch face drifting in balmy evening air under palm trees, was a light blue, in contrast with Jared's dark blue. The engineers who conjured such expensive *djia* or PETs (Personal Electronic Taskmates) usually programmed key features to order. If a pet had to be sold or otherwise transferred, those same peripherals (eye and hair color, overall proportions, etc) could be retweaked without harming the *djia*. Stella's source was Lyxa; that much Jared knew and accepted. He was fond of Stella, as her source, the Princess of Mercury, had once been the great love of his life. No longer, a let-down of cosmic proportions, like everything else that had happened since Lyxa had used her power and wiles to take over Jared's life as if he himself were a diaphanon. He had learned to live with his bitterness, but now sought the right moment to make an escape, once he could figure out what that might be.

Jared held out his hand. "Come, Stella, meet our nice new friends."

He felt her soft, dry hand firmly in his as she stood shimmering over him. "I am so pleased to meet you," she said in a faintly accented, softly lilting voice that was almost as exotic as the Sea Tea, almost a *Samba* of old Earth. He and Stella had joked that they might stay here, run away from Lyxa, who had given him this pet as a gift. Stella was a diaphane, just like Edzar—diaphanous, like a fly's wing, meaning see-through. They were constructs from 3/di holos of their human source's nervous system, rather drifting seaweeds of genes and minimal construct organs including every detail from skin to eyes to fingernails, but still just moving projections of could be, would be, should be. They were demi-humans and, by law, had souls meaning, for practical purposes, they had human rights except that freedom had been bred out of them.

Pets did not reproduce and were not sexual creatures. They had no physical organs for sex, and no instinct for how to perform something so alien to them. They did have powerful emotions since they were grown from human stem cells and holocopied nerve tissues including everything from the cranium and spine to the remotest finger cells. Jared sometimes, lying in bed at night and watching Stella walk nakedly (still mostly invisible) about the room before settling to sleep, would imagine she drifted about like a creature of finest ocean kelp. The finest *djia* were essentially creatures built of nerve fibers, like humans stripped of muscles, skin, veins, arteries, and the like. Her nerve trail had the softest greenish underwater glow in that hotel room light residue. It was actually somewhat horrifying to some people, and impossible to get used to, but once you came to see your *djia* as a demi-person it was like having a combination cat, butler, and best friend. A good *djia* could be the closest, most loyal friend you'd ever have. You got used to a face that resembled a slightly glowing (at night) ink sketch or a pencil sketch by day. It was far more suggestion than minutiae but the human brain was wired to fill in those details on the fly.

"Hello, my dear," said Hordibay as Stella stood modestly before them, with her hands demurely clasped before the Y of her dress, covering the area where a full human's thighs and frontal bottom met.

"Oh Stella, you are beautiful," Iada gushed, overcome even more by her than by Jared.

Edzar rose, or floated upright in rapt attention. *Djia* were either going to be instant friends or enemies for life, depending on their programming. In this case, it looked as if Edzar and Stella would get along just fine. Stella went to sit beside Edzar at Hordibay's feet, where they held hands, looked at each other, and communicated emotively (a step down from telepathic, but heartwarming to see when it wasn't an instant cat fight with pixels floating in all directions).

"Where did you get her?"

"From the royal family," Jared said obliquely, thinking privately: *From my lover Lyxa, whose pet I am.* Unlike Stella, he was fully human, of natural gene stock, but he might as well be a *djia* these days.

"After that run on the Victory Arch, you deserved the best," Iada said admiringly.

If Hordibay knew anything, he wasn't saying. Jared's fate had become a news item for a while, but so much scandal surrounded everyone in the city that the daily gossip media had already long since moved on to a million other stories.

Iada changed the subject. "Are you at all afraid to travel these days, lieutenant?"

Hordibay injected a slight explosion at his wife's question. "We came here to relax, dear."

"I know, Franjek, but we're in the company of an expert."

Jared had to laugh. "If you rely on my expertise, you're in a losing game."

Hordibay held his drink before him as if steadying it would steady his nerves. "There is talk of war everywhere. The aliens are moving in on a thousand fronts, and all our government does is bicker."

Iada made a face. "The UGO is worse than useless."

"What do you think?" Hordibay asked sharply.

Jared reluctantly told them the truth. "I am actually assigned to our delegation as a military liaison, and I don't know any more than you do right now."

Iada raised her fingers to her lips in a gesture that she knew she'd made a *faux pas*.

Hordibay declared sensibly, with an air of resignation, "You have all sorts of secret info going on, and I know you couldn't say anything if you wanted to."

"It's all right," Iada said, sitting back with her drink. "Let's just relax and enjoy ourselves."

"That's right," Hordibay said, "in a few days we have to get back to our lives in Mercury FPC. We are a house divided, and a house divided always falls."

"A dreadful thought," Jared said.

Iada added, "The way it is now, with rioting in the streets, and the Raskians and others undermining everyone, I'm not looking forward to going home."

"People who can are already fleeing from the capital," Hordibay said. "Anything to get away from what is coming. Anarchy, destruction, invasion."

Iada waved her glass in a wide arc. "To look at people here sunbathing, drinking, partying, you'd never know it may be the end of the world as we've known it."

Jared had seen certain intelligence briefings. What he could not tell these people was that things were far worse than anything they could imagine. He raised his glass. "Let's drink to peace and enjoying every moment we can."

All three raised their glasses in a cheer. Stella and Edzar each raised one hand in a silent hallelujah. *They'd make a cute couple if djia could be couples*, Jared thought.

In his few years with Stella, Jared and she had become fond of each other as much as a full human and a demi-human could ever be. In some ways, he loved her as if she were a sister or a daughter. He suspected that she had feelings for him also, in the complex way that *djias*' emotional lives were like humans in some areas and unlike humans in others.

He'd been gifted her by Lyxa, who was at the time deeply infatuated with her Olympian prize. By now, Lyxa kept him at arms' length, calling him to her when she needed him. He suspected there was a connection between Lyxa and Stella. After all, Stella had been grown from some extracts of Lyxa's genetic tree, which made the two almost sisters. Jared still had some feelings for Lyxa, and he supposed in a Platonic way that rubbed off on his interaction with the neuroclone. It was like having your cake and eating it too. He was only grateful that Lyxa had never had him neurocloned, or there might be a ghostly copy of himself floating around the palace in the Free Port City like sea kelp glowing on the obsolete castle ramparts at night.

Could he trust Stella? He wasn't sure, and so he never told her of his on again, off again plans to run away. That would mean abandoning her, along with his name, family, career, and education. He'd become a cipher on the galactic spaceways, a thought that always made him change his mind. She was totally sexless, but sometimes if they were cold she would wrap herself in a blanket and spoon with him, so they'd keep each other warm for the night. If his hand strayed to the blanket, her curvature and hip felt much like that of a fully human woman.

Jared did go out, did date attractive young women, did sleep with them, but he always returned to his bachelor life with Stella. He'd once loved Lyxa, and he had not truly loved another woman since. That was the major missing part of his life right now. He was not ready to settle down, and so he felt he must wait it out.

This situation, being on call for Lyxa, while serving as a military attaché to UGO President Cyrus Mbe, could not go on forever. It was an artificial job, threatening to become a real job as the political situation worsened. And Jared had always seen himself as a line officer, leading men and women in space combat as a fleet commander. Being stuck with a bunch of aging or aged civilians and all their bickering and intrigue was just not his taste in theater.

The Hordibays stayed for another drink, along with their *djia* Edzar.

Jared gestured to Stella, who rose in compliance. He excused himself, saying they must get some rest because they were to travel home to Mercury FPC the next day. After cheery goodbyes and well wishes, Jared and Stella sauntered through park-like surroundings, holding hands at times in an absent sort of sibling sign of affection, until they reached their decorative, turreted building overlooking beaches and ocean. There they slept the night away, full of uneasy dreams and portents while the planet's two large moons were full and gyrated glacially in the night sky. In the morning, their journey home would begin. He wasn't looking forward to it. And once again, he had not run away. He wondered if Stella understood that. And if she might be reporting or beaming the information to Lyxa back in the city.

Many of the scantily clad beach goers were on the so-called Summer Planet for early celebrations of the upcoming new year and new millennium. These were the last days of 4999 OC. More than just a calendar would make its millennial turn. An entire civilization teetered on the balance, and with it the survival of the human empire that sprawled across the galaxy.

Millions of partiers, surfers, swimmers, drunks, and orgiasts wanted desperately to ignore the chaos beginning to gnaw at the fringes of the human domain, now starting to cut uncomfortably toward the heart of the empire itself in its nearby capital city Cosmopolis and planet, Mercury FPC, orbiting the Aldeb sun.

Here, a just a few orbits away from the capital world, Jared could briefly escape the crowding, intrigues, and struggles of the City of the Universe. The republic was, as historians liked to say, another empire in all but name. Jared lived and worked in the center of the whirlpool, and saw it all first hand. A pretense of democracy continued, but all power was now in truth (a dark but blatantly obvious reality) in the hands of ruthless oligarchs who looted, who pillaged, who sold to foreigners whatever they did not want to acquire for themselves, who cared nothing about the civic religion of the holy ancestors. If the oligarchs had souls, they would sell their souls for more profits. The Assemblies (Interior and Exterior) were entirely under corporate control. It was a yard sale, and anything could be bought or stolen. Nothing was sacred anymore. The pretense of normalcy continued from day to day (what else could ordinary citizens do?) but time was running out for the republic and for humankind. Not only was the republic or empire (take your pick) being torn apart from inside, but vast hordes of formerly oppressed alien races had formed confederations whose fleets already approached human dromespace.

Here, briefly on vacation, Jared could escape from the tendrils of Lyxa's spy organization that poked into every aspect of Mercurian politics including the city's enemies (which were many). Lyxa was a survivor, the last princess of an extinct Vegan royal house that should have vanished a thousand years ago when Mercury became a republic. As Jared saw it from the inside, those people never went away. You could declare a republic and pretend to have a democracy, but the tyrants simply went underground. It was an eternal defect of the human race.

Jared's ideal, his youthful dream while finishing the Star Academy and becoming the world's champion torch runner on the Victory Arch, had been to earn for himself—by his own blood sweat and tears—a posting to some remote outpost. He dreamed of a place where he could lead troops in battle and build a career of adventure and glory for himself. At the moment of his triumph, Lyxa had seen him running the Arch with that torch, to the cheers of billions on a thousand worlds, and she'd claimed him for her own. She'd used her connections, her wiles, and raw desire to get him in her bed and assigned to her personal body staff. Only in the past year had she begun to move on to other pets, but she was not one to let go. So she had thwarted his dreams again, and gotten him assigned to a diplomatic post with the Starmeer in Mercury City. He hated it. It was better than being stuck in her palace with the eunuchs and other unfortunates, but it wasn't the remote posting either. He was on the staff of Exterior President Cyrus Mbe, as a military attaché, working for Colonel Jesse Bowman, and working with more senior military officers who all had the line and frontier experience he had so desperately wanted. Worse yet, some thought he had evaded duty or curried favor, so they despised him, which hurt all the more.

So Jared was always looking for that way out of Lyxa's clutches, away from his own beloved capital city, and out to the frontiers. He had no idea how he would achieve that without sacrificing everything. But he kept looking for that middle way—a way out, far out, to freedom.

2. Menkent Express

Today was nearly New Year's Eve 5000, Old Calendar (OC). Tomorrow the Year 5000 was going to begin. Man ruled the Galaxy, and it was going to be mankind's finest thousand years.

Jared Fallon took one last deep breath of summer evening air of Alda Meina III. Then he stepped into the spacecraft that would bear him back to Mercury City. He looked crisp and handsome in his uniform. With him moved a slender, graceful ghost—a hologram in motion—elegant, dressed for travel, almost resembling a wife or at least a feminine counterpart to his life, but as far away from that in actuality as possible. A swarm of molecules bound by deep physics particles around a 3/di holo of Lyxa's nervous system, Stella faded in and out from moment to moment, and in parts at that.

Vacation was over. When they entered the little solo vessel, Jared was once more a lieutenant in the Mercurian Star Fleets, wearing his white summer uniform with gold braid on the gray bill of his white saucer cap. He carried his black winter cloak over one arm. An orderly brought in his suitcase, saluted, and left with an appraising glance at Stella. Only wealthy persons owned *djia*, so Stella's presence at a young officer's side left a lot of questions unasked.

Jared turned on a small bedside lamp and settled on the bunk, in the passenger cubicle, looking out a small square window. Stella had brought along her cosmetic kit, and proceeded to do her eyebrows (peach blonde) and her lips (apricot pink) while they waited to lift off.

The craft trembled, vomiting radioactive waste into a cistern deep in the ground, and began to float weightless out of the atmosphere. The journey would take a little over one day at Li!2 velo in the Temporale, the motherverse transit world underlying time and space.

Jared made himself a sailor's grog when the vessel was under power and well away from Alda Meina III. The drink was a Menkent Express, sweet and fruity, but potent.

Jared settled back on the leather bunk, not bothering to put a sheet over it, and thought about his terrible dilemma. In his personal life, he'd been robbed of his potential for advancement, and become a uniformed pet of the queen's palace. It was sweet but bitter duty, and he would give anything to escape her clutches, rejoin the line fleet, and finally make his destiny among the stars. In his world,

Mercury Free Port City tottered on the brink of collapse, under assault by subject races on all sides, including hostile aliens who hated humankind.

"You look sad again," Stella said. Her beautiful features shimmered, flickering almost like the softest of neons by night. He'd gotten used to having a demi-human as his, well, now his best friend if you got down to it.

"I can't help it. You know why."

"Yes," Stella said with a sigh, without looking up from painting her nails. "Poor Jarry. I wish I could help you."

He made a wry mouth. "You are a good friend, and you help me greatly. I'm sorry to be such a bore."

She kept working and said matter-of-factly, "Oh no, I understand and I don't blame you." After a pause, she added: "Jarry?"

"Mmm?"

"When you do get free. I mean, find the woman you will love. What will become of me?"

"I'll take you along."

She gave him a melancholy look, as the fine golden pencil lines of her facial mask, normally agitated, now worked overtime at a crazy redrawing pace. "You know that won't work. I'm an echo of an old love. You need to get away. Fresh air."

The Menkent drink was too sweet, and he made a face, adding a few drops of very sour red lemon. "Stella, you shouldn't worry. I'm attached to you by now, and anyway, you're not a love in that sense because there cannot ever be anything physical between us. Just out of curiosity, did you get a contact for Edzar?"

"Why do you ask?" The pencil redraws on her face quickened, giving the impression of a wink. "Are you jealous?"

"No, I do want you to have friends. I just saw you two gazing into each other's eyes and holding hands."

"That's just how *djia* communicate. It doesn't mean anything much. We are more like cats. We don't make friends, just keep our solitary territories and eyeball each other."

"You could have fooled me, holding hands and all."

"We were *djia*loging about the weather, the beaches, the swimming. We do go swimming, you know. I love being in the water, and I'm a good swimmer. He said he's afraid of the water, and can't swim." Her pencil lines fragged. "Not my type of guy."

"Not your kind of guy then," Jared agreed. Stella had a blonde fierceness about her, a dramatic pout, a serious and unnerving stare that she'd inherited from Lyxa.

"Just a friend," she said.

"Would you fall in love, ever?"

She shrugged. "How do I know? I like holding hands. I like it when you hold my hand."

"You are a woman," Jared said fondly.

"Yes, I am. A demi-woman, but female through and through. Just as you are a man, and I like that about you."

"We're a pretty decent match after all."

"Yes we are. I am here for you, whereas Lyxa seems to be letting you go."

"You think so? Will she ever just give me my freedom back?

Stella finished her nails and inspected each hand carefully. "I don't know, Jarry. I don't emo with her like I do with another *djia*."

"I think we emo sometimes, you and I."

"We do, Jarry, but you need a real woman, and I am content being alone. My social context is you, or whoever shelters me and, well, owns me. That is logical, comfortable, and works for me. You humans are much more flighty and volatile."

Jared sipped at his first full glass of winey Menkent; there would be another before he fell asleep. He was glad to leave Alda Meina III. That was the standard vacation planet of junior officers, who crowded its beaches, vomited in its dingy hotel rooms, and crowded its venereal disease clinics. He'd been spared that indignity; it was one of the perks of being attached to both the royal household and the UGO president's staff.

He'd grown daily uneasier because there were foul rumors circulating about Mercury City, about assassination plots and popular unrest. It was possible to set those fears aside on the vacation world, but now the realities of life came flooding back.

He had at first enjoyed Alda Meina, trying to overlook its vile accommodations as he went swimming at the beach, and then stopped in a cabana here or there for sausage and beers. Young, smart officers from all parts of the Galaxy circulated among each other, passing on vital rumors and reports that made for a comprehensive picture of the status of the empire.

Jared's cover assignment was at the capital—Mercury Free Port City herself—as attaché with the Mercurian delegation to the United Galaxy Organization. His real mission was (or had been) between the sheets with Her Majesty the Princess. He'd been her favorite, but that could end any time at her whim. He wondered if she'd take Stella from him once she released him to the common stable of line officers. If that was what Lyxa had in mind; or was she selfish enough to just keep him dangling forever at her whim?

Stella finished her grooming, wrapped herself in a blanket, and after giving him a brief pat on the forehead (her way of kissing, usually) she crawled into bed behind him, facing the wall, and fell asleep. Soon, he could hear her snoring—a sibilant, broken but regular little whine, almost like a tiny engine. Like all else about her, she did not have straight-forward human lungs but she did breathe almost like a person. Oxygen mattered for her. He reached behind him and touched her forehead. Half asleep, she responded by gently squeezing his hand briefly in both of hers. Then, as sleep took her, her hands dropped away and he was left to his thoughts.

Two thousand years of peace and prosperity were the fleet's mandate. That was the real meaning of his lieutenancy in the Mercurian Star Fleets. Tomorrow the Year 5000 of humankind's ancient calendar would begin.

"Happy New Year," Jared Fallon said to a bright star outside his window. A second Menkent Express gurgled down his throat. He forgot about Stella and brooded about his fate.

"I'm still an athlete," he murmured drunkenly, pulling the coat up to his neck. He flexed a muscle to convince himself that his body was still lean and strong. Comforted, he cursed Lyxa (Li Sha), who had done this to him. He'd done the full ten-year officer training at the Academy of the Stars, become Olympic long-distance running champion in his last year at the Academy, kept his eyes trained on a commission in some far edge of the galaxy, perhaps even in the conquest of the rest of the galaxy, and had the misfortune to catch the eye of Lady Lyxa, Princess of Vega and Mercury, last member of a royal family living in exile on Mercury since the founding of the Republic of Vega in 4901. She'd been betrothed to the Procyonian throne-heir, but secretly had courted Jared and other young, handsome men (and women). Among the presents Lyxa bestowed on him was a commission as Lieutenant, attaché to the office of the Military Advisor of Mercury's UGO Delegate. He'd been 22, just out of school, and he loved her.

For a while, she was intent on him and him alone, the great Olympian athlete. After a while, she began to have different lovers without telling him. He'd raged, and she had shrugged while listening to his tirade. That was when he learned she had also become addicted to opium and other drugs. He had begged her to let him go, help him obtain a transfer to the Periphery, where he could be part of the human sprawl's defenses against the growing alien threat. Humans had treated the aliens they conquered pretty badly. In fact, humans had a habit of treating each other very badly. Finally, as the human sphere was starting to seriously fray from many internal conflicts, the alien races had begun to band together and offer growing resistance that was turning in to assault. The situation became more and more grave by every Mercurian day.

The commission never came. She'd bought it away, and he had to sleep with her until she grew tired of him. Now, she summoned him only occasionally. He was free of her stifling bed, her tantrums, and her drugs, but not of her money, which was said to be among the most substantial fortunes in private hands in the galaxy. Jared sighed deeply, remembering how it had been, and how it was now.

There was no despairing just yet. Alda Meina had taught him something. Alda Meina had thrust him red-faced among bronzed, strong young officers from the deserts and jungles of the Galaxy, and in their unhappiness he had seen nothing to long for.

Those from the Periphery spoke of aliens in near-revolution, of massacres, of hopeless official corruption. Those of the Heartland spoke bitterly, of intrigue, assassinations, corruption, and of a growing menace from the ancient, rival Raskia system.

Jared thought maybe these territorial officers had a clearer picture of world politics. He had learned that he understood as much as any of them, and that was sad, because he knew very little about day-to-day politics of the City. These men spoke an alien language, the language of small-officerdom and it was not what he had imagined it to be: Instead, they spoke dourly. They spoke of finishing their terms and settling on Periphery worlds. They spoke of impending war: *Raskia. Raskia. Raskia...*

Raskia was on everyone's tongue, in everyone's mind, everyone's life. Raskia was the enemy, swelling empire of hostile Ankh Lords bent on destroying Mercury City and making a religious empire of the Galaxy. They were fanatical followers of the prophet Ankh-e-met'aten from a remote world.

What the Ankh message was, Jared wasn't sure. Maybe no sane person knew, but while humans were tearing each other apart in the UGO and on battlefields around the human domain of the galaxy, alien confederations were moving in with a lot of grudges and motivation for payback.

The distant Ankh Lords preached a New Order, of Love, of Peace. A lieutenant in the Mercurian Star Fleets must see them differently. The Ankh Lords promised a New Order, but brought destruction and disorder. Promising love, they brought blast guns and inquisition. Promising peace, they were shattering a human empire that had endured over two thousand years in relative peace. Jared didn't understand the Ankh Lords, in short.

The alarm buzzed. The ship would be docking at TS I shortly. Jared leaned close to the window, steaming it with his breath.

Tomorrow would be Year 5000, Old Calendar (Earth). Who ruled? The question bit dangerously. Humankind, itself a mere periphery of the Milky Way, had as yet barely penetrated the center of the Galaxy. There, it was said, and the only source of information were the mythologies of the opium-smoking story tellers of Donnas and Robalta, lived a race of dogs who were blind but saw, and saw only, the brilliant star bath of the center of the Galaxy. There, it was said, were no night or day, no planets and no suns. There was only prime star matter, called dust, made of heavy nova fog, wherein dwelt the Gods. They were flaming spirit bodies, and no man could approach within a quarter-galaxy of that place. No race dared enter there.

Years ago one ship had entered the hearth of the galaxy. A ship, made of sound metal and cool plasts, had travelled into the center. No one ever found out how far the ship went in. Coming out, it speeded back to Mercury City with the solar winds at its back. It whispered through the realm without stopping anywhere.

And, before it touched the Mercurian atmosphere and burst into blue flame, the tracking dishes of the man-planets picked up these garbled words from the mutilated mouth of the dying captain: "The heat, the heat...they're dangerous…stay away from here…I am a blistered sponge…oh, the heat!" No other ship ever ventured there.

Humankind ruled the outer shell of the Galaxy. For a thousand years, the core of the Galaxy was unknown. *Terra Incognita: Stellata Aliena Manent.* And the young bronzed officers said that man knew little of the alien races he ruled. They said that man ruled nothing. To hop planets once every hundred years, looting and burning, was not to rule. They said many powerful ships were originating from unknown places and destroying human ships on sight. The ships were not of matter, and could not be destroyed. The Galaxy was in unstoppable rebellion, and it was only a matter of time before Mercury Free Port City fell under the terror and fury. These young bronzed officers were going to finish their terms and settle far out, where alien ships would not come for a lifetime yet.

As he thought these things, sleep overcame him at last and the glass slipped from his hands.

Jared awoke from a groggy slumber at the insistent buzzing of a faint, obnoxious alarm.

He rose and walked to the see-port (not a window, but a true repro of a scene outside, broadcast through the ship's neural skin as if it were a window or porthole).

Outside, TransSpace Station I gloried the stars with gleaming spider-laced expanse.

In the little spacecraft, another buzzer rang. Jared studied the display screen, but it remained a black aquarium of stars.

A voice, damp with electrical sparking, swam in the cabin air.

"Lieutenant."

"Yes?" Jared replied, watching the stars.

"Sir, with your permission I'd like to hold idling at one-m from TS I. The Commissariat has beamed a message saying they want to send an agent aboard. Will you receive the man?"

Jared shrugged. "Why—yes, or course. Carry on."

"Very well, sir." The crackling faded.

Puzzled, Jared straightened out his uniform to prepare.

Stella stirred in her sleep, and he shushed her by leaning over her and brushing her hair lightly with his hand. When she slept, she looked the most human of all—pale, blonde, almost totally visible with the electronic holo cloud at rest. She slept peacefully on.

It was unusual for the commissariat to hold up a UGO ship and send a bureaucrat of some type aboard. Jared paced up and down.

In the transparent pilot bubble forward of the ship, a hand moved efficiently toward a button. A finger penetrated into the brown glow of the flight lights. The surface of the button retracted into the shimmering instrument panel, making a momentary dark spot.

In the passenger compartment, Jared turned off the bed lamp. He found a stack of rations in the refrigerator, and warmed himself a nutritious soup that stilled the pangs in his gut. A shot of caffeinated hot tea helped clear the cobwebs away as well.

"Docking now, sir," the pilot's voice crackled. The maneuver was so gently executed that Jared's vessel did not even shudder slightly. Jared's eyes rested on a small black corsair, sleek and bloody-red-nosed, which cut off his view of TS I. The corsair was a ship of the Port Authority Police. The black-and-red ship was a reminder of the fiery days before the UGO. The corsair was a police ship, and it stood for trouble.

Jared touched the window, and the cold was like an electric shock.

"Police Commander Thanar Valk is in the passage, sir," said the pilot.

Moments later, Thanar Valk shook Jared's hand. Jared invited him into a small room off the sleeping quarters, so as not to disturb Stella. "Will you have a drink, Commander Valk?"

Valk was short and fat. His brown eyes were bloodshot. His black uniform and black leather belt seemed to be strangling him, for his unshaven blackish jowls were puffed out purple. When he spoke the words dragged out between his lips. "No, thank you." He produced a handkerchief and wiped the back of his head. "I have a spate of bad news, I'm afraid."

Jared was still being civil. "I figured as much," he said, making them each a new Menkent Express. He felt woozy all of a sudden, more from anxiety than a hangover. He dropped the lemon-half twice before squeezing it over the glass.

"Lieutenant, I've just come from Mercury City, bringing you a message." He presented digitals. "I'm here representing my superior, Admiral Vodir Llewdollyn actually. We have a new president—your boss, Cyrus Mbe."

Jared started with shock. "A new president?"

"Just a few hours ago. The brass isn't saying, but there's a pretty heavy rumor—if you know what I mean—it's yesterday's news that Interior President Liew Chao is dead."

"Dead? How?" Cold acid seemed to rain inside Jared. What now? Of course this would affect him not only as a loyal citizen and star fleet officer, but personally in the mess of his private life. Could Lyxa ever be far removed from any intrigue? *Hardly...*

3. Dawn Plot

A dark-skinned, white-haired man stood silently in the dark just before dawn on the beach and was a part of Mercury city's growing weariness. Mercury City was in its autumn orbit. The days were still quite sunny, but there were strange winds, and the wooded hillsides grew quiet.

The watcher on the beach knew of the plot, but could do nothing further now. He had come to witness the death of a leader of nations, and the unraveling of an empire with dark consequences for an entire galaxy. He was an elder, stately man, with heavy eyelids, and a dignified demeanor, yet nothing could veil the look of distress in his features.

Mercury City was a man-made planet, half sea, half land, built on the ruins of a mining station of the Earth Empire. The land was really a single round island in the sea. At land's center, the Arch of Triumph rose ten miles high and forty miles long over the Old City. Outside the atmospheric bubble covering the Old City lay the full majesty of Mercury City, the City of the Universe, the city of a billion people, the city that ruled the Galaxy. Beyond its central dome, the city tapered all around into suburbs, then the open lands of wealthy plantation owners, finally the sparse settlements along the uninhabitable coast. All this man had made, a five-thousand-mile wide button that made the Galaxy stop and go.

The sea, too, he had made, a blank-faced tumult of waves dotted with some small islands and many rotting archipelagos and bays chewed up by the salty tides.

Summer was over. The man on the beach stood watching. The waves crashed on the sand, and a small bubble-topped underwater skill nudged against the beach, tied with a long rope that stretched to a rock near the man-silhouette.

Autumn, the brief, wistfully beautiful Mercurian autumn, was on. Out on the sea horizon, a long string of lights stood out against a gathering cloud mass. The eyes of the man on the beach were full of rain. For a long time he had stood here watching the lights of the little village fishing boats. A storm was rising out of the sea, close on the heels of the line-of-day-and-night, and the little vessels were rushing among the offshore islands, full sail against the growing winds. Sometimes the wind brought a cry or a splash across the water to the ears of the watcher. The sea worked all night, gurgling and tossing fitfully. The watcher closed his eyes and was miles away, where the fishermen groaned and cursed, periodically hefting aboard their nets heavy with frightened fish and unwillingly receding masses of seething water. Often the fishermen looked from the boiling water to the inky sky and fretted under the drifting clouds. It was a last journey out, to gather up drifting nets, to squeeze the last rich loads of fish out of the sea for winter, before the autumn storms began venting their fury.

Night swung easily around its mid-balance, but gathered a growing tension as it sped toward daybreak, gathering a faint moon and morning stars. Already thunder grumbled far away, muffled by a hundred miles of clouds and fog riding low on the waves.

The eyes of the watcher opened, and a faint light made a jarring discolor in the gathering clouds and tantalized through the translucent, low god, and the sea sang some vague song about eternity and the ocean breezes carried the song inland and shook it off to fall with the dew on green leaf-stubble or stone-faced cliffs washed by spray and foam.

When the sea was empty of nets, the little fishing boats heeled and blossomed out in full sail and strained against their high-water lines to reach shore, a fine spray of rain at their backs.

Day grew, a mixture of sunshine and rolling black clouds. A false twinkling roved over the murky waters of a swampy archipelago that reached out not far from the beach where the man stood waiting for the inevitable.

Small birds twittered in occasional tree clusters on the archipelago. A crane splashed his head in the water, raised his head, tossed it, and made a glittering jewel at the end of his beak disappear. Minor splashes among the slimy, half-submerged tree roots marked the flight of a school of fish.

The sun, struggling against powerful darkness, grew slowly and grudgingly brighter. Clouds grew taller and darker, while the angry colors where the sun was trying to get through were becoming more and more intense. This mixture of (faded beyond recognition) lightening and darkening, it was as though dusk had failed to drown in the summer sea, but instead ran knife-waving and blood-screaming through the halls and chambers of the night to stab and tear and cut and flay the dawn as the sun put its soft white limbs out naked. The man on the beach waited, putting his hands to his hand, and sagged to his knees in the sand.

In the false daylight, the crane on the archipelago fluffed and beat his wings, and slowly rose dripping in the air, and the sea murmured, a frog chirruped, and leaves rustled.

A faint dot of fire dropped out of the sun, arrowplaned out of the sun, dropped into the bright yellow panes and black cloud walls.

"Death of nations," the man on the beach whispered. "Leader of nations."

The faint dot of fire grew larger, still too far and too high to be heard from the beach, and the sea murmured still louder, a frog chirruped, and leaves rustled, occasionally slapping a branch in the disturbed wind.

The crane glided at treetop level, eyes half-closed against the rushing wind with its smells of sea water and marshy plants, and its many pinprick droplets of drifting rain-birth. Abruptly, sensing 'predator,' the crane stopped at a tree branch and watched the growing sky-thing. It was big. It spewed fire. Its brilliant silver hull, in the sunlight high above the storm clouds, was now visible, and the crane watched it move, slow and silent, first behind one leaf, then another, and through the vacuum where the wind bent a leaf away.

The man kneeling on the beach watched the aircraft intently. Eyes wet, his dark face plastered with sand, he fixed his eyes to the sky.

A hundred miles inland, where it was still night, a small six-armed mammal woke in the trees at the sudden sound of thunder. Shaking off dew, it skittered farther up the tree and hid in a cluster of leaves. There it chattered loudly, surrounded by wet leaves. The roar and the light in the sky increased. 'Swooping hawk,' the little mammal sensed as thunder deepened by an octave.

In the richly carpeted control room a quiet voice said probingly: "Flight 1. This is Mercury Tower. What is your trouble?"

The pilot, bracing himself against the instrument board as the floor tilted crazily, cried out helplessly: "I have a working fire. I have a working fire. This ship is out of control." He finished his sentence and as he drew a breath for the next, the sun rose out of the floor, vaporizing everything.

A death panic frenzied the mammal in its tree. The fire of fifty suns flashed in the moisture of its eyes and in the all-coating dew. The sun-thing rolled overhead loud and hot, trailing miles of fire, and exploded somewhere on the deserted plains further inland.

Leader of nations. The Interior President, Chao, was dead, and on the faraway beach, where little of man's affairs every broached any significance, the flying crane settled once more and stared inland for a long time.

Watcher and boat disappeared form the beach. Sand and water rose in a great empty whirlwind as the sun faded and a hundred-miles-high wheel of black clouds rolled in out of the sea and broke the trees and gouged out the eyes of the eternal cliffs. For now, an illusion of peace again spread amid all this beauty—a hammer, waiting to drop.

Waiting to change history forever, as of this moment. And the watcher was prepared to do his part to save the world, now that the point of no return had been reached.

4. Memory

"I don't know how it happened," said Thanar Valk. He dabbed the back of his head furiously, pudgy hands warding off imaginary monsters of sweat in the air around him. "We learned of the air crash just today."

The enormity of the event rocked Jared's mind. He looked at Valk and wasn't drunk anymore. "Are you sure?"

"Yes, yes, actually, quite sure. I got my orders straight from Center House, only an hour ago. I only met you with lucky timing."

"Good work," Jared said while mentally still holding the grimy, sweaty little police officer at arms' length. "I assumed you are bringing me my orders."

Valk nodded, gulping, and reached into his coat. "Here." He handed over a black plastic envelope sealed with Cyrus Mbe's private seal.

Holding the envelope in one hand, Jared quickly scanned the seal with a small pocket isocounter. The scan showed that the seal was intact and authentic. He noticed that Valk bristled almost unobtrusively.

Mbe—the new acting president! Jared tore the letter open. Mbe was Exterior President—the Delegate to the UGO. Chao had been actual president of the City or Nation.

"Why is there not an election scheduled for a new Interior President, Commander Valk?"

"I can only guess, Fallon. Mbe considers the national situation so critical and serious, given the threats from Raskia and the aliens, that he is assuming the total presidency. No more dual magistrates. He has seized power, and nobody can stop him."

Jared was shocked, but hesitated to question his boss. Was this a coup? What would a reasonable person call this? Suddenly, Mbe had become the most powerful man in the human-centric universe. Jared felt especially pained, because Cyrus Mbe was his superior, which made this a delicate situation. As an educated citizen, as a trained and loyal military officer, he instantly felt a pang at the loss of the checks and balances built into the republic millennia ago. Having one man in charge of everything could only lead to dreadful consequences. He hadn't expected this of Mbe, whom he barely knew. Jared was assigned directly on the staff of Commander Bowman. Bowman in turn was the primary military advisor and attaché on Mbe's staff at the Starmeer (the ancient parliament, now also the United Galaxy Organization external government of what everyone acknowledged was already a commercial and cosmopolitical empire in all but name).

Mbe's letter read: "Lieutenant Fallon: Dear Colleague: I regret to inform you of the death of Interior President Liew Chao of Mercury Free Port City. Mr. Chao, a leader of nations, died yesterday morning in a plane crash of unknown cause over the savannah near Rodinburgh, MFPC. This information is classified and not to be released to or discussed with anyone. The bearer of this message is Rear Admiral Vodir Llewdollyn of the Home Fleet, Port Authority Division. (Picture below). He can be trusted."

Jared glanced up. Valk quickly said: "I have been appointed Admiral Llewdollyn's adjutant. I know, it's crazy. I'm with the federal police, but right now everything is in flux."

Jared shook his head and kept reading Mbe's message silently: "Your orders are to immediately bypass Trans-Space Station I and proceed directly to the restricted Port Authority space base in the Olympia Sector of the Old City. Be advised that Mercury City is in crisis. Confidentially, let me tell you that there have been three attempts of my life in the past two days. I believe a Raskian assassination ring operating out of the city's foreign quarter has launched a strong offensive. They are the ones most likely responsible for President Chao's death, which I am preparing to announce as an assassination. We will bring you under the tightest security. From the landing base, please move directly to the UGO Assembly Hall. The General Assembly is due to start bogus hearings on 'Mercurian imperialism and murder' at midnight tonight, led by the Ankh and by the Raskians colluding together while we have an enormous alien threat on our borders. I will meet with my entire delegation staff after the Assembly adjourns.

"Of necessity, I will be taking some exigencies with the system to ensure its survival in the struggle against the Ankh and the Raskians, among others. Since I have the power to transfer members of my own staff to the interior staff, and though that has never been done before because there has never been a situation like this, I will announce some promotions and dual interior-exterior posts.

"Remember, please, that this is a trying time for us all. Our nation must survive. The threat is that grave. Not only are we faced with the enemy without, but we have lost our president. The death of a leader of nations is a death of nations. In the present danger to our nation, and in the personal danger to us all, we must draw close together and fight as one to overcome the assassins and religious fanatics.

"I am assigning you directly to my personal staff, effective immediately. You are relieved of your billet with the Mercurian Star Fleets, and you will answer only to me, directly, until further notice."

Jared read the letter twice more, then folded it and jammed it into his pocket. For Mercury FPC, the situation had gone from bad to dreadful, and much worse was yet to come. Jared was sure of it. Still, in the back of his mind he thought: *here is a way out of Lyxa's claws for me.* His earlier billet in the city was as a member of Lyxa's official state guard. It was a nebulous portion of the star fleet that her dynastic house effectively owned and operated. At least he'd be free of that now, but he could only think his situation was going from bad to awful. The

General Assembly was the same thing as the ancient Starmeer, now the external branch of Mercurian government, and Mbe was now President of both. Something about all this seemed suspicious to Jared, maybe because he'd already seen so much intrigue going on around him.

Valk said: "The President on occasion refers to himself by the new title of Leader, having consolidated his various positions." He added urgently, "My orders are to accompany you to Mercury City. There, I'm to transport you to our Safron Geneff Police Station in the Dome, then transfer you to the Assembly Hall under tight security." Valk looked around. "Is there another cot? I've been traveling and I'm a bit tired."

"I think there's a cot that comes out of the wall. There—under the light."

"Oh, yes, here it is." Valk tried to pry the panel out of the wall. "It seems to be stuck." His stubby body struggled against the unyielding panel. Jared got up to help him, and together they eased the creaking bed out of the wall. They stood back silently. The bed was covered with dust. The metal had rusted away into a red, crumbly frosting. Llewdollyn shrugged. "This ship—a wreck. It looks as though it's been in storage for a few decades."

Jared sat back down on his window bunk. "Class M hauler, isn't it?"

Valk smiled coldly. "No. It looks like one of the old Class A ships. 3090's. They still use them occasionally. We have had ten of them in storage at Safron Geneff since the early 4500's."

Jared wrapped his arms around his knees. "They must be about the oldest ships we have."

Valk sat down and mopped his neck again. "No. It's about a median age."

"You're joking. What about those new supercarriers we hear about—Clusterkings?"

Valk shook his head and said: "The average battleship is five hundred years old. That means a battleship used in Aldeb space. For the Galaxy, I think the figure is about a thousand years. One ship came from the other side of the Galaxy ten years ago, from one of the rim Fleets, thirteen centuries old."

Jared laughed hysterically. "But that means we should be a thousand years behind the Raskians—or the aliens, for that matter."

Valk nodded. "I know the Comptroller of the Home Fleet. He told me the figures one night when we were all drunk. It seems incredible, doesn't it? But when you consider that we have about a million ships in the field, and that each takes a billion credits to build, and that a battleship really doesn't age—nor is it built to age—I guess the empire keeps going."

Jared pursed his lips. "Would you call us an empire?"

Valk bundled himself up by the window in his black cloak, and smiled. "I used to worry about that word. Mercury City is a republic. But there's only one word for an empire, and that's empire. There's nothing really wrong with that. It's been a long peace."

Jared nodded, also sitting back. Stella slept peacefully in the other cabin.

The ship plodded on through space. Valk's hauler had disappeared from the window, as had TS I. Space hung cold and glorious in the glass.

Jared felt drowsy and withdrew to the cabin, where he slipped into bed beside his *djia*. He felt overwhelmed. He thought of home, of many years ago, when he'd had a father and a mother and had gone to the arena at the Olympia House to watch the ball games. His parents had been a poor, austere family of old republican stock, completely opposed to the gladiatorial fights of the prisons.

Jared put his face in his hands. What he felt was nothing. He felt nothing. His entire being was nothingness. Nothingness propelled him back to old dead, lost memories.

His family lived on a small street called Eye Street. Eye Street had glittered in the snow on cold winter nights. The snow had come from the coast and rubbed the meadow towns white. In the summers the streets were dark and warm. Small boys had run through the dusky meadows and pressed their noses against the fence at the space base near Oudangad and watched bright ships float weightless into space. Space: So vast and cold but warmly swirling with stars, so beautiful to fly in.

As an adolescent, Jared told people he was from Lesht, one of the new middle-class suburbs. That drew smiles. To say he was from Oudangad would draw howls of laughter. He'd had his eyes set on the military academies. His father had shaken his head. His father was dead now, gone with the summer nights. His mother was gone now, dead with the stars and moths of those summer nights. They were gone, face-down, deep in the meadows of memory and dreams, and so was the president. As Jared Fallon slept, he dreamed of good but wistful memories.

5. City

When Jared's Temporale transport landed amid the ruddy glow of myriad lights in Mercury Free Port City, a Port Authority sedan took them into the city: a black-uniformed policeman driving; Stella in the front seat; and Jared in the rear with Thanar Valk. A rain storm had moved in from the sea and lashed the city with wind and water. Only the central dome loomed dry and darkly gleaming as ever—the Old City, where government operated, where Jared worked and played, where Lyxa had her main palace.

In the wind-whipped suburbs of Mercury City, the storm had moved on but in some places flood waters still flowed. In some places, land vehicles lay overturned. Low-level windows were gone from some of the darkly glowering stone buildings dating back a thousand years or more. Crews were everywhere amid flashing orange and blue lights, fixing and salvaging.

Jared and Thanar Valk sat in the back of a ground car driving away from the space base. Stella sat ephemerally in the front seat, surrounded by a smoky-looking electronic privacy shield against the chauffeur's prying looks. To Jared, she seemed steady-state as usual, although she was often unreadable. Her sketchy flickering seemed steady-state, but you never knew.

Valk had been staring at Stella as well. Only the very wealthy could afford to keep *djia*, and a commoner like Thanar Valk, even in the police, rarely got close to a prime *djia* like Stella. Valk interrupted Jared's thoughts. "We've arranged for you to stay in a suite at the bachelor officers' barracks near the Old City," he explained.

This looked like a deserted city, Jared thought. Usually millions of people were in the streets, night or day, and even then the city still looked deserted. It looked dead and deserted because it was too big even for a billion souls scattered across this continent. Some buildings were as much as two thousand years old.

Nevertheless, people still lived here. Millions of people, who had never known anything else, and now it was quite likely their world was about to fall apart around them.

Rain beat against the car windows, and the car cautiously drove into the wind.

Jared thought again of escape. His thoughts drifted back to an assignment he'd had during his blissful years of innocence at the Academy. His class had been sent to a remote farming planet called Lethe, far from the bustle and concerns of the galaxy's capital. The air had been sweet, the forests deep and dark, the fields fresh and windy. It was a place Jared longed to return to, now more than ever. If things continued at this pace, there would be no future for him here. And if the fleets and armies collapsed, nobody would bother looking for one missing junior officer. At least, one must hope there would not be a total collapse. It was all in the hands of President Cyrus Mbe now, and Jared hoped that his boss had a better idea then he himself had, about how to save the human range.

Stella leaned back and told him: "I've had a message from Lyxa. She knows you are back, and wishes you would come to see her." The *djia* had their beginnings long ago in many technologies—in the many ways that people could communicate through electronic or digital gadgets. The human brain itself had not yet been harnessed as a transmitter, but the *djia* had become effective transponders and personal assistants.

"Any particular reason?" Jared asked darkly.

Stella shook her head. "I have no other information."

Jared studied her. Her facial sketchings redrew in mostly neutral lines. If there was any underlying subtext, she was veiling it well. Jared knew his little *djia* well enough by now. She was a loyal friend, but with a devious dimension that no doubt tied in with her baseline grounded in Lyxa. Whether she spied on him for Lyxa was a question he never cared to pursue. He was all right with assuming that Lyxa only took an occasional interest in him as her whims dictated. He liked the *djia* too much to begin resenting or even fearing her. He preferred to see her as a woman, a sister maybe, or even a friend; not a lover, therefore not a seducer, and therefore not a strong interface for Lyxa other than to convey random messages.

6. Exalted

Cyrus Mbe convened a crisis meeting of his dual cabinet (interior and exterior). He knew it would be contentious. He now had to manage not only his own enemies in the Starmeer, including the radical and fanatical Ankhmen as well as the increasingly bold representatives of alien races across the galaxy. Here, at Interior, he must now also face Chao's long-time opponents including Ankh sympathizers and local surrogates of the powerful Raskian enemy.

"Center House isn't safe anymore," Cyrus overheard two ministers whisper between each other at the great rectangular table deep in the underground rooms of Olympia House.

The official building of the Interior government was Center House, whereas Exterior was housed at a vast complex half-in, half-out of the Dome, called Olympia House. This included not only the ancient Starmeer (now UGO or General Assembly) hall, but a prison complex with attached arena and amphitheater from the waning days of gladiator fighting—which was going out of vogue and Chao had hoped to ban it entirely during his administration.

Cyrus Mbe, a heavyset, middle-aged man rose, surveying the group at the table before him. Those he most needed and trusted were here, including Sselmore Shin, Advisor on Interpresidential Relations; the staff chiefs of his own delegation; and the ministers of the interior government, whose president he now was. The ministers could be trusted—they had to be trusted—but he wasn't too sure of their feelings about him. In fact, a bitter rival of his was present—Rooster Fardin, who always raised objections and opposition to any issue at hand, in a most scathing and acid tone.

Cyrus cleared his throat to speak: "Thank you for coming at this late and urgent hour. This meeting is top secret. No one is to know of it, never mind what is said at it." He paused and looked closely at the expectant faces surrounding him. "Yes, the President is dead." Almost as though this were a statement to bring relief, suspenseful silence yielded to whispers and strange looks. "For the moment, I have assumed his powers in addition to mine, until further notice." As executive delegate to the UGO, he was in effect the Exterior President. Now he was also Interior President in an unprecedented consolidation of powers. Most top officials were too scared to worry about such details now. They wanted to trust him to save the country, their families, and themselves.

"We have reason to believe that his death was caused by human hand." This statement drew a few curious looks; but it was not unexpected enough to cause any excitement. Many enough must have suspected. They all knew of assassination rumors; some of them, too, had already narrowly missed death.

Mbe continued, "There is a connection." He dialed up a document marked *Exalted* on his podium looksee. "I must reveal some classified information to you. Unknown to the public and even most government officials, interior and exterior, Mercury City's ally Lacryma and our rival Raskia some days ago were involved in an armed misunderstanding. Tonight's emergency session of the Starmeer, where I represent Lacryma pro tem, had already been called when the incident occurred. In fact, we called the session, you will recall, because we were getting sick and tired of seeing them gobble up land. They're a bloody empire, and they get bigger every day, chewing up our, ah, trading domain." He looked at his folder. "Unfortunately, they are going to have a strong case against us tonight."

"Just how damn big or small was this 'misunderstanding'?" Fardin demanded.

"It was a major space battle. We cannot deny it." Mbe had been expecting the Rooster to launch one of his typical attacks, sniping, looking for any opening of any kind to please his lynch mob base and increase his power.

Fardin slammed his hand on the table as heads met in a violent babble of voices. Lifting his arms, Mbe with difficulty restored silence.

"Just what exactly happened?" Fardin demanded.

Mbe kept his iron self-control: "Let me read this letter to you. It was written by our ambassador to the Mudsheaves, at Mudsheaves I, and will be submitted to the Starmeer tonight. I read: Three days ago, a space battle took place between Ankhman and Lacryman fleet units in Ankhfire territory. The incident happened while the Lacryman fleet was on maneuvers in Mudsheaves territory, though no Mudsheaves ships were involved. The—"

Fardin interrupted: "Its this the same fleet that was on maneuvers there a month ago?"

Mbe nodded. "They have been in the Mudsheaves a month and a half."

"Then why was the Mudsheaves fleet not involved?"

Mbe pressed his palms together. "The Mudsheaves fleet was ordered back by its commanders as our fleet entered Ankhfire. Now before you interrupt again, let me hasten to explain why our fleet entered Ankhfire."

Fardin sat back, with his arms folded high over his chest, and his face raised superciliously.

Mbe tapped his foot on the floor, reading: "The engines aboard the flagship of the Lacryman fleet, the *Exalted*, blew up while she was attempting to convert to light-one drive in an evasion tactic, strictly training purposes. The ship, one of our biggest, drifted helplessly into space claimed by Ankhfire. Fifteen battleships and carriers, making up the rest of the fleet, followed their flagship for protection. This is a mandatory maneuver in such cases, known as 'three-sixty-cubed defense.' The other ships, of course..."

"Monstrous!" bellowed Fardin. "Pray tell these people what policy we agreed on three months ago after we 'defended ourselves' from Ankhfire at Leborne!"

Mbe held out his hands almost beseechingly, looking for support from Fardin's enemies. "The ship in that incident was crippled by a space mine and drifted against the force field of their space fortress at Leborne. After the stink they raised, we agreed that a ship under those circumstances must be abandoned and then self-destruct."

Fardin commented acidly: "We agreed with our enemy that we would abandon our ships and blow them up rather than face conflict. That is a government policy I opposed then and oppose now. So why was our ship not abandoned and blown up?"

Cyrus said: "You'll have to ask the commanding officer of the *Exalted*, and he is dead."

"And no remote control could be exercised?"

"Perhaps the destruct became inoperable."

The Rooster cocked his head with a dirty smile: "Oh? I distinctly remember that the destruct system is fail-safe, and becomes fully operable only when something major, like an engine failure, happens."

Mbe shook his head. "What are you getting at, Mr. Fardin? You are not to interrogate me."

Rooster, at one time a chief prosecutor in the Olympia House, smashed his fist on the table, so that the men on either side reached over to restrain him. "Was our admiral a coward?" It was strictly a distraction, a destructive tactic to break up any line of reasoning.

Mbe said loudly: "Let us stick with the issue at hand. We need to consolidate the nation's defenses internally and externally as the alien threat to our very existence becomes worse and more terrifying by the hour."

The conference got out of hand, and Rooster Fardin kept shouting but was overruled by others yelling at him or among each other.

Finally, after two minutes of gaveling with the ceremonial ivory cube set on the podium for that purpose, Cyrus was able to refocus the conversation. "We have lost President Chao, and I am temporarily leading both top magistracies. We have another ongoing crisis among our human brotherhood while our alien enemies gather at the borders. As a famous politician long ago said, if we do not hang together, we shall hang separately, or words to that effect." The room quieted, and he continued: "We all understand that the Ankhmen have their eye on the grain-rich Mudsheave worlds. Believe it or not, they are the first nation in two-thousand-years to be vaguely capable of capturing the Mudsheaves in combat. The *Exalted* Incident, by virtue of its proximity to Ankhfire and origin in the Mudsheaves, could give them an excuse to bring their crusade into the Mudsheaves. What we face is a desperate need to either turn the Galaxy against the Ankhmen, or lose control to external enemies. For any number of reasons—whether they perceive themselves to be winning or losing, it doesn't matter to fanatics—the Ankhmen may see the moment to start a new military crusade soon. If they control the Mudsheaves, we are lost. Mudsheaves once more proves to be the fulcrum of our world. So, tonight will be a very important night. Ankhfire and Lacryma are going to fight for control of the Starmeer."

A babbling of voices arose. Even Rooster Fardin, a slim knife-like figure with pale skin and gray hair, sat back with his arms folded bellicosely, and for once kept silent.

A neutral observer asked: "What happens if the Ankh crusaders begin a war and control the Mudsheaves?"

Mbe looked at the minister who had asked the question. "Then, sir, there is the regrettable likelihood that the Ankhmen will have their crusade anyway, one way or another. They would likely then broaden their operations to take over all human governance across the galaxy, including here in the capital they hate so much. They can be expected to try destroying the Starmeer assembly hall, and much of the rest of our legitimate government. And then, my friends, we would expect them to engage in a final nihilist, all-out battle with the alien confederation which, unfortunately, we are almost certain to lose. Then we become a captive population of enemy empires including reptilians, avians, sea creatures, and all manner of life forms we have treated badly since our rise to galactic empire two thousand years ago—and who want revenge, as we know from crypto intercepts at the frontier systems."

Jesse Bowman, Cyrus's advisor on military affairs, had just arrived, taken a seat, and now broke in: "For the moment it seems like a strategic issue question. Diplomacy is already being replaced by warfare as the next option. I believe the Ankhmen will start a war in one of three areas very soon: the Periphery, at the Mudsheaves, or attack us at Lacryma City herself."

Mbe waved Bowman down. "Thank you, Jesse. Let's table that for our Top Command strategy session tomorrow. Let's deal with one crisis at a time.

Rooster Fardin spoke up. "We're not done jawing about the loss of *Exalted* and several thousand crew and officers of the Mercurian Star Fleet. Make no mistake, Mr. President. You will not get off the hook on any of your failures or Chao's failures for that matter."

Rather than rebut him, Cyrus waited for the poison to finish flowing. Fardin's constituents were the village idiots who hated and feared their own government, taking social programs and farm assistance in every form while biting the hand that fed them. Fardin was truly like this as a human being but as a politician, he had no choice but play into the small-mindedness of his constituents and their usually sectarian leaders and demagogues.

Rooster Fardin continued: "The Admiral of the Million Suns is a friend of mine. I want to chat with him about starting an investigation into your handling of the fleets of the exterior." He added pointedly: "Who killed the president, Mr. Mbe? Do we know?" He gave Cyrus a long, hard stare before walking from the room.

Mbe felt a great urge to order the man shot. But that would have been disastrous. He must stay on top of what was happening inside himself. It seemed that somehow, a mere elected president was no longer what was needed here. A dictator, perhaps. But Cyrus Mbe would rather shoot himself than see that happen to Mercury FPC. Then again, what did Fardin and his people really know about the events surrounding Chao's assassination? Cyrus felt a moment of confusion, a vision of dark skies and sea storms, a chill in the pit of his stomach.

*Silence, silence, silence…*Cyrus saw only leaden silences, tensions, exchanges of stares around him. He realized clearly that he had no real friends here. At best, allies of opportunity.

He thought: *The only possible winners can be the aliens. It is just a matter of time, and very little time at that. We won't even know the bitter pride of vanquishment, because we have never yet experienced bloody and murderous defeat if not extermination. Our nation, our race, will simply cease to exist.*

7. Stella Grateful

Valk dropped Jared and Stella off at the Bachelor Officers' Barracks in Old City.

Hustling through the last drizzle, with Jared shielding her under his coat, they rushed up stone steps that had coach lights and a beautiful, curving antique stone gateway. They entered the lobby, a modest hall under huge chandeliers, where they checked in at the robotic desk and concierge. Stella was able to plug in with her palm print and accomplish all this instantly

A cubby machine rolled beside them, carrying what little luggage they had. Most of Jared's meager possessions were still stored in a locker at Lyxa's palace.

On Lyxa's private credit, Jared managed to obtain a Colonel's lodgings (three rooms, private bath). "You wait for me here," he told Lyxa

"That's fine with me." She opened his dripping coat, revealing a sketchy figure and dark red dress.

He took the coat and hung it on the back of a chair. He didn't care if it dripped water onto the rough carpet. "I'll be back as soon as I can. Keep the door locked and stay safe."

"I will." She stepped closer. Something was brooding in the phantom squiggles of her face, the emo sine waves that rippled like auroras across her features. She placed a solid, firm hand on his shoulder and stood face to face. Their eyes intersected, and he read stars deep inside her skull through the eye sockets. Not stars, maybe, but flickering electrons. And yet there was a girl in there. "Thank you."

He felt emo himself. He took her hand in both of his and pressed it to his mouth. "So glad you are with me."

"You care," she said. "It means everything to me."

He let go of her hand and stepped back. "Me too." She didn't kiss or drink or make love. What was there? *Companionship.*

"Be safe, Jared." Her voice had that lilting, *Samba*-like mix of exotic and innocent.

"I will be safe," he promised. "Hide under the bed if you have to."

She stared at him, stony if a *djia* could look stony (or baffled), and he said: "Bad joke. Gotta run now. Lock yourself in."

"I will."

8. Father Mercury

On his way to the General Assembly or Starmeer to report to Cyrus Mbe, Jared resolved to take a short time and see Lyxa. He did not call an official car, in order to steal that hour or so from his duties. Instead, he walked the several blocks through the drying air, into the Dome.

He thought less about Lyxa than about Stella. Stella's reaction was enigmatic to read, as always. Sometimes he thought maybe she was deeply in love with him. A *djia* should not be able to have such feelings, and he should not have strong feelings for a *djia*. He had a strangely guilty feeling that she trusted him so much, and he dreaded that anything should happen to her through his fault; or that anything should happen to her at all, because she had become part of his life.

Rain drops picked shiny spots on the pavement in the narrow streets, and neon lights changed rhythmically. The festive air—it was the New Year spirit. After all, this was the new millennium.

He heard the noise before he saw the lights, the people, the dancing, and of course Father Mercury on his throne, a white-bearded chubby sot in a red suit, with a pretty girl on each knee. As mythology would have it, he emerged every New Year's Day as an infant in diapers—a myth dating to the pre-space age—and grew old through the months until he was an elderly Bacchus by year's end, at New Year's Eve, which was tonight. At midnight, the revelers would flee, and Death would come for Father Mercury. In the deserted square, he would be replaced by a terrifying hooded figure swinging a scythe, with a sickly glow about him and a stench of death. Jared had seen it once or twice on holos—you did not want to literally be anywhere near Victory Square during that still and morbid hour. Then, sometimes during the night, one of the city hospitals (it was always a lottery) would announce the glad tidings that the first baby of the new year had been born, and with him the spirit of New Year's Day. The revels would resume by dawn, the baby would be displayed and whisked away to anonymity, and the actor playing Father Mercury was probably by now naked and unconscious in some bodega after partying all night. It was all in good fun, and nobody really got hurt—but you never knew. It was best to play it safe, and Jared was glad he'd avoid the midnight hour.

He'd had a few drinks. Must stop now. His stomach was slightly upset.

Maybe, too, he didn't really give a damn. On New Year's eve a man should be able to walk on the streets of his own city without feeling uneasy.

Softly colored reflections changed rhythmically on puddles, as neon lights changed rhythmically in dark nooks at crazy angles high up in the gloomy walls of the ancient city.

Parts of the city were protected by airy transparent domes. Like rippling scarves, discarded cloth and dove-like shreds floated laxly in the high-up cool breezes of the air-regulators.

Jared walked in the rain. Down the street he could see a two-hundred-foot-high portal, one of the entrances to the bubble of the Old City. The City reminded him of an old, dying animal. It lay slumped on its belly in the spell of a mortal dizziness, with night-black skin draped over its tall, projecting bones...a bedragglement of wet lights and shining pavements. *I am being digested*, he thought.

Rain thinned. Cool winds blew scattered droplets away. Wreathed in mountainous shrouds of clouds, the city remained—silent and enduring as it had for over two thousand years. Towers loomed, whose broad, flat walls glittered with tiny windows glowering out of torture-browed concrete. *City of the Universe...*

He walked through the portal. The bubble lay open to him without comment. His feet padded softly on the street, where no rain had fallen in centuries. Different winds blew against his face. Music came to greet him.

Everywhere was loud music. The little streets between the canyon walls of the buildings were filled with a wild music. People ran in groups, near-naked and uncaringly happy. Flowers were everywhere. Jared smiled. It was good to be small, to walk among ordinary people. The grim walls were silent and drawn in upon themselves forbiddingly, but the streets had become a world of laughing, noisy people, happy people, happy music.

Walking through the small, blind side streets he knew so well, he recalled what he had seen in earlier years in Victory Square under the central dome, and tonight was a living replay.

Countless persons shrieked and laughed while tinny music flowed from a forest of loudspeakers and drink flowed freely from acres of dark-stacked barrels. The air had a heavy smell of roasting meat and nuts, of bread and onions, and all sorts of good things. He smelled wine, and brandy, and beer, and even coffee or tea (but nothing as precious or exotic as the Sea Tea of Alda Meina III. How nice that had been; he must take Stella there again. He laughed as he caught himself thinking of his diaphane or *djia* almost like a girlfriend or a wife. Maybe it was because she was demi-human and lacked much of what was so imperfect in a woman.

A portly, chalk-powdered, red-cheeked Father Mercury sat on his throne in the center of the square, wearing a skimpy toga and holding a gold scepter whose head flickered with the electronic illusion of a flame, and he slapped his thighs and howled approvingly.

Giddy young women threw themselves at him to pull his beard, and he rubbed their fannies. The noise all around was deafening.

Anything goes. Happy New Year's Eve.

Four huge, inflated halcyon nymphs turned obliviously round and round in a blizzard of confetti and scent-bubbles. The nymphs were of glastic, twenty feet in height, and their eyes were demure, their lips sweet, their hair loose.

Smiling young men and women danced around Jared as he walked. He accepted more than one sip from a mug of fresh, spicy beer, until he could feel himself growing tipsy. He welcomed the relief, trying not to think of the ordeal ahead.

He had to now visit the woman he still, somewhere in his core, loved, who had ruined his life and turned him into her own sort of *djia*. He had even wondered if he might be a *djia* himself and not know it, but that was impossible. He had all the dreams, failings, and strong points of a fully human man. Not a farmed girl or man, not a holo guy or a *djia* boy. He was a farm boy from Lesht and Oudangad, a laughable hick from the sticks, who had accomplished incredible feats in acing out the Academy ahead of many city slickers. He'd become the galaxy's most celebrated athlete for one short day, celebrated with his run over the Arch of Victory. He'd become a hot commodity, and had been purchased in the city's exchanges of lies and excuses, the propaganda (as he saw it) of *how great we are versus the reality of how low we have sunk because we walk with our shoes in mud and our brains in clouds of self-delusion.*

Jared nodded as people left a path open for him wherever he went, because he was in uniform. He wore a common, ash-gray greatcoat over the uniform to hide it and be less of a target with all the crazies out tonight, but he still looked different. He was not a reveler but an important looking, dignified and handsome young man hurrying on a mission.

As he hastened along over the trash-strewn streets, the mercurial laughter of children closed unheedingly behind him. One street scene after another fell behind him. Each street corner seemed to have its own ongoing fiesta.

Victory Square still lay a few long city blocks ahead, along narrow streets loomed over by dark buildings and shuttered windows.

He came to the palace, which occupied a whole city block. Even the royal honor guard, who daily marched up and down in their Vegan and Mercurial livery, were gone for the night. They had locked up the watchmen's posts, taken in the flags and pennants, and locked the doors.

Jared stepped before a brass-bound wooden door. Amber coach lights out of a previous century flickered on either side, burning real *halom* oil from the fields of rural Vega.

He raised his palm and let a discreet scanner read it.

A mechanical voice said: "Welcome, Jared. You are expected."

With that, the door swung open, and he entered the palace.

9. Lyxa

He stood for a moment in the great entrance hall, whose cathedral ceiling soared several stories high amid stained glass and Gothic-style fluted pillars. It was a scene borrowed from the long-ago past, a snapshot of life in a lost world, a memory of the royal past in the Vega System. The floors were covered in flagstones. Broad stone staircases rose among the pillars on all sides.

He'd been here many times in the last few years since she'd changed his life forever. If anything was different, it was that he saw servants laboring at moving furniture and large trunks and wagons of costly dinnerware far away at the ends of long corridors. Was she moving? Something was afoot. But of course, all Mercury City was in an uproar.

A herald in gold braid over white silk, wearing a black tri-cornered hat with a cockade (green-white-black) in one corner, ushered him toward her quarters on the second étage in this maze and warren of corridors, rooms, doorways, balconies, crossings, transepts, nooks, and lantern posts.

Bemused, and wonderingly as always, he ascended great, hushed spiraling stone steps. Royal servants bowed around him, insular and unobtrusive, occupied with their individual duties and finely dressed according to their rank.

The eunuch Garth, Lord High Usher of the Royal House of Vega, wordlessly swept ahead of Jared. He was much taller than Jared, elderly but robust, and carried a sort of bishop's crook and walked with both speed and dignity. He indicated with a flick of a finger that he would lead Jared to Lyxa. As they turned corners, Jared marveled at Garth's craggy brow, and Garth's yellow-white fanned-out beard. What man would allow himself to be castrated in the modern world in order to be the usher in a charade of long-ago tyranny? Or was tyranny back in vogue?

There was a silence here in the palace—a muffling of all but the iron gut vibrations of ancient hallway clocks. Jared felt soggy and uncomfortable in his rumpled uniform and heavy boots. He was not of the people outside. Nor was he of this place. He did not want to be here, but Lyxa had summoned. As always, he hoped maybe this would be the day she'd set him free.

Garth swept on, monolithic, swathed in robes braided in darkening gold, with one knotty hand clutching up the cloth at his knee.

The palace was as old as the city. As old as the Olympia House, whose lowest levels had once been mine shafts, some of which ran right under and into the deep cellars of the Vegan palace.

Lyxa was crown princess of the Vegan monarchy, which had ceased to exist centuries before. She lived in the palace where once Polarian and Procyonian, and, before them, Imperial Terran administrators had lived. Her ancestors had come to Mercury City in 4901. They had been welcomed as 'a New Order' in that long-ago day. They had been welcomed to a city 'where everyone ruled,' meaning democracy. Fleeing for their lives, they had accepted a sham of becoming commoners like everyone else, while maintaining their connections and their untold zillions in wealth.

How they must have smiled (or cynically grinned) as they were welcomed to 'a rulership greater than that which they had previously enjoyed.' As the Hon. Lern Wilson had told the Galaxy's delegates in the Starmeer nine hundred years ago, 'We are a city that looks to the future.' Such nations are meant to rule universes, he'd told the delegates. Jared had seen holos of the delegates long ago, sitting and listening with their chins in their hands. Nations looked only to their greater future, never their lesser past. This nation, Jared reflected, produced space troopers like himself, star-struck children who became the officers of the mighty fleets that spanned the Galaxy. *Now where are we?* he asked himself behind Garth's rigid back. *Lyxa's people are packing to leave. That's got to be a bad sign.*

He still had some slight feelings for her. Lyxa was a sensitive, lonely young woman. Jared had fallen in love. He was drawn deeper and deeper into her world of a past she had no contact with, but she had nothing in the present, and certainly no future to grasp instead. Hers was a world he did not belong in. Perhaps, he thought, pausing with Garth before her chamber, he belonged at the beginning of what she would die with: A thousand years or more of civilization separated her from the star-struck spacer from Eye Street in Lesht. She'd been sleeping with many a man (and pretty girl) who crossed her doorstep, but he did not know this at the time.

He could forgive her many things, and almost feel sorry for her that she inhabited this shadow world of pretense in an ancient dead palace, where she medicated herself with sex and opium. She'd preempted his life at the very crowning moment as he ran above the city carrying the Olympic torch. He was celebrated (his brief moment of fame) in the media, toasted in taverns on a thousand worlds, and given a hundred great awards by important committees of men with tight little mustaches and women with stiff cleavage at ceremonies in libraries and such. Lyxa's possession of him was just a part of all that, and he didn't see it coming until the noose with tight and he had no escape. He was dazzled and deliriously in love with her, with her power and the whole panoply of royal pretense,

He had slept with her for a few exhilarating weeks, after which she had had him transferred to the lieutenancy of the palace guard. By then, it was becoming clear that she was moving on to other conquests. He even met one or two former lovers of hers who drank too much (on her credit, which was bottomless) and welcomed him to the losers' club. He ran from them, refusing to be a loser like they'd become. It was his stubborn pride, his endurance, his refusal to surrender, apparently, that kept her coming back to him for more. In between lovers, she would come to him, or have him come to her, and he found himself in a strange sort of equilibrium if not equality with her, at least when they were naked in bed together. She was a beautiful young woman, and the sex was deliriously passionate and overwhelming. She knew tricks he'd never heard of, like having them suffocate each other with silken scarves so their orgasms became truly a little death and resurrection. Even all of that now tired him. He wanted to find a real woman, not a queen or a phantom, and be a man in love, a man with his sleeves rolled up, making war or tilling fields or slamming beer mugs on tavern tables with other men.

During that initial let-down and break up, he'd had left her angrily, in a big tirade (from both of them to each other). Through Academy connections, despite her will and behind her back, he'd managed, against all her machinations, to resume study for an added year at the Academy of the Universe. Then he had shipped out for a year's maneuvers to a heady little corner of the universe where there was peace.

To accomplish this, he'd taken advantage of his reassignment under a decent officer named Jardin, the Military Policy advisor of the Mercurian delegation to the UGO. In that time, he had been skipped from the rank of rear ensign to senior staff lieutenant—ten years' progress, never realizing she was behind it all. She did love him, in her possessive and megalomaniacal fashion—always the tyrant's hand, with a velvet glove.

He'd enjoyed a wonderful year stationed at a rural frontier world named Lethe, where he'd finally gotten his chance to live as a normal junior line officer on some small vessel. He'd visited the planet a number of times, and fallen in love with its dark forests swept by fresh winds; its miles of green fields; its quaint towns and small cities; and of course its fresh-cheeked, beautiful young women. Before he was able to get serious with a few girls he started dating, he'd been recalled to Mercury City. He realized Lyxa controlled even that assignment. He had bitterly resigned himself to making the best of his situation while enjoying all of its perks but always looking for that moment of escape. You could run away any time, he supposed, but you lost everything and became a common vagrant with no past or future. He even considered buying a commission as a merchanter's third mate to escape. But—he'd worked too hard to give up his accomplishments, including Academy and Victory run. There must be a way, and he'd find it. Meanwhile, he must play nice. And, as long as he played nice, she appeared to love him in some strange manner.

Garth knocked on the door with his staff. A servant opened the door to Lyxa's fifty-room suite. Garth left silently.

Entering the main door, Jared felt her cloying, overwhelming presence as always. The air had a tinge of the finest perfumes. The walls were creamy white and gold with fine, tiny hints of lavender here, mauve there, blue iris other places. The floors were richly carpeted, and she had illusindoes (like the virtual ports on starships) showing happy green summer scenes from far places and remote times.

Lyxa came in a cloud of mink. She was tall, with long dark hair in glossy curls bouncing on her pale shoulders. Her skin was milky and pampered. It was said that the finest diamonds are genuine because they contain imperfections or inclusions. Just so, Lyxa (Li Sha, Elizabeth) had a few delightful strawberry freckles across her perfect nose, and some chocolate beauty marks in the skin of her arms and (only Jared knew) a mole by her pink opening.

She wore a long silken gown that shone, gilded, in the soft light among all this ritzy furniture. She opened her fuzzy mink wrap to reveal a slender body with small, hungry little breasts. "Lethean mink," she said—the first thing she said, to tease him a bit mean-spiritedly, to show her power over him.

Lethe...that was the name of the place...the little quiet planet...where he longed to escape again, this time forever. To hell with a career in the fleet. For the first time, that moment, seeing the sham of her beauty, the mortality amid all of her pretense and power, he dared to think: *the city is lost. It's just a short time. Even this woman is already packing, and when the princes flee, the kingdom is about to fall.* He did not share his thoughts with her, but waited for her to speak. He knew what would happen between them next. Her eyes said the same. She had dark, liquescent eyes as filled with passion as the pure whites around her pupils radiated strength and health. If she was using drugs much, it didn't show in her eyes. But then she had the finest doctors in the galaxy to keep her strong. Her body was perfect for him. It was soft and firm in just the right ways, curvy without excess, lean without losing that bit of fullness here and there like in her strong thighs and ripe belly. Her breasts were those of a girl, never having filled with milk. She'd never had offspring physically, but somewhere a young prince was being groomed to become her son and heir, nursed by women and machines owned by the palace. Nothing was denied her which was why he remained her supreme prize: the man who would not surrender. Or, who had surrendered, and she'd betrayed him, and he would never trust her again. He could still taste her, take her, rock her, make her delirious for a few hours, and apparently that was all she needed. So he gave that to her, and she gave many things to him. Only she'd never really given him herself, and she had no idea about that sort of thing, so she remained puzzled at his strength, his ferocity, his individualism. That intrigued her more than all the money and spices and genetic monkeys and other indulgences in her world. She owned everything she wanted, so that only thing left was to grasp someone or something she could not possess.

Her eyelids had been kohled and blued a dark shade mauve, lightly and in good taste. Her fingernails and toenails were square and perfect and glossed that same shade of mauve or violet.

He opened his arms, and she ran to him, threw himself against him, and he clasped her to his body as he swung her gently this way and that. Already she sighed with anticipation, moaned with passion, as she pressed her soft cheek and bony face against his own. She wrapped her arms around him and let him know of the naked surfaces waiting for him to touch. As always, he felt a stirring in his lower half, the hardness, the straining, the yearning, the need to fuck her. For those moments as they sailed toward orgasm together, he was the lord and she was his nothing.

She started peeling his clothes off in feverish motions, while licking her lips and regarding him with hungry eyes.

"I have to go soon," he whispered.

"The mess at the Starmeer?"

"Yes. The whole city is in turmoil."

"I want." She felt before him, taking him in her mouth. She held his bare buttocks in eager hands while sucking him.

He closed his eyes ecstatically, rolling his eyeballs upward. Why was this always so good? And why did he want to escape? She was an addiction, like her opium.

She took him out of her mouth and licked her lips, nodding as she stared at the glistening head. She growled in a girl voice: "I want." She popped it back in. She rocked her head back and forth, loudly and furiously working her mouth around him.

He held her head in his hands, enjoying the gritty crispy feel of her combed dark hair, while her mouth pumped him back and forth, until he felt himself letting go. He danced from one arched foot to the other, while her head shoved around between his legs. She held his jewels with delicate fingertips so they would not hurt while she mauled his font tenderly and lovingly.

When he thought he would lose his balance (and consciousness) she pulled him down onto the thick, soft carpet, on top of her, and breathed: "In me."

He was ready. She had stripped him and he was naked, hard and stiff and wet from her spit. She fumbled with trembling fingers, but he didn't need guidance. His wet found its way into her wet. She threw her head back with gritted teeth and gave a short, barking yell. As he hovered between her pale, soft, spread thighs, and slammed against her wet nothing, she raised herself up on her elbows, looked into his face savagely, and pumped. She pumped and slammed her Venus mound upward, meeting the force of his fast, slapping, slamming motions. Their impact filled the room.

He slipped his arms around her legs and raised her, so her knees were folded over his powerful, wiry forearms, and her feet dangled behind him, flying up and down as he slammed her. The room filled with wet slapping noises.

At some point, she turned to one side, pulled away, and presented her naked ass to him. He entered back into that wet warm yeah and hammered her while she rested with her elbows on the ground and started making moaning, crying sounds like someone in pain. It was the sound she made as she sailed into orgasm bay under full sail with all flags and pennants fluttering in a brisk sea wind. He piled up against her, pressing her, dominating and mastering her, while she cried out to be taken and mastered, to be manned like a ship and sailed to her orgasm.

He piled her and drove her, shoving and manhandling her, while she whooped and cried for *more, harder, faster, yeah, big, I want...*

They rested a few minutes. She lay under him spread-eagled and breathless, while he lay panting on top and held those frail little tits and sucked their purple cone-shaped nipples, violent with passion, from one to the other back, clutching them in his fists and she raised herself up holding each tit and forcing it in to his mouth as he flicked his tongue in circles.

She was hungry again and slammed herself up so he was inside her. She pulled on his knees, pulling his legs to her, which lowered his rear, so that he was in her deep. He fought with her, pinned her arms back mastered her while she shook her head from side to side and implored him with sick eyes to just fuck her *more, more, more harder...*

He took her again and again, in all of her holes, while she pushed herself and pulled him. She wrestled and wrapped long strong slender legs around him. At one point, she had his head in a thigh-lock, sideways, while he sucked at her fons. And so it went, until they were spent...

Wrapped in her dress and her stole again, she kissed him passionately and laughed. "There is no escape for you, is there?"

He had to admit: "Whatever it is you do to me, it is a good price for being a prisoner. Until I walk out the door."

She dropped onto a couch and gestured for him to sit. "Thank you my love."

He kissed her, while resenting her and wanting to be free, but he said: "Thank you."

"That was so great." She looked at him pertly, reclining to one side, not a princess now but a simple young perky girlfriend. "There is no man in the world like you."

He shrugged, feeling drained and good and momentarily in woolly paradise. The feeling would not last, he knew. "I have to go soon."

"I know," she murmured sympathetically. "Wouldn't you rather stay while I suck you?"

"Yes." *Honestly, yes. But honestly, no.*

"You need your freedom," she said in answer to her own question. "Have you meet my Lelli?"

Before he could answer, she raised a delicate, feminine hand and snapped her fingers. In answer to that flash of mauve, that snap, a shadow detached herself from a wall nook. "Meet Lelli."

The *djia* stood before them demurely, as Stella might. Lelli's pleasantly penciled phantom face redrew in pleased, wiggling lines. It registered the ghost of a wide, pretty smile. "So pleased to meet you."

"She was watching us," Lyxa said, ever to be provocative.

"They don't understand sex," Jared said as he lay back, winded and rubbed his forehead with both hands. Session over. Life to resume.

"I had her printed from my neural kelp tree 3/di," Lyxa said. "Didn't I, baby?"

"Yes, Lyxa."

"She will be my standby since you took my Stella away." Lyxa pouted.

"You gave me Stella," Jared said. "And you cannot have her back."

"They are adorable, aren't they?"

Jared didn't answer. For a moment he had a dreadful feeling that she might take Stella away, and he would not be able to stop her. The *djia* were programmed in certain ways, and of course Lyxa had ordered Stella made to obey Jared but so she, Lyxa, could override Jared's commands if she wanted to.

Lyxa took Jared's cheeks in both soft palms as she stared into his eyes. "I wouldn't think of taking her from you." At that moment, more than any other, Jared realized that his lover was totally insane. "That is why I had this dear baby Lelli made to be my shadow."

With growing horror, Jared pushed her gently away.

Lyxa seemed not to notice. She had a long habit of teasing or angering him, and then ignoring his temper. "Lelli is there to protect me."

Jared shook her wrists gently. "Is that why Stella is there? To protect me?"

Lyxa shook her head faintly, while smiling a dazzling, distant smile. "No, she would not be there for you to step into."

He shook the poor crazy rich girl's wrists. "What do you mean?"

"Silly. If I get hurt or die, I simply step into her. She becomes me, and I resume life as if nothing had happened. I will look just like my old self, and you'd never know."

Jared let go of her wrists and laughed. "I would not want to become you or Stella."

"Stella is me," Lyxa whispered. "I am with you at all times."

He shook his head. "If you were with me, we'd be fucking night and day. Stella hasn't got a clue."

"But if I stepped into her, she'd become me."

"I don't get it."

Lyxa sat up. "Progress. New technology. Watch." She raised her hand and snapped her fingers again.

Lelli approached, dropping her flimsy gown so that she became a statue of flickering ashen lights with a vaguely sketched face; a cartoon figure; a mannequin; a femmequin; a hallucination; a diaphane. Jared swallowed hard, feeling his lunch rising in his gorge. As with Stella, Jared noticed that the *djia* were the same height and general appearance as Lyxa, though they were half invisible, and the visible part was a sort of staticky (but silent) pencil sketch that kept redrawing. Beautiful in a spectral, haunting, cartoonish sort of way.

Lelli stood by as Lyxa dropped her clothes and nakedly approached her. Lyxa said over her shoulder, "Watch this."

Jared was paralyzed with shock as Lyxa stepped into Lelli as if running into her on the street. What happened was over in a fraction of a second. Lelli reached around Lyxa to embrace her. At the same time, Lyxa's dead body slipped like a boneless bag of rubber to the carpet and lay sprawled. Instantly, Lelli's flickering sine waves and pencil lines resolved into a perfect analog of Lyxa's features. She'd become Lyxa.

"See?" Lyxa-Lelli said. The voice was exactly the same. Everything was the same.

"I could live on forever in this new body, and if that dies, I'll have another replacement ready."

Jared rose, feeling sickened. He didn't want to say this: *It isn't natural. And they become demi-humans with all the rights we have, except for their freedom. We are not legally allowed to hurt them, kill them, or in any way to be cruel to them.* The look he gave Lyxa should have said it all, but she was beyond cognition.

Lyxa-Lelli spread her arms in a vague gesture and said: "I'm not ready to be dead so I'll just get back into my old body that I'm used to." She bent forward, spread-eagled the crumpled body on its back, and got on her knees between its legs. "Although this feels just like my old body. It might as well be my old body." So saying, she spread her arms and swan-dove into the dead woman in a belly flop.

Instantly, the dead girl shoved the pencil-girl away and rose. Lelli staggered to one side, righted herself, an in a few seconds looked like her normal redrawing self, all random flickering and dancing sketch-lines and sine waves.

Lyxa laughed and rose, doing a quick jig as if at the gym. She flailed her arms crosswise a few times to restore circulation. "See? Good as new."

"I have never seen anything like it in my life," Jared said. More than ever, he wanted to run from here and never come back.

As he dressed, she lit a small opium pipe, offering him some. He shook his head.

"Don't be a stranger my love."

I have to move on with my life. His eyes were shouting, but he did not say it.

"Take good care of Lelli."

Smoke trickled from her mouth into the air as she regarded him with feigned surprise. "Really. And I am nothing? Jared, you hurt my feelings." She pouted a little bit.

He sat beside her. "I love you. I have loved you from the time you took my life away. I am as much a prisoner as Lelli or Stella in my own way."

She giggled. Her eyes looked half closed, but she managed to continue expertly to torment him. "You are too strong a man, Jared. I can't let you go, so I am your prisoner as well." She reached out with one hand and grasped his chin almost painfully. "Do you have any idea how it torments me not to have you by my side and in my bed every day? I know that will never work. But don't you see? I could have anything done to you, including murder; you could even become a eunuch like Garth." Seeing his look of horror, she laughed. "But then I wouldn't have that powerful motorcycle cock to suck. I like it when you treat me like a rag. Nobody else has the courage to act like my equal. Only you, in this entire galaxy, and I love you for it. That's why I gave you Stella, and I'll give you anything else you want. Just not your freedom. But you are way better off than you would be in Lesht, you peasant, or in some dirty old attack cruiser risking your life, for what, so rich playboys and playgirls can have everything they want and you die for them. Trust me, my love, you don't know how good you have it. This world is going to end soon."

Jared finished dressing. "I see you're moving the dinnerware out. Where to?"

"That's a secret, my love. Time to kiss this ancient pile goodbye. I get all the intel, you know. I have spies everywhere. The Ankhmen will ravage the human sector. The Raskian idiots think they can take over, kill the Ankhmen, and replace your old Mercurian order. Make me laugh. I know what's coming. A thousand alien species are waiting to run through the streets here, killing any humans they find. Time to die, my friend. Time to die or move on. If you're smart, you'll come along."

Jared was ready to walk out. He was dressed, and pinned to the ground before her only by the urgency and insanity of what she was saying. In the marrow of his bones, she felt she was speaking truth. Only the question remained: would one die as a free man, or save one's skin by surrendering into slavery with this foreign princess?

"Go, darling." She sucked on her pipe. "You'll come to your senses when reality hits. We'll be in touch soon. I promise. *Ta-ta*."

"So long, Lyxa." He whirled and started for the door.

"Jarry."

He stopped, turned, and looked at her.

"And what about my dear little surrogate Stella? How is she treating you? How are you treating her?"

"We get along. We are friends, as far as that may go."

More smoke. "She is a demi-woman copied from my template. I gave her to you, Jared. You should feel honored. And you are ahead of your graduating class in rank, pay, privileges, everything. Plus you get to make love with me, and I treat you like my lord. You have much to be grateful for."

"You're right," Jared lied. "Be well, my dear."

"You too, lover. I'll call for you soon. Bring me Stella so I can have a chat with her and see how she is doing." Lyxa added pointedly. "How you are treating her."

"She is happy with me," Jared said, while Lelli rushed to open the door for him. This had not gone as planned, nor any better then previous visits. It was always the same old stalemate.

Leaving her, with those dazed looking eyes as she sagged slightly to one side, Jared stepped into the hall, where Garth waited. Jared followed Garth, without a word exchanged between them.

Jared rushed down the endless, winding ancient palace steps, and emerged on the streets outside with a sigh of relief.

At that moment, the clocks in a thousand bell towers around the city tolled, signaling that the old year was dead and the new year had just been born. It was 5000 OC, a new millennium, and much change lay in store for everyone.

10. Death

Now Jared must really hurry to reach Cyrus Mbe at the Starmeer or UGO.

The street was empty, more so than usual—almost scary, and he stepped back in bewilderment for a second—until he remembered the tradition: At midnight of the old year, streets must be empty, because now comes Death, to take away the old year and let in the new. Anyone caught on the streets between midnight and dawn of the year's first day would be struck dead. That was the ancient superstition.

Now all was still. Jared walked as though he were in a dream. Loosening his coat because sweat plastered his hair and shirt, he let his feet walk of their own accord. "I was a child once," he said to the ghosts around him. The cobblestones, flattened by long use, sounded hollow and muffled under his boots. Not a soul anywhere in the streets.

Death, with his scythe and his moldy robes, once frightened him. *I was a child once.* He had stood before a fence and watched a ship laden with ether food for the Voranniair-5 godpeople take off. He forgot where he had seen that. He had wanted so, so much to become one of the starmen. He had dreamed of shooting through a grand net of stars, in command of a great, silent vessel.

As in a dream, the cockpit lights would flicker and flash silently, and quiet radio traffic would crackle with routine self-assurance. He would fly among the stars, touching on planets here and there, maybe merging his dreams with those of beautiful, angelic humanoids making love amid alien fields.

He would sit on his shipmaster's throne in the middle of the command module. Below him would be officers and crew of all ranks, milling about in orderly confusion, stern-quiet, while running a starship. He would let his throne rise high up, and all around him would be only a transparent bubble, and all he would see would be stars. There would be a bath of stars. *Starbath.* Stars and stars and stars, like a vast ocean. He would travel so fast that he would be bucking among the waves, and the stars would be like molecules, so tiny: But, in reality, suns, mighty, thundering suns. Waves would be hundreds of millions of light years high. There would be no measuring the might of a sea that could slap together such waves, but which were negligible compared to the depths of that fathomless, radio-torn sea.

Even more, though, he dreamed of being alone with the stars. He saw himself in a tiny ship hurtling among the galaxies. In his vision, he was seated alone in a command chair, looking at a window filled with stars. Inside the ship was only contented, quiet gloom. He saw soft buzzing and clicking of machinery, like music. He saw a red light blinking slowly, steadily, in a corner. Starshine, soft and dreamlike, touched random shimmering metal, softening surfaces to make them like rippled cloth. Starlight would shed not a light but a soft glow through the dark. That red light would seem distant and shrouded in fog.

He had never, though, been able to figure out just what sort of ship he had imagined. It seemed almost to be an extension of his very body. The red light was like life, almost, he wasn't sure: It blinked slowly, and in the symphony of silences it had a deep, probing quality, like the insistent booming of a foghorn over a mist-shrouded sea. It seemed to sing of something invisible, something reaching like an interminable plumb line, and, again, like a cork rising forever and fast, from the depths of the subconscious to the air and the surface of the mind.

He snapped out of his reverie as he approached a street corner ahead.

The side street opened up into the wide emptiness of Olympic Avenue. The corner was close at hand, and Jared grew apprehensive; childish, but true.

Trash lay scattered and windblown on Olympic Avenue. This nameless street emptying on to the galaxy's Sacra Via—its sacred way or capital street—was small. Weathered wall-masses leaned around it imposingly. Austere arches crossed and recrossed far overhead in the narrow chasm. Jared left the side street and stepped out onto the deathly still expanse of the avenue.

A fifteen minute walk ahead, he could see the broad, low portal where you entered the bubble dome. Olympic Avenue stretched through that portal, and ran on and on toward the ever-surrounding sea. Looking the other way an equal distance on the Avenue, he saw the park. He began walking. At the end of Olympic Avenue was a line of trees, where the periphery of the park began.

A vague childhood horror at his back, he mounted the curb and walked in the win between two tree giants. When religions were strong, people had been killed for doing what he was doing. "This is today, in the modern world," he said, without conviction, looking at the broad, grassy plain surrounded by distant, hulking forest masses. No longer was there a black army in the forest, to come out and kill people, as legend said happened once during the early kingdom, by chance on a New Year's night. That was where the legend, and the tradition, had come from, but this was today. Today the army wore white, and flew among the stars.

Slowly, Jared walked over the grass. He would be glad to reach the under rail, which would take him right to the Assembly Hall. Quickening his step, he thought he could see the dry, white lights of the station among the trees.

He stopped dead in his tracks because someone was standing in the path of the light, someone standing very still and swaying softly from side to side. In the act of stopping, Jared stumbled over something. He looked down, and it was a bit of broken wood. Strewn all around him lay the wreckage of the monstrous feast. Jared spotted one of the immense nymphs, now deflated, sickle-slashed, flattened on the ground under the trash and broken chairs. There was a heavy stench of spilt wine. It rose to Jared's head, and, in a convulsive wave of fear, he stared at Death.

Death, small and bony, poked about in the scattered trash. His garments blew in the wind, and his scythe moved like a dark, slow pendulum. Jared was no longer sweating; the sweat had chilled and grew icy on his back and around his neck. Death was there. Night light played around his feet like an aqueous current, pool of star flakes. Death moved about the deserted platform where Father Mercury had roared and slapped his thighs. A soft wind stirred his cold, mildew robes the way the wind stirs old curtains in and out of an open window.

Jared stepped past, remembering that he must make his appearance at the Assembly Hall. But he couldn't take his eyes off Death. He thought of his lover, the princess. Lyxa would be oblivious by now. Opium hit her mind, rising up, tingling in a brief wave of exhilaration, and then there was peace. Dreams came. Not so for Jared, who sought action rather than escape.

The sky was filled with moving shapes: Ferries, liners, warships, barges of gas and metal…Stars, planets, space vessels docked in the bathing brilliance of stationary-orbiting platforms. Life went on, outside the mythology of death and rebirth.

The collective light of heaven blended into a soft gas enshrouding all objects salient over the darkness in a vague, ethereal light. Death glowed over of the darkness, a tiny scary form apart from both the dark earth and the light-filled sky.

Jared and Death stared at each other, in just one threshold moment between the old and the new. They stood suspended in time, between earth and sky. Jared could not, did not want to see the face, but stared at the bony hands that held the sickle. Probably some alien hired by the Recreation Committee. Jared gave a nervous wave of the hand, backing away. Then he wheeled and jogged to the subway, not to be late for the Assembly.

This evening, he'd seen Lyxa, and he'd seen death. He wasn't sure which was scarier—or more real. He passed through crowds of protesters outside the great hall. People were kept apart by police, who could barely restrain the fanatical Ankh mobs on one side, partisans of the Raskia federation on another side, and beyond them supporters of traditional democratic values that seemed to be vacuumed up by the hate and heat of lunatics seeking brutality in their demagogues, easy answers, quick fixes, hot talk, lies, and of course more violence. Simple, stupid people understood nothing about checks and balances. They comprehended nothing about tolerance or multiplicity. They only understood taking up cudgels and following a strong, brutal leader, a liar and a megalomaniac, a malignant narcissist, who had the gift of being a radio to communicate persuasively with their inner ox.

Jared commandeered a police escort, and entered the hall. There, he found a confrontation in progress that was yet more frightening, as his superior, President Cyrus Mbe, struggled to face down his opponents in the Starmeer.

11. Ankhfire

Cyrus Mbe sat in the Assembly Hall as all hell broke loose.

The Assembly Hall was, floor to roof, cold design. A thousand people now sat here silently to decide the fate of the universe. A thousand people sat at their seats in ten tiered circles of the tall, round building, and with them their delegation staffs, and the stars were visible through the transparent ceiling. Cold design: A massive buttress rose from floor to ceiling, splitting at the base to enclose an imposing portal, and on a balcony projecting from the face of the buttress high up sat the chairman of the UGO with his staff: cold design: taking even murder into account; the arrangement was meant to protect the chairman from assassination during meetings open to the public.

The stars shone down on the thousand delegates, and many souls across the human galaxy prayed over these thousand.

A small man rose at his seat and said loudly: "I defy you. I damn you, Lacryma, City of Tears." He was Alan Chase, of Ankhfire, shouting at the delegation of Lacryma, a Mercurian ally.

A thousand faces made a sea of expressions, and their eyes made lights of worry, glistening in sweat: That, so far from their homes, they should have come to watch a battle of giants.

Stasis was mutating, and Cyrus felt the pain of it. There were angry faces among those of Lacryma's delegation. Mercury's delegation were pent and silent, but red-faced as if they were going to cut loose with yelling and fist waving at any moment. Cyrus glanced toward Jared Fallon, one of his military advisors, but the young officer's back was turned. It was the moment of calm before an unstoppable storm.

The new Assembly Chair, Thor Eystrigg of Veredig, let Chase finish some opening remarks. "Very well, Mr. Delegate, proceed. You may make your initial claim for a hearing at this time."

Chase launched into a harangue without thanking the chairman. "I choose not to call this an initial claim because it is not. It is an indictment. It is a plea for justice. This Lacryman (he pointed at a delegate, who made no sign of emotion) has robbed thousands of followers of Ankhfire of their voice. The Lacryman war machine has crushed and killed them, and I am here to speak for them. They have started it, and this means war!" A shocked babble of voices broke out, but Eystrigg beat it to silence.

"Yes, quite frankly," Chase continued, "war!" He looked around with gravitas. "A month ago, Ankhfire and her holy allies have been at war since attacked by Lacryma. Behind them stands Mercury, the host nation of this charade, so we condemn Mercury Free Port City as well. Eternal damnation! The gods are with us. You are finished."

"Throw the son of a bitch out!" someone shouted. The gavel dropped before the mike, and there was silence. Chase yelled words about a holy war of good against evil: "It is the sacred battle of Ankhfire against them who challenge his will."

Cyrus rolled his eyes up. How could he intervene? Mercury City was the most powerful of nations, but against this alliance of madness and fanaticism he felt oddly powerless. Unreason and insanity were laws of nature, like gravity or evolution.

At this point a man jumped out of the multitude and, in the middle of one of the ramps leading into the pit of the Assembly Hall, raised a dagger to his chest. Crying out loudly, "Ankhfire is love, not war," he stabbed himself. The huge fan of blood spurting and pulsing from his chest as he fell instantly confirmed his death. The Ankhmen, fools that they were, could not have staged it better. And their manipulators, the Raskians, must be quietly gloating all the more.

Delegates rose in alarm as the mortally wounded Ankhman fell to the ground.

As delegates deteriorated into a herd of panic-stricken sheep, Eystrigg's gavel crashed and the echoes reverberated louder than voice or masses outcry. "Back to your seats!" he bellowed, but the rioting continued and only grew more violent.

Ankhmen in a mass carried the martyr's body toward the exit portal.

National Police in forest-green uniforms appeared. Others, with clubs swinging loosely at their hips, appeared in a thin line in the pit, looking up into the expanse of seats. They might protect Cyrus and others on the dais, but they were powerless to control the raging mob that had once been the orderly assembly of Starmeer delegates—the external government of Mercury.

"Ankhfire," Chase bellowed. His voice resounded with the holy name, powering each syllable of it: "Ankhfire is will."

A woman rose with a wail like the pain-cry of a wounded animal, but green uniforms and thrashing clubs brought her down before she could harm herself. Some of the saner delegates prepared to leave. Cyrus clutched the railing before him sickly and grimaced in Jared's direction, thinking: Why this? Why am I here at all?

12. Year Of The Bread Ships (5000 CE)

The Magnon of the Mudsheaves raised his wand and a million ships fired up a million miles away in orbit of Mudsheave I.

The Magnon nodded to himself. The Bread Ships were a worthy gesture, good for trade.

It was 12 a.m., Lacryma Standard Time, and the year 5000 began. Long ago there had been great upheavals, and many ships had taken Bread from the Mudsheaves to the starving galaxy.

Now was a time of peace, though the Ankhmen threatened at every turn. But the Mudsheave Worlds were the Bread mother of all mankind. They would always survive. Lacryma, perhaps not. The Magnon lowered his eyes in great piety. He saw himself in the position of a fifth-millennium grandee, allying Ankhfire with the Mudsheaves. Bread and ships, a natural combination of powers for greatness. Yes, the Magnon thought to himself, perhaps it would be good if Mercury City fell and Lacryma lost the war. None would dare destroy the Mudsheaves. The Mudsheaves wed Ankhfire, and another two thousand years of peace would ensue. He, Onych IX, Magnon of All The Mudsheaves, would be remembered with past great leaders.

The Bread Ships, gathered from every nation for a great journey to the planets of the man-galaxy, were a sea of stars in the Mudsheave sky, and they moved slowly outward in a great arc, with the Lacryman League standard, revived after millennia of disuse, emblazoned on the flagship *Lacryma Pacifer*. The journey had begun. The Magnon smiled to himself. He had seen to it that they would first travel to the Ankhfire nations. The result would be a holy war.

13. Dreams Gone

It started out wrong: There was that oppressive morning atmosphere, polar wasteland, bleak abyss of frigid hell.

Jared walked nervously. A small white dot hovered momentarily behind a grimy window. It was a human face, narrow with suspicion. Jared quickly looked away. His gaze fell upon the forbidding monster drum: The looming North Wing of the Olympia House, thundering in the silence by its sheer size.

Someone shrieked. Jared whirled.

It was a clothesline, pulled by a fat, pasty arm. Jared walked on; what was there to fear, except Mbe's secret police? He now thought of the uniform less agents of the National Police. Was Mbe making good use of them?

Gunshot! Jared tensed, ready to throw himself on the ground. But it was merely a door. Other doors banged. A voice uttered a slurred, unintelligible curse.

Shadowy figures, of little substance in the wan light, stepped into the cold morning.

A whistle shrilled in the thin air, loud as a rocket making a dead fall.

None of the people walking with Jared looked at him. To them he was probably just another derelict drifting in and out on the strong legs of a fast-dying youth Perhaps, a drifter from Kublec or Daltonia or some other ill-famed destitution world, who had found a woman in the tenements and would stay a few weeks before moving on.

At the intersection of Victory and Olympic he ran from the oppressive shadow men, clambered up an embankment. A vac train rushed him away into thick traffic and he tried to forget what he had seen.

All was finished.

Jared walked to the Starmeer, fought his way in through rioters, got into the hall, but was unable to even get close to his boss, President Cyrus Mbe.

Jared saw, as the one delegate went down in a spate of blood, that Ankhfire had just achieved an most important propaganda victory. Those among the followers of Ankhfire who would throw their lives gladly and deliriously away for their faith had just witnessed their inspiration. The Ankhmen, the warriors, had destroyed the UGO order, and now ruled a tide of war. Fools that they were, Jared thought, they were manipulated by the Raskians, but those in turn were fools for not understanding that they had just sentenced themselves and everyone else in the human galaxy to death and slavery at the hands of a thousand vengeful alien races.

"People of the galaxy!" Chase screamed. "We are at war! Join us in the holy war! Help us overthrow this vast, rotting empire, which refuses to change, refuses to rightfully dissolve the empire formed under the guise of protection in the early days after the revolutions!"

Jared looked across the aisles, to the dais, and saw the new look of determination on Cyrus Mbe's dark face. There was no alternative: Mbe must take control of the government right now, right here, or they were all doomed.

Agony of agonies.

Something moved with a dull, loud roar against the portal from outside, and when Jared looked, he saw a great crowd of people pressed against the thick glass. The body of the suicidal Ankhman lay on a litter, surrounded by policemen and Ankhmen. "Ankh, Ankh!" came the cry of the growing masses outside and Ankh sympathizers inside the hall.

More delegates walked out, and Eystrigg sounded hoarse yelling, trying to get them to stay.

Jared thought Eystrigg must hurt himself pounding that ivory block.

Alan Chase, followed by a phalanx of Ankhmen, moved down the ramps. Policemen and delegates stayed out of his way.

"Ankh, Ankh," came the massive roar of the people.

Alan Chase stood before the Ark of Convention in the pit, erect and angry before the bristling hooded microphones. His face was white, tinged with scarlet mottle at its knife-sharp folds. Silence surrounded him, made everyone stop and look at Chase, while the distant crowd crowed: "Ankh, Ankh!" and the eternal stars, tiny flames, silent and watchful, nodding unintelligible messages with blurry faces, hung suspended as time itself. Chase blazed at the chairman: "We can no longer live side-by-side with this Monster of Iniquity!" as he pointed toward Cyrus Mbe and the Mercury delegation.

Don't do this, Jared pleaded inwardly. *Not now, not with alien fleets heading our way.*

Chase and his Ankhmen strode away through a small door leading to private chambers.

Echoes rolled around the hall: *-iquity, -iquity, -iquity...*

The main portal groaned and people around the dead man jumped back.

A second thundering groan came as the macroton glass portal bulged. The crowd outside roared ever more loudly:

Ankh! Ankh! Ankh! Ankh!

The body disappeared from the litter. Noise beyond noise. It all happened quickly. The floor and the walls shook, and Jared was knocked to the ground but quickly rose again to clutch a banister.

The portal was down. That had made the deep, pounding noise.

Ankh. Ankh. Ankh. The holy name. The holy litany. The litter, the body, the uniforms and the Lacrymans were lost among a tidal wave.

Ankh, Ankh, they shouted, and a man with blood on his face ran past Jared. The man yelled something, but Jared could only hear *Ankh, Ankh*, the blood cry of the rabble, cry of sacrifice and martyrdom, all in service of the ruthless, invisible manipulators who were really orchestrating the fall of democracy for their own short-term profits and power. This Ankhfire madness was only the beginning of the end for Mercury Free Port City and the entire human status quo as dominant force in the Hither Galaxy.

Now shots rang out.

Looking over his shoulder, Cyrus saw Eystrigg go down as a man with a weapon stood over him at the dais, emptying the gun into the dying Chairman's twitching body.

It was the beginning of the end. By now, not only the Raskians but the aliens as well would know that Mercury FPC and the UGO were coming apart at the seams.

14. On The Run

Jared managed to slip out of the assembly hall amid a group of police in riot gear. He made his way to an island of safety, where police were marshaling ground vehicles. Air cars came and went in a chatter of engines, flashing of lights, rushing of wind. Riot squads hastily gathered and formed ranks on the corners.

Jared knew his first duty was to be with Mbe at Center House. The police were busy and distracted. He was not even a delegate, but a simple staffer. He was unable to cage a ride, so he began jogging—his greatest skill in this universe, even greater than having sex with Lyxa.

The streets grew quieter as he put distance between himself and the seats of government. Behind him lay the Starmeer and Olympia House, Mbe's office building as Exterior President. Not far away, still under the Dome, hulked the Interior Presidency, where Mbe also now held sway; or was 'ruled' the better term now?

Jared ran with purposeful strides, washed in cold and emptiness. The new millennium was a few hours old, and the world was going to hell. Cosmopolis—City of the Universe! It was starting to look like a hollow anthem.

Jared rested against a door frame. He wasn't winded, but knew to conserve energy. He slid down and sat on the door step and folded his hands between his knees and thought, *where have all my dreams gone?* He thought, *people's lives are the mutation of their childhood dreams.*

Why do I think in terms of millennia? Is death what they say it is? Is it peace and rest? What is life? Once, long ago, he had dreamed of moving through empty space at great speed, an Astral, a space sailor. *But now I have a vastness and emptiness, and it is inside me, and it hurts. Is Ankhfire the answer? Is it blood, hot and unthinking, a death in itself?*

No, he thought. *No. This city was built by men greater than men. Greater than themselves. Curious.*

He had filled himself with an empty dream, and when the dream disappeared, the emptiness remained.

He sat in the doorway and the doorway was the mouth of a dragon, stretched into a breathless O that might snap shut at any moment. Jared sat gingerly on the flat brown teeth-steps. What if there was a great war now. The new-millennium people would be dead.

The flat teeth were especially made to grind against each other. Jared tasted dread. If it happened, neither he nor any other human being would be left alive.

Quasar bombs would rip the fabric of the galaxy asunder. Nothing would be left. The huge dragon loomed evilly in the night, glowering in the bleach-blue undertone of untruth of the dark sky.

Night was full of strange winds. Cold air blew out of interstellar space, cold of the parsecs and light years, cold of the stars and oceanic dust clouds.

Jared rose, looking upward. There were the stars, still. The horror of the Assembly Hall was passed, and there were the stars still.

A wind chilled his bones, a wind derived from no earthly source, a wind shallower than life, and for an instant Jared relived that childhood dream on the breast of the mind-sweeping cold: A vision of being an Astral, of moving through space at great speeds, of living in a small cabin alone in infinity, with the noises of soft machinery, with the light of the stars in the dark cabin otherwise lit only by a dim red transit light.

Instead, *reality*. He walked.

The days of the Academy of the Stars had been days of pomp and splendor…marching through alien cities under wild and stranger suns…maneuvers in the fields where grew all the breath and warmth of alien life. Lethe, Lethe, lost deep amid the star fields of denial.

Green, green, were the fields and forests of wonderful Lethe.

The days as a student in the Old City had been warm and hopeful. They had marched and laughed. Nothing like sunshine on a concrete expanse rippling with flags and white uniforms. There had been the eternal present of pompous military and civilian honors passing between gloved hands on the steps of this or that immense building.

Night was black and forbidding. The Olympia House stood in to the heavens, shrouding everything with its shadows, Olympia House of the prisoners; and gladiators not so long ago, and fights to the death.

Jared paused before a sign, Olympia House. The words were beaten faded into bronze. He touched the icy metal, ages old and black and eroded.

Dreams gone, here was the raw, green, ageless face of time on an empty street where the wind blew a piece of paper along the gutter and somewhere a pauper skulked near a trashcan unmindful of death and here and there a cat crossed the silent street.

Lowering his head the slightest bit as though he were diving into the sea, he pushed the door open and walked in. This was the Olympia House. Here he had once trained for the great sports that Mercury City had to win. The toughening given him here had put the victory Torch in his hand and sent him off over the Arch of triumph, running, the winner, for a little while a great name. He walked, and as he walked, he was walking in the past. He walked by silent, dark arenas, by gymnasia that smelled in their black, fathomless, whispering immensity of sweat and sawdust. Here, all was stone and metal and beaten leather.

Passing the pens, he heard the clangor of metal on metal, but he didn't look inside because those had to be robots. Humans had gone out of vogue. Robots were the craze, because they hit harder and they smoked and burned and roared nicely while killing each other.

He stopped before a door that said No Admittance but his mind wasn't on the door, it was on that day of all days when, during the galaxy-bright Mercurian night, he had run the Arch. Zillions had cheered his victory run from below, and the sterling stars had beamed down their unguessable messages.

Metal rang on metal.

He opened the forbidden door and stood within Olympia House.

15. Olympia House

Inside Olympia House, Jared stood in darkness. Where to? He seemed to remember there being a way out near here. But how could he find it in this darkness?

Too late, he caught sight of the door closing and locking behind him. Then he was blinded by an intense light. A loudspeaker boomed out:

"Do not move. Raise your hands. You are being searched for weapons. The door is presently an electrical conductor; you will die if you touch it. Stand and wait to be apprehended."

Before he could turn to run, before the metallic voice had reverberated away down the corridor, he was pinioned by some invisible force.

The light softened. Jared turned toward the tramp of heavy feet, and shook with fear. Robots, hard and cruel, accompanied by two guards. The two robots locked Jared between them. One of the guards slapped Jared across the mouth. "What are you doing here?" Jared remonstrated, but the guard cut him off. "I don't want to hear it."

They took Jared to a lift. Glowing platforms of energy passes perpetually down through floor after floor, coming out of the ceiling, going down through the floor. While sinking out of sight, Jared caught a last glimpse of the blind, circular little hallway he'd been captured in, which was mystifying because both its beginning and its end circled around out of sight. A group of robots were passing: Battered metal hulks, smoking, burning frames, moving along with a clank of heavy feet and a clatter of mangled limbs. A large robot, with a tower and hose, was spraying a robot that had begun to smoke. The smell of scorched rubber and torn brain cases faded as they passed floors going down.

They took him to a small office where a man in a sergeant's uniform sat behind a desk, cleaning his fingernails. A corporal was just entering a door marked Men. A youth in a colorful kimono, Dubhean style, held the detached arm of an automaton who sat silent and unmoving in a corner. The boy said, "Come, fool," and the automaton rose to let him screw the arm back on.

The sergeant pointed his nail file at Jared. "Who's this?"

"We caught a TP," the guard growled. *Trespasser.*

The sergeant's face darkened. He grunted, throwing the file in a steel drawer. It clattered jarringly. "So." He sat back, tipping his chair against the wall. "So, a tp."

"Give him hell, Sarge," the boy said.

The sergeant didn't answer. Looking off into space he sighed, "Can't you people read signs? I don't know why you were in there, but they'll never believe anything but sabotage. Well…" He turned toward the man who had accompanied Jared down: "Get his papers."

The guard easily fished Jared's wallet from his pocket. "It better be good," the sergeant said, taking out his nail file again.

"Sergeant, I am an officer in the star fleets, assigned to duty with the President's staff."

Several men laughed. One said: "Yeah really, and I'm the Queen of Vega."

The irony of this heckling had best remain discreetly not pointed out to these fools, Jared thought.

"You here to hurt the robots?" one man asked.

It dawned on Jared that a former athlete might be a very likely person to want to destroy robots.

"I'll tell you—what's your name? Jared—If I lose one robot, the entire Galaxy would start war. And in any case, I'd be dead. Malean, what did you find? Malean!!"

"I'm right here," the guard growled, and Jared was astounded at this insubordination. Malean shook his head. "Jared Fallon. He was once an Olympic runner—I remember him: The last year a human ran."

"Where's he work?"

"He's an officer in the star fleets."

The sergeant's face was clouded by a funny look. "You know," he said softly, "none of that sounds like it's going to get you off the hook too well here." Nevertheless, he looked somehow impressed.

The boy's voice called out again from somewhere: "Give him hell!"

A muffled voice came out of the room marked Men. There was the sound of water rushing, and the door sprang open, and the corporal popped out. "Fix him, Sarge." The corporal stood by, watching eagerly.

The sergeant glared. Time passed.

"You're—how old?"

Jared told him; probably far too young to be believable.

"You're with the UGO?"

"Yes," Jared said, surprised.

"Get out of here," Sonlo whispered. Just get out. Don't even look back…" He looked as though he would say more, but seemed to choke on the words. And Jared sprinted past the silent, grasping figure in the doorway, back to freedom's agony.

16. Starbath

Moments later Jared Fallon stood amid roaring traffic on the City's main street, Olympic Avenue. Here some people stood on the sidewalks, talking. Bars and restaurants were full, holiday-full, though it was still night, but New Year's Day was coming into full swing around the city.

Though lost in a crowd, Jared felt lost as if he were the only human being on the planet. He stood for a while, sweating on a curb. It had been a close brush. Although he was sure he would never really understand fully what pushed the events in the city along their track, he felt its mystery and its evil, something unholy, something more powerful and earthy than all the power and the codes and the ideals of the Galactic Union or the Star Fleets.

He must call Mbe, and he had no tech assist, not to mention *djia*. He hoped Stella was all right. Time for a drink. He spied a sign, Bar, and pressed his way over through the jostling people. He put in a call with the automat, then stopped at the bar while waiting for a return call.

Soon, the bartender, an Achernarian with a gold-striped gown of white silk and a turban, whispered in Jared's ear with a smacking, sour-smelling voice: "Telefox."

Jared turned, holding his drink. "But who would know to reach me here?" He took the man by the arm. "Who is it that wants me?"

"A Mr. Abebe, Sir."

"Oh. Oh yes, of course. Did he mention my name?" Jared tried to sound as casual as possible. He put a furtive hand to his eyes; they were wet and his face red, but he did not look to suspiciously upset.

"He asked for a Mr. Jared Fallon, Sur; described this Mr. Jared as a young gentleman of your description, dressed in uniform as you are, and wearing a long black coat, as you are."

Who is tracking me? "Let me talk to him."

They handed Jared a com button, and he spoke to the man on the other end. Of all people, it was Mbe. "Situation is desperate."

Jared's stomach dropped out; had war been declared?

"Jared, report for duty at my office, in Center House, immediately. Big trouble. I can't and don't want to talk now. Mobs are tearing the Assembly apart. We've lost Exterior, I'm afraid. Hurry. Meet me at a little funeral ceremony for Eystrigg. We're gathering there now."

Jared virtually fled from the bar, out into the street.

Night scent and dew and mystery and earth on a quiet back street. Somehow, his spirit was relaxed and detached. He hung over a trap door by the strands of what he had been conditioned to desire—life, advancement, and so on—while what he really wanted was to let go and drop through that trap door entering into the world beyond it.

He looked up and saw the stars above.

To be a star! To burst forth, like a supernova, streaking across the heavens with fire, one creature in a sea of many others, all moving along their self-lit paths of darkness, moving with the speed of darting fish, except in human eyes that saw them as fixed dots of light!

Trees and shrubs were settled into the night all about. To be a plant, and share in that slow silent motion and be unmoving to human eyes only—to be great, as a human is to the darting ant, only greater and faster on a scale of light years. A bush, like a wave frozen before the delving bow, the corner of a house; a tree, running slim from the earth, expanding and blooming all in one fast motion, and quickly returning to its primeval dust, all in the span of many poor human lives; a thin-stemmed flower, moving at the beck and call of the winds in the night darkly near the earth…

The air was crisp. The wind blew cool, faint, fragrant breaths like perfectly-mixed liquors or precious snow jewels. Cool-sided grass blades on hard ground tickled Jared's hands. They touched his neck and the back of his ears softly.

Jared was still. He was a silent, crusted rock at

Starbath. Dreams of escape, of peace…

the bottom of a dark, voiceless sea, amid waving dancing shapes, while the gods swam about oblivious to him and to themselves, the gods of here and then, the gods of then and there, gods of past, present, and future, gods of many pasts, many presents, many futures. He lay there, letting his roots sink deeper, deeper into the ground. His mind rose on a thin stalk into the high waters, and he was wondering when the stalk would break so that he could be free, but it would not break, and he knew then that he would have to get up and keep his appointment.

17. Dust

Behind Jared Fallon an air cab took off with a slight soughing sound in the near-evening cemetery. They had told him Eystrigg's funeral was to be here. Mbe must be here; those State cars outside…

Raskians stood all about the bier. Mbe was the only Mercurian there. At first he seemed not to recognize Jared; a light dawned small in the tired yellowing eyes, and he motioned to Jared to stand behind him. Jared did so.

A lector was reading something in the soft, sadly sibilant tongue of Rasalhague. Crickets wẹre beginning to chirp. A bird warbled among the towering mountains of green all around, the last of the famed Hearthclimber trees of Mercury. Another bird squawked somewhere, disturbed in its sleep. The air was soft and fragrant.

Auburn sun glow in gathering gloom; the days were turning cold, Jared decided slowly; in these times. A sad autumn was descending on the City of the Universe as it swung outward in its orbit of Aldebaran. Winter was coming deep and eternal. Jared wondered if, ages before, some man might not have stood among the uncoffered amber of the evening woods, watching sadly as the dying of the warm months rhymed with the swelling litanies for the dying in the waning of the world he had always known. Had he dreamed, dared to hope for, rebirth?

The service was over.

Chase and his followers briskly made their way out of the cemetery. They walked ahead, old men and somber young, dressed darkly, in a line across the breadth of the gravel walk. The austere faith of Chenner clung about them like frosty breath.

Mbe and Jared and some plainclothesmen followed, looking wilted in the face of unspoken epithets.

Mbe drew back with Jared. "Lieutenant, you are the only one of my men who showed up today. Thank you. What happed last night?"

"I was ill, and…I couldn't move."

"Hm; I hope you're well today; well, anyway…" he nodded, engrossed…"Perez, Van Eyck, Jardin…Why didn't they come?" He snapped a finger. "Jared, something's afoot. They know something…They're keeping clear of me for a reason. They know something I don't."

"Our lives," Jared asked, "are we in danger now?"

"No, of course not," Mbe said quickly. He looked strangely at Jared for an instant. He smiled reassuringly. "Won't worry, Lieutenant. I'm still in control here, and I have my agents. I'll handle this situation in a few hours. What I want you to do, meanwhile, is to go to the Center House for me. I'll be there in about an hour."

"Yes?" He was a bit hesitant, but Nothing.

"Go to my office. You'll have to get the keys from my secretary. Take out the files on the brush wars on Shaula 09, and go over them in a general way. Have a broad resume ready for me when I get there. I know there isn't much time, but it's very important." Mbe nodded and slapped him on the shoulder.

Mbe spoke briefly with the other Mercurians, and they nodded. A state car waited. The Raskians had already left. Instead of getting into the great, polished vehicle, Mbe told Jared to take the car and hurry back to Olympia House. Jared said to himself, the Delegate's brusque manner was understandable, but annoying. Nevertheless, he entered the vehicle without further question and the driver jumped it into the air rapidly. They left Mbe and his plainclothesmen behind in a small, close group and headed uptown through the heavy traffic, with the broad, long expanse of Olympic Avenue rolling beneath them.

18. Betrayal

Brush wars on Shaula 09?

It dawned on Jared soon enough: there had never been any.

For the second time that night, Jared found himself in the vast expanse of Olympia House, this time more tired, baffled, and frazzled than the first time.

There were no planets in the system Shaula. Perhaps if he searched a more specific index. But how strange. Something was wrong. He knew before the door opened behind him that he had been somehow deceived. Angrily he whirled.

He whirled and faced the drawn guns of several of Mbe's closest: Perez, Kilmer, others. He backed away. Perez and Kilmer turned to each other. "Who is this?"

"A new delegate maybe," Perez suggested.

"Maybe Mbe got wise to us," another scoffed.

Kilmer steeped forward. "This is Fallon, an assistant of Mbe on Bowman's military attaché staff. We can't afford to let him walk."

Jared said: "Don't do this."

"Sorry, Fallon, but we have new plans for you."

"Damn you."

Kilmer patted Jared on the cheek infuriatingly. "Look, we're going to let you live. We won't kill you. We'll just lock you up for a while until we're done with our project."

Jared stared at the man. "What project?"

Kilmer made a foul-looking grin, and Jared knew the answer. They weren't working for the aliens, to be sure; and they didn't look like stupid Ankh fanatics; so they must be Raskian agents.

Kilmer snarled in Jared's face, "Where's Mbe! Quick!"

Looking into a gun pointed at his face, Jared came to a sudden insight. So this was what Mbe had wanted him to do—to fall into a trap. He had been used as a probing device. Someone had been tracking him all along, since the Assembly, which was why Mbe had been able to reach him in the bar. That was why he'd been sent in Mbe's car!

Mbe had betrayed him. His boss had sold him down the river, not caring if he lived or died.

To hell with Mbe and this entire show. There was nothing left for him here. Mbe had probably suspected worse…a bomb, or a shooting the way Eystrigg had been killed, in his own car. It was every man for himself now. He threw a quick punch that knocked Kilmer backwards.

“Ho-ho!” Perez said. “Little gravy bird, he’s going crazy.”

Several men wrestled Jared under control. Kilmer rose, holding a gun in one hand and his wounded eye with the other hand.

“Don’t shoot him,” Perez ordered. “Let’s lock him up down deep in case we need him later.”

Kilmer abruptly said, “All right, we’ll put him away for later. We haven’t got time to waste with him now.” He glared at Jared as if to say, we’ll deal with you later.

Something struck Jared on the back of the head and he lost consciousness.

19. Raskia

Cyrus Mbe was starting to grow desperate, fighting for his political and maybe soon his blood life. He'd never realized how alone a lifetime of climbing the ranks at any cost had left him.

"Mr. Chairman, the Delegate from Mercury Free Port City pleads that, on behalf of the people of the Galaxy, he be permitted to speak on the matter of the Bread Fleet."

Mbe's secretary was reading the plea before the packed Assembly Hall.

"No," a cynical voice interrupted from Raskia. "Just on behalf of the Mercurians."

Mbe wiped the palms of his hands with his handkerchief, under the podium where no one should see, so that they wouldn't know he was frightened and nervous.

Malecan Bohr deliberated. He had to. He was new, and he did not want to make any mistakes. Mbe saw him reading from the Orders of Assembly. Oh god. Mbe himself had been instrumental in seeing a ridiculously incompetent figure elected, because in a showdown between Mercury and Raskia, where hopefully Mercury was the more powerful in the Hall, there was no place for a strong neutral chairman who might bend either way. Now he was apprehensive. He began to feel the battle was impossible to win.

True to expectations, Bohr asked the question that should be asked according to prescribed form, but which had been voted out years before: "Are there any objections to our hearing Mr. Mbe?"

YES YES YES YES YES YES

YES YES

The stars above shone unperturbed: The eyes that knew, and were not touched. The cold eyes of the Universe.

From all over the Assembly House the shouting rang out. A pulsing chant.

Ankh, Ankh, Ankh...

Cyrus could see the stony faced Raskians' eyes filled with gloating that their will was being carried out for them by these suicidal, sectarian fools. He'd sacrificed Fallon, and he'd sent Bowman to Procyon as an admiral to try and save the fleet and the whole situation.

No cost was too great now to save Mercury FPC. What had to be done had to be done.

Poor Bowman. Poor Fallon.

20. Underworld

Jared woke in a dark cell somewhere deep underground, feeling a headache.

Olympia House. Must be.

All was dark. Where was he? His mouth was gagged with a (rag?) coarse and oily and tight-hard as an iron clamp. It stretched his lips back until it seemed they must split. And if they had split he was too numb to feel it. His hand sand feet were bound behind his back. Glowering violet lights floated before his eyes. He strained to see, but black nothingness revealed nothing.

He began to panic, sweating profusely. He lay as flat as possible, afraid perhaps he as on top of a thin tower in an underground building that rustled with winds from cold, deathly regions. If he moved he would roll off, into the pincers of a giant crab five miles below waiting to devour his mangled, fallen body. Or perhaps he was on a platform on top of a chopstick-obelisk, turning as the Plutonian winds commanded, like a child's toy: A human propeller atop a stick.

In his imaginings in the darkness he was distorting shapes and figures, and his fear-driven mind he leapt to a new proposition: That he lay at the edge of a trap, ready to fall in, and he listened for the sounds of the beast-devourer.

Still worse, he heard sounds. His cheeks were numb from the gag. He remembered wildly that drowning people often swallow their tongues, and his heart beat, and he fought to breathe. The darkness pressed in around him like a stifling mold, and breath became more and more difficult.

He tried to cry out, but no words would leave his throat. He had already forgotten the gag. A lump in his throat was choking him. Gradually he felt himself sinking into a stupor. His struggles ceased under a nightmarish euphoria of pain and terror and death-fear. Like a small child crying itself to sleep in the dark room, Jared began to sleep.

In the unfathomable gloom a hand crawled down Jared's back. Immediately he was fully alert. His hair stood on end, and he sweated. Droplets gathered under his eyes and nose. He dared not move.

Icy wet flesh came to rest on the flesh of his own bound hands. He shut his eyes in revulsion and gritted his teeth, praying for delivery.

The hand began to pry at his bonds.

At the same time, a soft light flickered on.

A woman's voice said: "Are you all right?"

Jared whirled. "Stella." He felt a wash of relief, looking into her peacefully flickering clouds of neuro facial features. Sine waves, randomized flickering, blots and comets flying from cheek area to cheek area, even the suggestion of a broad smile and warm eyes. Her underlying blondeness shone through. She carried genes from a variety pack of some type. Lyxa was dark-haired. So the people who cloned these *djia* people carefully programmed in variety to add genetic strength.

"I am here to free you, Jared."

"How did you find me?"

"Lelli."

Jared thought for a moment. Of course, Lyxa's *djia.* They communicated via some ether cloud of their own, as Stella had done by holding hands and schmoozing with Edzar at poolside.

Jared sat up, free now, and rubbed his wrists. "So glad to see you." They were still in danger, but he wasn't alone anymore, and at least he saw more hope now.

"I am pleased to see you also, Jared." Her voice was warmer than her formal words were.

"How did Lelli know where to find me?"

"Lyxa has a tracker on you that you do not know about. She had it embedded in your neural tree."

He stretched his aching limbs one way, then the other. "That must make me part *djia*, eh?"

Damn, she knows every move I make, and she never told me.

She rested her hands on his shoulders, and he felt a wave of fondness emanating from her. Deep, warm fondness that filled him with love for her, which he was not sure she could reciprocate—at least not in the same way. Not on the same wavelength. He put his hands over hers and squeezed gently. "Thanks, Stella."

"I'm happy to serve you." She added. "I am happy to be with you." She nearly came closer to hug him—he could tell—but she hesitated and drew back.

He kissed each of her hands. "I am happy that you came."

She said: "I had a contact from Lelli, asking about you. Lyxa wanted to know if you were all right. I was at the apartment in the BOQ where you told me to stay."

"Oh my god. I was worried about you, Stella. Were you scared?"

"We don't scare easily, Jared. I had enough to keep me going."

She had explained to him once, in their late night conversations, that she did not eat or drink like humans, but consumed energy. She was phototropic, like a plant, and could absorb sunlight. Or she could wipe static electricity from walls and charge up that way. There were many ways she could draw energy to replenish her charges. She also absorbed nutrients out of air, and she could stick her hands into water and they acted like tree roots, pulling molecules of this and that into her system. She would have had enough to keep her going.

"Did you feel alone?"

She hesitated. "I was alone."

"I know. You are sometimes so literal minded. Were you scared?"

"There is fighting in the city. I heard bombers and explosions outside the Dome." She paused, narrowing the focus to her immediate surroundings where he had left her. "I was worried when I heard men yelling but they were simply drunk, I think. I relied on my faith in you. That you would come be with me again."

"Oh my dear." He nearly cried at the thought of her child-like loyalty. "You are loyal, aren't you?"

"We are made to be loyal and to serve. If that is what love is, then I love you with all my being."

"I love you also, Stella. A man could not have a truer friend."

"I would give my life for you, Jared."

He squeezed her hands together and held them to his chin, where he kissed them two or three times. "I would die for you too, Stella." The difference was that in her, it was programmed, though the logic was complex and fuzzy and of a much higher order than a simple automaton's. In his case, as a fully human man, he could not imagine all the permutations whereby he might or might not throw himself under a land car for her, or something drastic like that. It wasn't worth making a lengthy truth table of it. They were in the moment, reunited, a man and his *djia*, and what more could he ask?

"Lelli tracked you, and reported her findings to Lyxa, who ordered Lelli to tell me to come find you. So here I am. Now we must escape and go see Lyxa."

"I can just imagine," Jared said drily. "Right about now, that sounds like a very good option."

21. Sun King

Cyrus wearily tried to managed the circus that had until recently been the UGO Starmeer or General Assembly. He still controlled the Interior government to some extent, but Exterior, to which he had devoted his best years as Delegate, was slipping away from him. Killing Chao had been a terrible mistake. How had he allowed that? Oh yes, *delusions...*

Raskia was tired of waiting. Chase popped up. "Mr. Chairman!"

"Yes."

"Raskia retracts any objection. Let the Delegate from Mercury City cease these inanities and make his statement—a sensible one, I hope."

Acting Chairman Alger Bohr, delegate of Ramatam in the Aldeb system, bit his lip, holding a hand to his ear.

Mbe watched in growing frustration and anger. Bohr listened... to someone on his earpiece... Then he said: "You may proceed, Mr. Mbe. Begin your statement. Raskia has waived her objection."

Mbe grabbed a policeman sitting idly in the seat of one of the advisors. "Go find that guy who's talking to Bohr and shut him up. Kill him if you have to!" The policemen gaped uncomprehendingly. Mbe gestured angrily: "The man that's telling Bohr how to—"

"Mr. Mbe!" Chase screamed. Bohr banged his gavel once, weakly, but sat frozen when Chase stared at him.

"Excuse me, Mr. Chairman," Cyrus said, directing his apology well past the Raskian. "Ladies, gentlemen, what I have to say to you is brief and simple. I won't even go to the Pit to say it. I just wish to clarify the position of Mercury City and her allies about losing the warship *Exalted* and other matters. Now, as in the past, forever we stand as simple servants... (Cyrus' attention faded in and out after two days with minimal sleep) ...Certainly the most outrageous accusation! How have we ever infringed on Raskian integrity? Have we blocked the path to the Assembly Hall? No! Their answer is to invade and devastate our ally Procyon...

On and on he talked, writing a message on a scrap of paper. He addressed it to the National Police Chief. He gave it to the policeman, and the policeman ran. Save him...

Seeing the policeman run off, Chase jumped to his feet. "Mr. Chairman!"

"Now, Mr. Chase..."

"Nossir! Delegate is talking to stall for time."

"Mr. Chase, you are out of order."

"Nossir! This is illegal!"

"He is entitled to one hour of speaking before…"

"Nossir! He has been speaking for more than ten hours this session, and said absolutely nothing!"

"Chase," Bohr screamed, rising, "sit the hell down and shut your fat ugly mouth."

The Hall burst into laughter, while Chase rushed forward in a swirl of fanciful white Regulean linen. Half the delegates had not appeared, and dozens were walking out. "I demand that Mercury be silenced permanently!"

Bohr pounded his gavel.

Mbe anxiously sent prayers after the policeman

Chase declared, quoting Ankh scriptures: "I am here on behalf of the people of divine Raskia to free you and your loved homelands from *frater frater* the demon who mocks and scorns you and calls you while holding behind his back the whip, the shackles, and the cockles!!!"

Silence resigned. This was Chase's proclamation over the din. Sifting out of the confusion among the standing delegates and out of the galleries dark phantom figures moved, and shots rang out.

Mbe sat stunned. The Hall quieted slowly down in a sheer, fascinated horror. Silence was like a heavy weight while the Raskian henchmen took strategic positions unnoticed: The silence was general and instinctive, and there was only Chase:

Chase had torn off his billowing white garment. Now he stood resplendent in the scarlet-and-gold uniform of an ancient Denebean Sun King, his jeweled aegis radiant with deep lights, his feathered golden helmet topped by a golden disc like the sun itself.

A great eagle—a pet Scarlet Monarch, probably from Ramoor A—rose behind him and soared in glorious circles around the Hall and when it could find no way out, beat about angrily before landing in the Pit and strutting slowly, threateningly, here and there. Chase approached it cautiously and stroked its head, his voice once more loud:

Eat no more burrs, nor drink vinegar in his barren land!

Cyrus sat motionless, staring with misty fascination at the guns leveled at his face. The chairman was alone on the Bridge. His head lay backwards over his seat, and his exposed neck was scarlet; he was dead.

A shout rang out behind Cyrus, cutting through the fog. "Mr. Mbe! To the floor!" The Delegate, seeing the startled expressions on the gun men's faces, turned dreamily.

A battery of fire erupted and Raskians crumpled all over the Assembly Hall. Many delegates also fell. Cyrus felt himself lifted, carried through the din, and let his eyes rest relieved on the arms that held him: The forest green of the National Police. He was manhandled until he lost all awareness, slipping out of range, in a hail of glimmering lights.

So died Cyrus Mbe, leader of nations.

With him died any last hope for Mercury Free Port City, and the human order in the galaxy that Mercury had led for a thousand years.

22. Surrender of Procyon

Jesse Bowman sat by a window in a field command outpost in a desert on one of the Procyon planets. A chill wind blew through thin air outside.

Bowman, formerly aide to Cyrus Mbe, but now an admiral of the star fleets, clutched the papers in his hand, feeling them get soggier and soggier with sweat. He was about to surrender the entire allied military fleets to the victorious Ankhmen and their Raskian underwriters. Bowman sat with thirty Procyonian generals in a large, wood-floor room. In one corner, three female officers were hurriedly burning some remaining bundles of documents.

Jesse cast a glance over his shoulder at the Procyonians. Old grizzled veterans of ancient space wars whose very names were legendary: Zemelman, Pochin, Tiehfahr, Vitane. They were of the same burnt color as the dark-brown tobacco they chewed, burned by the light-streams of a trillion stars. Two or three junior officers sat with their heads in their arms. Many had committed suicide. The old ones waited for the final indignity, hum-hawing or smoking or snoring, collapsed like old sacks in their chairs. A few appeared drugged.

Waiting.

The capital city was in flames on the horizon. Its dull death rumble drifted across the jumbled slums and sleeping suburbs to the proud old redoubt at the edge of the Mountain of the Gods.

Waiting.

Jesse looked out. The window sill wood was covered with dust and flaking paint. It had been raining out, and a moist, cold air blew in. Sounds rose and fell heart-shakingly over the general clamor of explosions and air screams and vehicles. The light was poor. He smelled dingy walls and wet, gravelly back-courts. Outside, ground cars drew up with loud engines and banging doors and a brief fusillade of gunfire. Then only voices yelling, feet pounding, wood splintering, hallway echoes. Jesse shivered as he held the surrender papers.

23. Underworld

"What are you thinking, Jared?" asked Stella.

They sat facing each other on the floor in the gloomy cell deep in the underworld beneath Olympia House.

"I'm wondering if we should risk making a run for it."

"I was worried, but my focus was on tracking you."

"What did you encounter?"

She folded her hands together in her lap and looked down at them, as if gazing into a cloud of memories. "I went down, down, down. Sometimes the stairs were broken. Everything here is very ancient. A thousand years, I would guess. In some places I had to hide because scary creatures went stalking by."

"Like what?"

"Fighters from other worlds. Things that looked like dinosaur chickens with faces from hell, and long deadly claws. I feared for my life. More than that, I feared that you would lose me so I couldn't help you."

"You poor sweet thing. Those must be the combatants for the arena."

"So I would guess. Others were android or robotic. I was able to model their electron flow configurations and calculate how to disable them if necessary."

"Did you have to disable any?"

"One."

"How did that go?"

"He was a very large, lumbering wetbot made from animal cells and steel parts. He smelled me, I think, and snarled and came running toward me in a dark corridor full of hazy light. He had big teeth and yelled very loudly. I could see down his throat. His mouth was red inside, and wet with hunger and saliva. I was able to scan his instruction boards and de-instruct him."

"And?"

"He fell down dead and started burning and sparking."

"Brave girl."

"I was scared."

"You were."

"I was."

"I am proud of you."

"I will help you if you want to leave here."

Jared rose and hugged her. "We'll do it together."

"I will go with you."

It was so Stella. What did that mean? *I will go with you...*

A thousand things. *I trust you. I am loyal to you. I am yours...*

I love you.

Time down here was meaningless because there was neither day nor night—just eternal darkness since ages ago.

Stella had found him, had managed to pick the lock using her holoprobing fingertips, and had opened the cell where he had been left to die of hunger and thirst. Those goons were never going to return.

Hand in hand, they started walking on the dry, dusty stone floors.

Some areas were pitch-dark. Others were illumined by sickly green phosphor mushrooms growing in crevices.

The huge flooring blocks were dotted with bits of rock that had crumbled over centuries.

They were in the underworld.

Beasts howled constantly in the distance. It was a death-wail from another world. A great carnivore, stolen from its jungle or canyon somewhere in the galaxy, made this sonorous, endless mourning song that reverberated and picked up the death songs of other doomed living things.

At one point, cautiously taking one step after another, he thought: Orpheus with no Eurydice. Then he realized that she was there beside him, a demi-human right out of mythology. This time they would either leave the underworld together, or perish together while trying.

In some places there was a lot of pressure. His head pounded, and he seemed to hallucinate. The mourning song of beasts ebbed and flowed as they passed from one region to another.

Glowing things fluttered by. A flaming bat flashed past. Evolutionary adaptations to ocean bottom. Did the universe still exist? Was his past life real, or was the only reality this stinking hole, with eternal fear and acid boredom? Had he perhaps grown out of the walls here, with a set of dreamlike memories of a never-never life built into him?

"I'm cracking!"

She held his hand all the more firmly, squeezing it.

"Can you get a signal from outside?" he asked.

Her facial waves contorted, then relaxed. She shook her head. "Too deep." She strained once more. "Not even Lelli."

They passed through intermediary rooms of unknown purpose. In one of them, a desiccated, mummified dinosaur creature lay slumped in a corner, as if it had died while trying to stand on its huge hind claws one last time. All creatures were desperate to save their lives.

He shuddered at the thought of the mountainous bulk of the Olympia House surrounding him. If but one of these hundred-ton blocks (and they were in the myriads) should fall...

At times the pressure eased, and he was relieved to feel a cold breeze, though tainted with a smell of animal manure and rotting meat or blood.

He tried to clear his mind of such thoughts. Once more Jared turned to his stack of books. He knew them too well to be captivated in any way, and let them fall from him. Nonsense words about a nonsense world that did not exist for him here.

Still squeezing his hand timorously, Stella said: “I hear water.”

“Oh no. What now?” Jared whispered.

They stopped and listened.

A waterfall?

Olympia House was flooding rapidly.

Jared looked at the walls in this sector.

“Corridor level has been going faintly downhill,” Stella said.

The ancient Olympia house walls had many deep-gouged holes. The walls had once been white perhaps, but now they were corroded by urine and furrowed by huge claws, and had merged into an overall tone of blackish desiccation-film. The stone surfaces were coated with a hardened black sludge like dried oil, stinking, out of which grew mosses and lichens, even tiny ferns among which colonies of fireflies drifted.

She touched a spot. Her finger, she showed him, came away glittering wet. “Fresh water.”

Clear water ran down the walls, onto the floor, and the rotten black glistened with motion. Jared looked closer. It was water, struggling with impurities, moving slow, but seeming to increase slowly in speed.

The gouge marks spoke of many struggles, marks old as antiquity. Perhaps some small scratch might attest to the fact that once had lived a Jared Fallon, and died here in small struggle against the onrushing waters.

Somewhere, water had broken loose and was fighting its way through the dead burrows of the Olympia house.

Maybe someone had broken a huge feed pipe above. Or bombs had destroyed a section of the complex.

In the uncountable cells and halls and arenas underneath Olympia House, an ocean circulated. An ocean was circulating in the death house. There must be this much water, gathered in rain pools and cisterns to sustain fighters and animals. The water was held apart by pipes centuries old but the end promised to be a final, fatal brackish unity drowning everything.

Jared pictured him and Stella being tiny dots, insects, helpless atoms, sixty floors below the surface of the earth, among the beasts and gladiators, as the waters closed over him, this soupy sea.

They’d be dead even as their eyes slipped shut while the tide crushed them in its dark arms against studded walls.

The sea would tear to pieces the age-old horror that had made a galaxy shudder…

Somewhere sounded a dull, thunderous POO**OO**MM as a billion tons of stone shifted weight by a fraction of an inch. The monster was buckling.

Now the ceiling was sweating thin drops. Mother of the City! No time for caution now!

Jared and Stella, holding hands, ran for their lives.

"This way," she said, pointing to a slight up-slope in a wide side corridor.

The cosmic mourning song, the death dirge of dying monsters, crooned on and on.

A door crashed down nearby.

Thousands of bestial screams echoed through the stone corridors.

GO! GO! Jared's mind screamed.

Now far down the hall, standing on splintered wood and piled stone, hulked something out of a nightmare, momentarily looking the other way, outlined in a steam of body heat.

GO GO GO.

Jared pulled Stella in a different direction, in this maze of corridors. He was dismayed by the loud slapping of their shoes on slimy cobbles.

Stella fell once, slithered into a rough wall, but he pulled her gently up with both hands and they ran on.

Images pursued him: Terror images of water and fear and beasts and even brought a cry from his throat. But he forced himself to the stairs and clambered up on his hands and knees until the savage battle ceased and he stood up. Stella swept silently along behind him. He put his hand to the wall to steady himself, but felt a sharp sting and drew his hand away. It was bloody. The wall was studded with glass blades. How cruel this Olympia House was!

A few feet away something bellowed thunderously as they just barely made it past a set of long blackish horn claws reaching out in fear and hunger.

Jared and Stella ran on and on, never pausing, never looking back.

Many little corridors led off to the sides, foul and black, with hell alone knew what hideous creatures might be wallowing in their filth…maybe there was no way out? *Panic…*

Many false hopes kept them going. Once the ground changed, became cry, sloping up.

"Watch for dead ends and blind passages," she said, sounding winded.

"We have no other choice but to keep going."

So they continued on, still holding hands.

They hurried up the dry slope, around corners, until they came to steps. These led them another two flights up. There he faced a dead end.

Sorrowful at the loss of hope and precious moments, they retraced their path.

"Some of these are illusions," she said in a burst of sudden insight.

"What do you mean?"

"They made a house of mirrors to fool escaping prisoners and animals."

What fiendish planners! He realized that in some places the walls looked strange, like digital constructs with poorly, vaguely planned fibers and pixels.

Some areas that looked like walls were actually empty air with illusions painted in, and mixed up with phosphor fungi and biolume colonies of tiny things that looked as if they were floating in underwater currents.

Is there such a thing as underair?

How deep are we here anyway?

"Got to keep moving," he said. Their hands slipped apart as they grew weary. "Stay by me."

"I stay by you," she said in that strange, lilting tropical *Samba* tone.

Pleasing to the end... like a song...

He fell to his knees and for a moment lost hope.

Stella helped him stagger back up, and they moved on, slower now.

How dry... The air was flat and dead. Pressure hammered at Jared's temples, trying to drive him back. But he held his to his temples and stumbled forward.

Amid mounting vertigo, Jared saw open cage doors in a corridor.

Oily slowness paralyzed him, almost a death wish. *Get it over with. Surrender...*

Once again, Stella put her hands on his waist, his hips, as if lifting him along.

They passed cages with long ago missing gratings that had fallen outward. In the cages, they glimpsed mounds of dry, unbleached bones, tufted with hair and bits of leathery skin, on strewings of bone-hard manure and blackened straw.

Too dry! Such a stench and heat and pressure amid that endless howling, echoing, crooning of dying creatures slipping into dark sea water to swim home among the stars…

Death song of the universe...

As they moved through this underworld, Jared became all the more conscious of life, and death, and truth all around him. His galaxy, his cosmos, had been founded as an empire of greed and power. Maybe that was the way of all things—the struggle to survive, the constant combat, displays of power, the games on gladiator sands…

Humans had taken the atomic stuff of life itself, their own DNA, and fashioned playthings for themselves or to sell to the idle rich. Brains grown to fly starships but never to taste or feel or smell, but perhaps to despair for centuries pushing cargo and settlers among the stars. Brain boxes, they were called. Or a casual sketch like Lelli or Stella… was that really lawful?

Somehow, there was justice in the overthrowing of that human order. Were the aliens any better, or merely another form of predator that would do anything to survive and protect its brood? Philosophy and anoxia and melancholia and phantasmagoria seemed to grow around him like throbbing fungi in the walls. *I am losing my mind...*

That firm, loving hand grasped his own hand and kept pulling him along.

So cold!

He looked up, shivering. They'd stumbled into a different region of the subterranean labyrinth somehow, and now stood side by side leaning against a white-washed wall.

Cold all around. Strange new light here. Instinctively Jared looked up. Light—good, hard, cold sky light—shone through the ventilation grills, one grill over the other, story over story, losing themselves toward the distant daylight.

Stella looked up also. "That's the way out."

"Yes. We just need to get there before we drown down here, or the beasts get us."

It was still a wan light. It was more depressing than no light at all, because it seemed so far away, tantalizing and unreachable.

The strange cistern smell drew deeper horror into his soul. Walking in the eerie light of bacterial lights dying after these after these centuries of neglect, Jared began to hear a steady slapping sound. Stella, taking his hand again, also looked puzzled. Louder and louder the sound grew, until he knew it was water, falling in torrents from the ceiling and gushing out of the unmortised walls. Farther on the corridor dipped downward, and water flowed hard down there.

He and Stella Impulsively turned and ran another way.

An overwhelming vapor of water was in the air like a death sentence. Water murmured distantly, dripping in cascades from ceilings throughout the Olympia House.

Once he tripped over something in the middle of the floor. Gingerly he probed with his hands, unable to see. His fingers tightened around a thick bar of metal. It was a grill. That meant there were more floors below, and they would have to fill with water before it could ascend to this level.

Jared listened as water swirled below him, and he smelled something like cold breath brought in with a November wind.

The water was less than six inches below him already. He saw a momentary dull glitter and it was instantly extinguished by filth, or possibly drifting fur.

"It's dead," Stella said with quiet finality.

If they didn't get out soon, they'd be drifting along the ceiling just like that poor beast! He closed his eyes at the brief vision of a heavy, motionless body drifting swaying along the corridor below, along the water-filled canal, already far, far away in the subterranean current.

Those huge, invisible alien animals resumed howling their grief-stricken, heart-broken funeral dirge. It rose into a blood-curdling, terrible chorus. They sang their death chant somewhere—maybe while feasting on the grisly remains of their keepers?

All that rage against the system... against the dying city that had done this to them...

Now they were walking uphill again, passing cells that showed some signs of life.

There came a shrill wailing of women prisoners.

"We're closer to the human side of the prison now," Stella said. She held her head, looked upward, and strained the circling, dancing yellow and blue geometries of her face. Then she stopped, shook her head, and said: "Still no signal."

They continued on.

They stood before a stairway, and for a minute or so didn't know it was a stairway.

Jared and Stella climbed on, and climbed up until they lost all sense of direction except upward. He all sense of time, all sense of distance. They climbed through dark areas and lighter areas until at last they began to perceive a dim shimmering around the corner, up another flight of stairs.

Coming to a landing, they knew they were on the right path.

The lights here were very bright in comparison to those below, and the walls were newer, though just as filthy…these were not black, just excrement-brown, and lacking the gougings.

An endless wide corridor stretched ahead. On either side were very large cages, and in the cages were the lowest human being Jared had ever seen. He saw them in the dimness of the recesses, bodies filthy and hair-choked, flaming with disease. As Jared passed slowly, they cried out in a tongue that achingly recalled the nearly forgotten language of the living. Jared began to run the gauntlet, holding Stella's hand. She ducked and made her profile as small as she could, staying close behind him as he towed her along.

Here a gray face implored, there a red-eyed face cursed him, here a terror-filled face peered out of darkness, there a gloomy mute glowered at him. Filthy, crippled hands reached out to them from behind bars. Huge eyes implored…

Jared ran until he fell and breathed flecks of blood on a concrete stair.

Stella sounded lumbering and winded behind him. How long could she go on?

Metal crashed behind him. There were howls of joy, as a number of half-men broke out. Jared pushed Stella ahead to protect her. He heaved himself up with a last effort and stumbled up the few remaining stairs. *Where now?*

Ahead, walls.

An open door, sagging at the hinges.

Freedom…

Jared held Stella close as they jumped out among them into a wind of clean air and ran in the darkness.

Gunfire broke out somewhere, and guards shouted to each other.

Lights flared up and engines raced as the prison force rallied to close their horror back up, to keep the underworld in its place.

Animals howled—faintly now, because Jared and Stella had found their way back to the world of the living.

Their breathless, terrified running stopped when his head bumped against something.

What? He stood holding his head, and laughed.

He had bumped his head on the bottom of a seat. There were tens of thousands of these seats, attached to metal and concrete, overlooking an empty arena.

Jared hauled himself up into the high, cold, busy night of the light-filled city. It was a homecoming after generations. He stood among the high bleachers and the wild wind was music in his head. He pulled Stella up with him, and they sat marveling, side by side.

Their run of terror was over. They had made it alive out of the underworld of Mercury FPC. They had encountered brutal truth and faced it heroically. Now they could resume normal, tiny lives out here in the real world, even as it was falling apart but was a long way from the horror they had seen in the depths.

He looked down into the giant arena. It was empty, the perfect picture of a prison at night. In the center was the pit, the combat area.

He looked with detachment at the glittering silver tongue of water extending like heavy, molten metal to the center of the arena. It was an empty-vessel arena, discarded, tilted and half-wet, half-dry like an old can. Something—maybe a huge bomb somewhere in the city, dropped by Raskian orbital subs, had rocked the earth, shifted the ground, and tilted this arena. It had dislodged the sea of water circulating in the O House, and caused massive flooding.

The gleaming dangerous half-moon of water on the sands below seemed almost solid, so still was it. But Jared knew that, inch by inch, the cohesive teeth of water were extending themselves across the sand. A drowning world, tape spinning off its silent reel, moving outward from the strengthless sun of lost youth…

Where to go?

Nowhere.

It was a good night for the stars, looking beyond the occasional combat raider, swinging search lights, ragged clouds and gleaming moon. High above the city hung the glowing discs of the superlevels, small cities in their own right, shining in the drifting, patchy clouds of pinfire. The many moons of Mercury hung waxen, surrounded by heavy traffic, traffic high and purposeful. And Jared wished he could be part of all that highness and purposefulness.

Somewhere out here was Aldebaran II, a barren hulk of acid seas and deadly gases. There was Raskia, ever watchful evil eye of a Cyclops, glaring into the very bowels of her arch-enemy as a madman might look into a jar in which lay exposed the working innards of his victim…

24. Arena

Jared sat exhaustedly on a stone wall overlooking the great round expanse of sand below—one of the arenas, the sands—overlooked by tens of thousands of seats now empty except for patchy, scudding moonlight amid rain squalls.

The sky was filled with oscillating searchlights. Aircraft with blinking lights moved this way and that. Distant explosions could be heard, unintelligible faint crowds screaming down in the city, and frequent rattles of gunfire.

Stella stood motionlessly. "I am in touch with Lelli."

"What does she have to say?"

"Lyxa wants us to travel with her."

Jared looked about, heartbroken. His city, his dreams, his everything:

Forever gone...

"What choice do we have?" He shrugged. "I want you to be safe. And there is nothing left for me here. Where is she going?"

"The Holy House is evacuating to Arcturus."

Jared nodded. Of course. That had been the meaning of the servants moving luggage in the palace. They'd already been evacuating. Lyxa was always ahead of the game.

"Will we go?" Stella stood facing him.

He regarded her, overcome by her loyalty. She didn't ask if he were going, or what he thought she should do. It was entirely up to him. She was his *djia*, his personal assistant, his demi-woman, his diaphane.

"Yes, we'll go."

"I am telling Lelli." She paused to receive. "Lelli says Lyxa is glad."

"Tell Lelli to tell Lyxa we are grateful."

A moment passed. "Lyxa tells Lelli that you must carry the Torch for her."

Jared looked out over the city, patting his palm absently on the heavy, lichenous rampart high up over Olympia House. "Tell her I will carry the Torch for her. Stay with me Stella so you'll be safe. We have someplace to go."

They made their way down into the arena, to cross the sand and emerge on public streets through a stone gate he could see dimly ahead.

Despite distant explosions and gunfire, here twilight shimmered in the stillness among stone pillars and metal girders. A cold, clean wind blowing around him as he realized sadly that the City of the Universe was swinging outward in its orbit toward winter. This would be eternal winter.

Phantom leaves brushed drily against the girders and drifted endlessly to come to rest at various elevations with the gentle tic of an egg shell breaking.

Jared squeezed Stella's hand as they walked with assurance now, no longer running in terror for their lives. They felt night's timeless caresses.

The wind was turning colder. A wind bringing this and that longing.

Memories...

He put one arm around her solid woman waist and pulled her closer. She pressed against him as they shared warmth in the brisk air.

His mind was far, far away…

Lethe...

Forgetfulness, a planet, a river, a crossing of eternal peace beyond reach from these trials…

25. Attack

Jared and Stella made their way along deserted, shadowy city streets. On either side loomed the decorative house fronts with shuttered windows. Ivy and gargoyles, baby angels and ancient forest gods with pointy beards—all of humankind's venerable mythology crawled on the walls here amid purplish-ashen shadows seeping across age-darkened stucco surfaces.

One moment, there was only the crowded sky full of lights.

Then, out of nowhere, came black ships: First, darting, thrusting beams from nothing; then exploding or crippled vehicles sinking to earth on flames slow as crumpling, listless flames; then the coal-black, space-colored ships flitting distance-silent like shadows obscuring the stars.

Finally, only silence.

The ships were gone.

In the heavens the moving lights ran running amuck, scattered fireflies in voiceless panic.

In the City was distant, mute burning.

Who could ever have imagined the City of the Universe so crippled, now dying?

It was something Jared only half-perceived, and only half understood. It was a thing of the eyes only, until the wind brought scorch smells to his nose, diluted by distance.

Wind keened around sharp corners, stirred up by the turbulence of distant burning.

Particles flew erratically in warm, chaotic breezes.

Jared led Stella along these familiar streets, which now looked almost foreign, if not alien.

They walked on broad, proud Olympic Avenue.

The crowds now were panicky, not festive. Vanished forever were Father Mercury and his halcyon nymphs. This mass of bodies surged in anger and fear about the air raid, about their growing hunger, the lack of drinking water, the breakdown of society. They shouted, waved fists, overturned ground cars, smashed windows, fought among each other, killed anyone who looked different. They behaved as their kind had in every society since humans had first walked upright.

Jared quickly led Stella along. She had her face veiled so the mob could not see she was different. In a moment, the ignorant fools might blame her, turn on her, kill her as a scapegoat to take out their frenzy before moving on to other victims, other destruction.

Three exceedingly tall monks from alien Aleazar stood at crowd's edge, their slender wine-red robes blowing in the wind. They took no notice of him. They watched the sky, blank-eyed, sharp-browed, swaying slightly with the rhythm of their vagaries.

"Wipe out the rebels," a fresh sign read, plastered on the wall. "Support your government."

One group tore the sign down. Another group tried to rescue the sign.

Then the various factions began slugging and stabbing each other.

With Stella in tow, Jared got past these mob scenes, through quiet streets, and made his way to an unexpected place.

Across deserted fields that made the city lights seem distant, he and Stella walked briskly and with purpose.

The smell of grass, wind-blown in these vacant lots, brought back a memory. Jared remembered Lethe, the green summer planet at the fringe of the man-galaxy. Sit all day smoking *tuma* leaves in perfect tranquility and wooded grove became stained-glass cathedral, bird-and-insect choir, sheeps' dirty pelts like a creamy fragrance…

Far from this place…

They came to a bench in Victory Park in the heart of the City. Above soared the Arch of Triumph, out of darkness near the earth like a delicate wire thing, crossing the stars with five thousand flashing air-lights, in a ten-mile arc from which Jared had once descended crowned with victory and lifted on the people's shoulders and carried over the crossroads of the galaxy, Victory and Olympic Avenues, in a glory that had gone but lived on somewhere…

Somewhere…

"Lelli calls," Stella said.

Jared and rested for a moment side by side on the stone bench.

"Lelli says that Lyxa awaits us."

Jared nodded. "Tell them we are coming."

They walked again among decaying brick buildings, unkempt grasses and wild scrubby trees. Trash littered the park that had once been so proudly kept. Back in the days when humans still ran in the races, and carried the Torch. He'd been the last.

They came to a small metal gate unevenly closed upon an entrance in a long brick wall.

Jared banged on the steel with his fist, and listened for signs of life.

Soon enough, the gate opened on rusty hinges. A confused, bedraggled figure peered out cautiously.

"Do you remember who I am?" Jared called out.

"What in hell do you think you're doing here?"

"I'm Jared Fallon. I ran the Arch once. You handed me the torch. Remember?"

"Hm. So you did. Ran the Arch? Hm. Can't say that I remember your face. Course, we both wore uniforms then." The elderly man squinted at Jared. "When did you run?"

"Just a few years ago."

The old man's eyes narrowed suspiciously. "Are you sure you ain't from the police? I ain't done a thing!"

"No, I'm not from the police. But let me in. Please? I'd like very much to see the inside of the Arch again."

"I'm not supposed to."

"No one cares anymore."

"No, I'm not supposed to."

"Who gave you your orders?"

"Olympia House."

"They don't exist anymore. It's just an empty, flooded hulk. The guards don't exist anymore. And I'm…I was…" Jared didn't finish the thought. "Tell me, how many years has it been since anyone ran the Arch?"

"Umh…let's see—now, of course, only those goddamn machines run the victory lap." He glared defiantly: "I don't talk to them, and they don't talk to me. It's all just lights and music and drama for stupid people hanging in bars, who'll cheer at anything."

Jared said, "I feel the same way."

The old man reflected. His eyes seemed to be looking through the Arch and into the past. "The Torch, now, it seems a long time since any of you fellows has come to run the Arch…"

"Not so many years."

"And moving fast. I'll be gone, and this thing will fall down or…"

Jared quickened. "The Torch? You still have it?"

"What? Oh, the Torch. Yes, of course. The Torch…" he chuckled. His smile was illumined by the remaining lights still lit along the bottom of the Arch. Half the lights were out now, shattered and dark. The night was icy cold, especially high up in the thin air.

Jared elbowed his way past the man, into the little courtyard, where the Arch loomed close and massive overhead. Its end pillars were concrete, while its slender curve was metallic.

Jared patted his bony arm, feeling loose flesh. "Do you think I might see the Torch?"

"The Torch? My old legs…won't let me fetch things the way I used to."

"No, no! Let me get it! You just wait here." Jared walked briskly to the old man's shack. It was a little wood-frame house. The paint was all gone; gray, dry wood hung sadly, stirring but not stirring in the night air, as bones might seem to because of the memory of the life they had once held, but certainly the wind is like the breathlessness of a corpse on these nights, a face as though asleep not dead and hardly able to stir bones. *Desolation.*

The old man had probably long been forgotten. Probably lived by begging on Olympic Avenue. This was his home, amid the ghost of what had once seemed a glamorous position.

Inside was the smell of sweat and dirty clothes and burning wood. Jared's eyes roved in search of the Torch. He saw a bed, a shelf, a night table, a sprawl of clothes on the floor, a wood-burning stove.

Ah—there!

The Torch lay on a dusty, tiny wooden shelf over a bed of rumpled yellow flannel sheets. The Torch shone golden, probably polished once a day by its addled old keeper.

Jared hefted it. Its feel brought back the past. Jared weighed its lightness, gauged its thinness, its half-meter length, its ornature. It fit easily into his hand, and rested against his shoulder as if he'd never handed it back years ago.

Back outside, the old man tore it from his hands and held it to his chest. "You can't have it!"

Jared held out money. "For a little while?"

"No!"

Jared tugged at the Torch. He pulled out of the man's grasp and the old one flailed at him. "Give it to me! It's mine!"

Stella, veiled and mysterious, stood nearby with her garments fluttering slowly, like a ghost.

"Old man, it belongs to the city. It belongs to the victorious. You can't sit here in the darkness and hold it to you like your only comfort. Always someone new has to have it."

"But," the old one wailed, "let them have their own Torches!"

Jared shoved him away angrily. "Damn you, old leper. You handed it to me once, you'll hand it to me again! I'm still winning! I'm taking it over the Arch with me!"

"But bring it back!" Tears in his eyes, the old man implored: "I beg you. Bring it back!"

"I will," Jared said. But his mind said, Perhaps…but even that was a lie, because he knew he would never return.

"Come back! Bring me my Torch!" the old man cried loudly as Jared climbed into the Arch through a broken window. "It's forbidden!" he cried out.

"Meet me on the other side," Jared said. "I'll hand it back to you for safekeeping. Nobody will probably ever come to bother you again."

Jared's mind was filled with the cheering of millions.

"There's no turning back," he told Stella.

"Take me with you," she said in her lilting *Samba* voice.

As if he would go without her. He reached out, and she put her hand in his.

Together, carrying the glorious eagle and light, they began to alternately walk and jog up the slope of the Victory Arch in its glassy tube that rose hundreds of meters over the city skyline.

The plastic-concrete floor was still intact.

Stella stayed with him, running a meter behind to leave him in front with his glory.

Tiny grains of matter crackled under his feet as he ran.

Drape-like ghosts of memory whispered and faintly cheered him on from the shadow-hung braces running around the tube-like Arch. Smiles followed him in the drifting water-shadows of warps in the transparent upper hemisphere of the tube, and from puddles in the cracked floor.

Slowly the Torch made its ascent, unlit but glinting with a million borrowed lights.

Wind tattered softly all around him.

Stella kept up silently behind.

Tides of the great atmosphere sea rolled around him. The wind's great power made the streamlined body of the Arch tremble, creak, and groan.

He ran upward on the narrow thread, high and higher, over the air and to the stars.

Jared stumbled a few times, but always caught himself. He was a bit out of shape, and breathless as the curve brought him close to the stars amid thinner and colder air.

He paused at the top to rest and regard the city one last time. Stella stood nearby, enigmatic and silent in her wind-stirred veils.

He felt phantoms of his past strength return. He recalled the men and women who had run, jumped, hurled discus, swum, wrestled, a hundred great sports. He'd been the showpiece, the kilometer man, talk of the tabloids and master of the media in his brief moment of fame.

Always, the popular hunger moved on to the next sensation, and he'd been forgotten a day or two later. Then the media had picked him up again as the dashing, dark-haired companion of the extinct monarchy's last glamorous queen in waiting. Soon, that also had passed into history and forgetfulness.

"Ready. Let's move on." He resumed his run, with the Torch resting imperiously against one shoulder. He couldn't see the bottom yet, but it would be in sight soon.

There were no way signs, no distance markers, just a few delinquent rock fragments.

Silence.

Wind blew against the sides of the Arch.

"Are you with me?"

Jared's voice was lost in vastness. Wind and sky absorbed his tiny sound.

"I am always with you." Stella's voice was calm and flat, but she added: "Forever."

He did not descend into that waiting night with joy. His mind, wishing to be free, lost itself in a dream. He left behind the memory of cheering millions and light-banners crawling in the sky. His hunger, thirst, exhaustion, and the cold got to him suddenly…

As he trotted on erratically, he mind-wandered…He would roll himself in a ball and roll and bounce pastel-happy and drift into the waiting arms…

For a few minutes he was a being in space, a commander of his own ship, and finally realizing his childhood dream. He sat in the cockpit, comfortable in his bulky pressure suit with bubble helmet, and managed the controls as his ship sailed among stars and nebulae. There was no happier place than this. Lights winked in erratic musical rhythms and assorted dimly glowing colors. The display screens showed stars, stars, and more stars…

26. Dawn

Nothing can bring back the past and its lost dreams...

Dawn was just beginning to discolor the night a cold gray when Jared softly laid the little dead torch down before the iron gate leading out of the Arch of Triumph.

The gate was rusty and fall into the sand with a sound as Jared pushed on the iron.

The sand. There it was again, the sand on Victory Avenue. *Arena.*

Jared stared in the grim, dirty light. Once long ago they had waited for him here by the thousands. Millions had thronged the gate, and other millions had borne him on their shoulders up Victory Avenue to Olympic Avenue.

But what had become of Victory Avenue?

The wide street had been divided into three narrow alleys running between great, ugly tenement houses showing their raw, stained rears. Rusty fences penned in narrow, sterile lots of sand and wisps of trampled grass.

Behind Jared, the Arch leapt into the sky. It too was starting to show wear and neglect.

Where the hinges of the broken gate had been, a long, thin red line trailed into the sand. Jared leaned the gate against the doorway.

He walked out onto the former street of glory, now a wasteland of poverty, crime, and hopelessness, and soon to sink further as the galaxy's capital city fell under enemy assaults yet to come. He walked toward the waiting ground car. Behind him came his *djia*. He kicked the litter on Victory Avenue with his foot.

Sand, washed by rain, formed long, damp lagoons that extended into the street, with gritty humps where sand ran over discarded papers and over rocks. Children's footprints were everywhere. Children who ran barefoot here, because they never had shoes.

Parked by the curb were three powerful and impressive looking black cars that had officialness stamped all around them. Outside the middle of these armored cruisers stood Lyxa, who might once have been queen of all this. Beside her stood the ghostly figure of Lelli. Arrayed on either side were armed guards in merlot and brown livery, flaunting dark weapons and wearing black helmets.

"I'm glad to see you," Lyxa said with a broad, welcoming smile

He was, for once, happy to see her as he had not been in well over a year.

She waited to embrace him.

He slowed as Stella walked straight past into the presence of Lelli, who stepped forward. The two enigmatic figures stood face to face, screen to screen, and held hands communing in their silent world.

"You brought me my Stella back," Lyxa said fondly.

Jared stepped into her embrace, relieved and happy to be there. Whatever had happened, whatever was going to happen, nothing could be as grim or to run from as what he had been through the past day or two. In the short time since he'd returned from Alda Meina III, the world had fallen apart around him. Everything had changed.

Lyxa embraced him. She wore a luxurious wine-dark cloak for this *nostos*, this homecoming, which she draped over his shoulders so they were both smothered in its warmth and communion. "I have never stopped loving you," she said looking up at him with that dazzling girl smile, a look of innocent joy that was in the moment and not to be translated any further. Jared knew that, she knew that, and they accepted their fate together.

"Will you come to Arcturus with us?" she whispered.

"Yes," he said, squeezing her tightly to him.

The cloak fell away, the princess turned and raised her arm to command, and all the soldiers and officers around them snapped to attention. "Take us to the ferry port. We're on our way."

Jared turned for a last look at the Victory Arch. The old man had stumbled along to collect the Torch that Jared left for him. When Jared waved good bye, the old man waved thanks. The night was over, its deeds done, its compacts sealed, and the stars were veiled from revealing the fate of those who stood down below.

Lyxa kept a firm, loving grip on Jared's arm. She guided him into the rear lounge of her land cruiser. Footmen helped Lelli and Stella aboard. The two *djia* sat together with their veils down, holding each other by one hand, as they continued to handshake terrarrets of information. About what, Jared could only guess. Maybe they sang songs of eternal calculus together, in an ocean of exogravitation, the key to eternal time and infinite space where countless universes pulsed their brief lives before fading and making way for more short-lived universes flicking with auroras and compass point lights like the two demi-girls' digitally beautiful features. *No matter...*

All boarded and bristling with defensive weaponry, the three land cruisers rolled through the slums of Mercury Free Port City. "I think these will be the last places bombed," Lyxa said in a melancholy tone.

"The least desirable," Jared said as he watched people sitting intoxicated on doorsteps from the night before, doors marked with street art and violent signs, and always the half-naked children running innocently amid the trash and ruins of their broken dreams. Ahead lay the ferry port. Lyxa's private dock could hold six orbital courier ships.

"We'll outrun it," Lyxa said. "Outrun the end of the world."

"You're good at that," Jared jibed as he sat pressed close by her, thigh against thigh, like a pair of schmoozing *djia*. They held hands, very much like Lelli and Stella who sat opposite on benches. That's mostly what the coach was—benches, nicely upholstered in a faded royal blue, and a rich carpet, on which a dark mahogany table gleamed under a thick, green-edged glass top. Glasses, a vase with one yellow rose, a case for Lyxa's opium and pipe, and a decorative fauxbook or two made up all the moveables.

"Queen on the run," Lyxa said with a comfortable giggle as she burrowed her elbow and hip closer, as close as she could. He felt the old want for her, the heat. "I could make you a prince," she said. "Or no, a baron. How's that? A count. A duke."

He squeezed her hand. "We'll take it a day at a time." He was in the moment, while knowing nothing would ever change. At least he'd found some sort of status amid a disintegrating world. "Maybe I can just be your military attaché."

"Hmm," she said, which was a deep, sexual groan of interest and anticipation. "How attaché do you intend to be?"

He played with her net of conceits. "How close can I get?"

"I will let you into my secrets."

"I've seen them, and I always come back in to look again."

And so they bantered, holding hands, until they kissed and began passionately petting in the privacy of Her Royal Majesty's personal coach. The *djia* continued to hold hands and sit side by side across the compartment. If they noticed or cared, they did not let on. For all anyone knew, Lelli was chattering to Stella about the birds on Melliform IV, or Stella was regaling Lelli with algebraic formulae regarding the opening of rose blossoms on the first day of spring.

For now, Jared felt safe and contented.

For now...

27. Winter

Mercury was hushed.

In the silent streets stood wordless people waiting for some sign…

Military police stood before every store front. Some of the shops showed signs of looting. One or two were burned out.

The ground cars showed official livery and played Martin's Horn sirens. The cops waved them through one checkpoint after another under gray, sullen skies.

Lyxa had pulled out a large blanket from under the seat, and wrapped herself and Jared in it. They were toasty and drowsy together, too dazed and tired to explore what lay under their hungry fingertips and open palms.

No one stopped Jared as he brazened his way into his hotel. One suitcase full; the rest down the incinerator.

Outside, winter deepened.

The cold grew. The temperature was dropping steadily, and the dryness of the air could mean but one thing: Snow, and soon.

Heavily armed astral units trooped down the street. Armed and armored, they headed for the military space port down the street toward the upclimbing horizon. Jared saw units of every description, from active reserves to strangely dressed legionaries from the farthest-flung garrisons of the galaxy. Some were fully human, others not quite.

Jared had learned of Mbe's death, and wondered who was now ruler of the city and the nation. Of an empire, there was no longer much to talk about. Ankhmen and Raskian fleets had defeated the star fleets, and now circled in for the kill. Behind them, cargo and troop movers brought legions of fanatics on the one hand, and storm troopers on the other hand under Raskian flag.

The convoy with Jared and his fellow travelers moved slowly but surely through many side streets toward the luxurious, exclusive executive section of the civilian ferry port.

Nearly all activity Jared saw was military. Ferries loaded with departing troops rose and fell thickly as orbiting starships awaited the last of Mercury FPC's defenders who were traveling to the remaining frontier worlds still in UGO hands.

Jared watched a troop of 20-meter robot, camo-crazied Marines lumber by, towering above many of the buildings among which they loomed on their way to the war.

Roads were clogged with military traffic. The death crisis was in the open now. Nobody even tried to lie or hide the truth any longer. Those who could, who had some money or just crazy courage and determination, were trying to evacuate.

No one offered any slogans anymore. *Only cold, mud, and silence...*

In the back of his mind, Jared kept alive the faint and wild notion that he would still somehow escape to that paradise world where he'd served as a cadet: Lethe.

Lyxa was right. In times like these, everyone must live for the moment. We must be grateful for whatever small thing we have, like food, drink, a warm place to sleep, love with the right lover. As Lyxa—premier survivor of a house of royal survivors—had suggested: *We are outrunning the war front...*

Lethe would be good. Jared's heart warmed to the thought. On Lethe there would be time. Time to live. Certainly the annihilation and death would not reach there, and if it did, it would be borne on some cosmic wind a million years old, a million civilizations old.

Could Lethe last that long? Jared wondered. Somehow it didn't seem too important.

Ahead lay the orderly bubble of Lyxa's executive travel port, where everything seemed normal as if nothing worrisome were going on. The convoy pulled up at a loading ramp.

Lyxa pulled the blanket aside. "Ladies," she said.

Lelli and Stella let go of each other with diaphanous, shadowy arms. They raised their veils and became individual young demi-girls again. "We serve," they said in unison. They rose, in their ghostly dresses, and climbed out as an orderly held the door open. Men with weapons stood all around, ready to guard the royal entourage with their lives.

Lyxa took Jared's hand. "Come, lover. Be with me."

He ran a hand lightly down her back to reassure her. Or, he thought, this side of her personality. The other side was tough as a combat marine, whom you did not comfort, but got out of her way and simply obeyed or ran away from her. Right now, she was vulnerable and open and reciprocal. He resolved to enjoy this side of her for every moment it was available. Who among the scared masses could be anywhere as fortunate as he was right now.

Rising out of the atmosphere toward orbit, Jared sat in Lyxa's luxurious shuttle.

She had graciously permitted some twenty refugees to take free passage on their way to the civilian orbital station. The peaceful air inside the shuttle was therefore clouded with the sobbing of men and women, and the cries of hungry or scared children.

He looked out the porthole at his side. The traffic-filled ugly gray sky hung overhead like an udder ready to shed oceans of snow. The City of the Universe was traveling outward on its long journey, borne on a barge of growing silence into the shadows of time. Jared sensed the jaws of a cosmic ice cave closing around him, and he shuddered.

Arcturus has the reputation of another summer planet like Alda Meina III. It will be good to roll lazily in the surf, playing with Lyxa or, knowing her, if she's gone off with someone else again, with some young woman. His heart ached in hope that Stella would still be with him, maybe sitting on the sand and watching impassively behind her electron-cloud face, that digital swarm of enigma, as he pursued some happy new moment in the foamy surf.

Jared caught sight of the mist-shrouded Olympia House a few miles away on the ground, like a blot among the scribbled buildings.

The ferry's exhaust flared up briefly as the radiation grid puked forth its deadly contents deep into the earth.

At each step in the journey, the grateful though scared refugees in their shabby clothes would emit a loud communal cry as they watched their home and everything they owned disappear forever.

The ferry began to climb slowly, gravity-free, as the ground turned salty with snow.

The last vision he had of Mercury City was of emergency defensive construction. One giant robot, over thirty meters tall with only one huge arm, lifted a train load of sand and earth onto a lorry large as a house. Instead of a head, the robot had a cab with about ten operators inside, revolving on its shoulders. Around this dirt-encrusted black hulk darted life on a smaller scale: smaller robots, smaller lorries, and men.

The lift ferry first rocked, swayed, drifted in the wind, then steadied, and began a definite climb.

A floating truck clattered through the sky on a metal chain a thousand feet up, dropping a mist of sand.

Snow fell ever more thickly as the scene faded from Jared's vision.

Soon they were climbing faster.

Now there was only the open sky, with snow.

They entered clouds. They rode on and on, up and up, and the sun broke out on the surface of the cloud sea.

The refugees became still. Faces wet from crying peered out of portholes all around the craft.

Jared felt the exhilaration. Everything was going smoothly. The sun was blinding. All was beautiful.

The ferry lingered there well over an hour.

The vessel drifted high up, trailing a thin hose of cloud, drifting like a feather over snow-topped mountains.

It hung like a plumb, turning slowly on its axis while the planet, the clouds, the whole universe, all rolled around it.

Sleep reigned, and silence.

Jared was awake. Lyxa sat beside him, holding his hand. Lelli and Stella (could they ever be far?) sat in the seats behind them, ready to provide companionship or service.

Gradually the sky was growing dark, the whiteness dissipating.

The flaming orb of Aldebaran was beginning to obscure itself over the horizon. Jared inhaled cigar smoke. Evening; he tasted dryness.

A single shaft of sunlight stood in water.

The ocean was below.

The sunlight shaft faded, too. The cloud masses grew distant and dim. The refugees slept close together.

Darkness enveloped Jared. He rested. They were in space now. The calm wink of a red light told him they were driving through emptiness.

Silently the crowded vessel swept along, a motionless point in the vault of the sea it sailed. The toilet had been plugged but then fixed and the air was deodorized. A typical night flight. A pleasant gloom hung in the ship: *Silence, blessed silence.*

Free?

Yes. The Knowledge was overwhelming. The dream remained. He was free. A fish out of his sea, suspended in eternity in a fragile bubble. Jared's hands shook. He felt the weight of Lyxa's sleeping head on his shoulder, and the relaxed drop of her hand in his lap as she let go.

First he would voyage to Arcturus, but that was just a way station.

He was going to Lethe, where a man could be free and happy at last.

Lethe, land of long summers, the fragrance of the meadows with heather and wild flowers.

Part II

ARCTURUS

Sun Flare and Golden Girl

On a planet named Vellallo in a system in a galaxy in a far universe, Larth Atuuinl stood beside his sleeping mate Ramtha, gazing up at eternity and infinity in a black sky filled with stars.

Balmy breezes stirred grass all around like a sea of waves. The wind bore fragrances of wild *sherii* and other blooms, with a chill of green ice vapors from towering mountains far away across these fertile plains.

As Larth savored the growing coolness of night, he felt something new and alien. He looked around with some anxiety, but couldn't make out the cause of his vague alarm. Something wasn't right. He sat up, with his hands joined, and his elbows resting on his knees.

What's coming over me?

The stars remained frozen in their whirlpool, but something was strangely different.

Was it the vague intimation of a stirring in the wind, a change in the breeze?

Was it the sense that a new consciousness had drifted in from space and now flew silently and swiftly as an arrow, just nicking the tops of the wheat sheaves without actually touching them?

Larth stood holding his head in both hands, terrified and yet amazed at the glorious and beautiful vision of a ghostly cockpit whose glowing interior surrounded him with its light and joy and melancholy freedom.

A ghostly ship filled with ghosts, dead spacemen and space women from another time and space called Mercury City, Earth, the human race, whatever those things might mean.

He understood instantly that the dead people in that ship had found sleep and forgetfulness, and now flew in dreams without end. Whatever they had suffered, they were free now and exhilarated as they rushed through the Temporale, the interstices between time and space, unbound and unshackled forever…

28. Sun

Traveling in Lyxa's private star liner, which was compact but gave him enough privacy and peace, Jared had time to reflect. The journey took several days along Temporale space (the interstice of time and space, exogravitation). During that time, he spent passionate hours alone with Lyxa.

If one day he decided to move on to Lethe, he would have to pass through a transit node at Arcturus. The Temporale would take him on its transit realm outside time and space, and deliver him at Lethe, or wherever he wanted to go. That day now seemed far off.

In all honesty, he was once again captive to Lyxa for real. Call it love? It was infatuation at least. If maybe she did not keep betraying him, he might find it within himself to make some time with her; to say nothing of a life together; but that was reaching for too much right now.

Coming to Arcturus I after the chaos in Mercury FPC reminded Jared of his brief but wonderful vacation with Stella on Alda Meina III.

For the time being, when Lyxa settled with her small household on Arcturus, she purchased a palatial estate in a suburb of Arcturus. This was the suburb of Imber, ironically meaning Rain or Showers, more from nostalgia than for any actual rain since most of Arcturus was a temperate, mild desert world like Alda Meina III.

She'd left behind most of her thousand staff, who had families they could not desert. Lyxa did not propose to alter Arcturian immigration laws (which would require much payola) so she accepted the notion of starting over. Her ancestors had done the same at least two or three times in the past thousand years. She brought with her Garth and about twenty of his closest house staff and their families.

Lyxa also brought with her Lelli, Stella, and Jared. If there were one or two other hidden lovers, she kept that secret from Jared, and he didn't want to know. One thing at a time. One crisis at a time was plenty to deal with. He wanted to take some time off to rest, tan, soak, and figure out his best career move. Maybe the Arcturian home defense force needed a young officer? He would see, all in good time.

As diplomatically as he could, he worked out a deal with his lover that he would stay part of the week at her estate, and part in the city (on the theory that he would begin developing work connections). He had virtually unlimited resources, and she readily gave in to his wishes—as long as he was hers to call upon several days a week as needed—so he rented a spacious flat with an ocean view in a small coastal town an hour's airskim from her estate.

As before, Lyxa kept Lelli by her side at Imber, and sent Stella with Jared.

He had no doubt she was using Stella to spy on him, especially by means of Lelli. He was looking for the right moment to confront her about the neurotransponder Stella had told him about. At the moment, he liked things just as they were, and didn't want to complain. In the end, Lyxa has stolen his career and his future from him, and with her limitless wealth and influence, he did not feel guilty about carving out a few crumbs of the pie for his own sake. And, as a final resort, he kept the dream of Lethe alive in the back of his mind. *If all else fails...*

29. Battle Of Suns

New refugees brought fresh rumors with them from the Aldeb system and from Mercury FPC, or what remained of her.

Raskia had destroyed the capital of the old Protectorate of Aldebaran. An initial alien invasion had failed, with space battles that cost millions of lives and destroyed entire solar systems, leaving the City of the Universe exposed on one flank after another.

A Battle of the Suns was rumored, that had involved over three million ships, had crippled both Raskia and Mercury's navies, isolated the Ankh fanatics in their remote hinterlands, and left much of the human race starving. The human sphere was now on its knees and waiting for the coup de grace from a confederation of more than one thousand alien fleets—small, each, but together a formidable foe that would render humankind at the verge of extinction; or at least usher in two thousand years of being the galaxy's rodents to be hunted and killed at will, or enslaved.

Last word from Mercury was that the FPC allowed no more travel in and out of the Aldeb system, so the City was in a stage of virtual siege while the remnants of her fleets battled on, dispersed and withering among the stars.

Few Mercurians had come as far as Arcturus. Most of Arcturus' Mercurians were the wealthy, and most of these were concentrated in the rich old town of Imber, on Arcturus. That was where Lyxa had set down her household, including a separate apartment for Jared in addition to his toiletry kit in her private bathing suite. And of course he was busy moving in at his new apartment on the fifteenth floor of a luxury building overlooking the city and the sea.

30. Rainbow

Jared chose his apartment in the largest city, Arco, whose full name in the lilting Arcturian language was Arcopluviale, or Rainbow.

With Stella at hand, he wasn't lonely. She was a good companion, needing little and desiring less. She slept in his bed with him—Platonically, since she had no orifices, no instincts for what a human might need in the dark of night, and no conception of love in the human sense. She had a range of emotions, to which he responded with kindness and sensitivity, as he would be conscious of any woman's feelings. She, in turn, was loyal above all, and kind, and a good friend to the extent that she could understand his thoughts and emotions. It always came back down to loyalty. She was in some ways an extension of Lyxa, though Lelli had replaced her as Lyxa's personal assistant. The *djia* seemed a lot like cats to Jared. They were solitary creatures, content with their lunch and their territory. Like cats, they might either get along (and schmooze as Stella did with Edzar or Lelli) or they might fight so the electronic fur flew. Jared had not yet seen Stella in a negative relationship like that. What puzzled him, until he learned the genetic engineering reasons, was her underlying difference in phenotype (outward appearance) from her template, Lyxa. The princess was dark-haired, whereas what shone through Stella's nebularity was blondeness. Jared often wondered what Stella would be like if she ever turned into a real girl, but that was out of the question. *Djia* had numerous built-in safeguards, including death-destruct if anyone tried a Pinocchio move (turning a wooden boy into a live one). In fact, the genetic kill switch built into every *djia* was called the Checkmate. A *djia* could give its life for its source (as Lyxa had demonstrated using Lelli back in the palace in Mercury FPC), but the reverse was by design seriously impossible. That was to prevent a *djia* from getting ideas, and killing its source by a reverse takeover.

In a sensitive moment, Lyxa had asked Jared if he wanted his own *djia*. Then, she said, he would have a male(ish) companion to talk with, do all those man things with that she didn't know or want to know. Jared had been repelled by the idea of creating an analog of himself out of ghostly electrons and sine waves and boreal lights. He thought it would be cruel, but he didn't say that to Lyxa. Instead, he accepted her own analog, Stella, and he rather loved having a female around all the time. She was good company for what she was. He had not created the situation but he would make the best of it. *Yes, I am wishy-washy,* he thought at the time. But I would not be part of creating a *djia*, and I will treat her with the greatest love and kindness. So that was that.

During his first weeks Arco, he liked to walk around. Sometimes Lyxa and Lelli came to visit, and they took Stella along for walks. The *djia* remained veiled during these outings, but locals were used to all sorts of tourist aberrations including farmed girls or boys, chimera dogs, and all sorts of other genetic cruelties that had become common place though at best in dubious legal twilight on all but the most radical worlds. The *djia* seemed to enjoy window shopping, but asked for nothing much. A pretty necklace maybe, or a golden bracelet, or a delicately patterned dress in the current just below the knee mode; Jared or Lyxa provided those little desires for them. Lyxa was a conservative shopper, surprisingly, and Jared found shopping a bore. They enjoyed a light lunch of local seafood or avian fare (roast quail *em fajiole* for example). All in all, after the hell of Mercury FPC in its declining days, life here was quiet and sunny, peaceful and safe. Those who had lived through madness and cruelty knew how to be grateful.

Lyxa liked to go native, and called little attention to herself so as to blend in and enjoy life without calling attention to herself. The usual gossip media were busier at Imber, and not so much in Arco (who would go there?). In their own separate ways, Arco became a getaway for both Jared and Lyxa. In a different way, tiny but upscale Imber with its sunny white malls and fragrant hives of lunch and desert, and a wealth of gift shops and galleries, was a natural hunting ground for reporters. You took that for granted. The Princess Vega, as she was known here, was a sensation to be sure. Sometimes she was holoformed walking with Jared, or just with Lelli, or with one of the palace staff. If she wanted the publicity (she did not) she would have had to compete with a thousand crazy expats and emigrés (kings, generals, actors, male or female) and their even crazier spoiled and drug-addicted children. All in all, Imber media quickly became bored with Jared and Lyxa, and they even more quickly became bored with Imber's press snoops. Often enough, drone spies disguised as seagulls would fly over the pool area of Lyxa's estate in Imber. It was comical. The next door neighbor, an exiled zillionaire from the Procyon system, kept a simple wood and plaxtif slingshot to wound the drones—not kill them, but wing them so to speak, always hoping not to cripple a real bird. Fortunately, said zillionaire liked to drink the potent beachy *cantamucho* liquor, and almost always missed his target. His projectiles, garden pebbles, sometimes landed in Lyxa's swimming pool. *Oh well,* Jared thought. *Life goes on no matter where you are, until it doesn't, and then who cares?* That was actually a line from a minor Mercurian comedian, rather a perpetual nuisance on late night holofare, who had fled to parts unknown as the war started. *Good riddance*, Jared thought.

31. Arco

Jared more often than not left Stella at the apartment so he could spend an hour or two at the beach without attracting overly much attention. The *djia* was still a bit of a sensation around here; she'd been that on Mercury FPC already, but here he sought peace and anonymity.

He developed a routine by which he spent a quarter hour communing with her to make her feel wanted. He'd take her out on the balcony, where she could absorb the plentiful sunshine, and he could eat breakfast, local style, meaning salt quail, creamed gull eggs, diced-fried *chaxuro* (a kind of starchy root, said to be from Old Earth, of a yellowish color), and strings of red *hashi* beets. This was best followed with a black cup of café *duro* lightened with raw *scare* and a drizzle of just enough *ungulatte* (cow cream) to take the bitterness off the top. Café *duro* was a staple on Arcturus, along with the cantamucho served during rowdy evenings, and a few other treats of the leisurely life.

Schmoozing with Stella, he'd hold her hands the way he'd seen her do with Lelli, and he'd speak with her in gentle and loving terms, talking about her beauty and her sweet nature. She'd hold his hands with a certain dry, strong, firmness that was the only way he could really gauge her reaction. She wanted it, and enjoyed it. What creature did not enjoy being petted and care for and soothed? When he asked her if she felt lonely when he was away, he was surprised (just for a moment) when she told him she could schmooze with Lelli any time (remotely) or with some other wealthy expat *djia* that lived in Imber or Arco or some hideaway beach towns.

That comforted him, and he made a habit of his morning balcony sessions with Stella, but did not worry about her so much after that.

What did worry him was the growing sense that he was being watched. By whom, and why, he had no idea. He brought the subject up with Lyxa one day when he stayed with her at Imber, and Stella went away to commune with Lelli (of course) like two silently chattering schoolgirls—or praying nuns in their veils for that matter.

"What makes you think so?" Lyxa asked as they sat by her pool, sharing a sort of iced local Sea Tea reminiscent of Alda Meina III. A servant brought cheese, crackers, quail eggs *algotta*, and other snacks of local custom.

He told her: "I was walking from my apartment to the beach yesterday, and I noticed a man following me."

"Are you sure?" She kept a neutral face, but he could tell she was secretly interested. Nothing much escaped Lyxa's attention. She was a survivor for good reason. Her dark hair was wrapped in a high towel turban (they'd made love, then swum in the pool, followed by a shower). Her fair skin glistened with solar creams to hasten a tan and block deadly ionoforms.

"He was acting suspicious."

"What sort of man?"

"One of the locals, you know, *Samba* strummers, whatever. Opportunists, only this guy looked urban and sleek. His fingernails weren't dirty and he wore expensive shoes that no beach *gallante* could afford unless he'd rolled someone."

She said carefully: "I have people watching out for me. I wasn't worried about you, but now I'll put someone on it."

He stared at her incredulously. "Nothing ever changes."

She gave him a faint, almost sinister smile that radiated survivorship.

"We have a good workable situation," he said carefully. In his thoughts, he was already shredding the last of his naïve ideas. Lyxa was a self-made zillionaire in addition to having inherited a timeless and measureless fortune. But such fortunes could evaporate over generations, and Jared was certain that was not the case with Lyxa's.

"Trust me, my love."

"I do," he lied. It wasn't totally a lie. Maybe seventy or eighty percent. He could never trust her again after she'd taken lovers behind his back and treated him like a human *djia.* Maybe that was one reason why he felt so protective and loving toward Stella.

"Very well." She sat up, sipped from a *cocoval* ball (local fruit), and folded her arms instructively. "Jared, I have a hundred different things going on here. I am negotiating business ventures that you wouldn't be interested in knowing about."

He bit his lip. Was she being condescending? No, he thought, she did not want to harm their relationship by making him one of her managers or stewards. It wasn't an insult, really. She wanted him for relaxation, for sex, for passion, for escape from the pressures of her zillionaire life. He'd come to accept that she must spontaneously relate with all sorts of people, including very nasty ones, to bridge enormous business deals that would continue vast seas of money flowing through her nets and banks and what not. She had this great talent that he did not. She could meet a wealthy stranger and in one hour be setting up a business deal. It was as natural as weather for people like Lyxa and other zillionaires. Jared was a straightforward farm boy, as he liked to think of it, from the remote towns of Lesht and Oudangad, where you could smell manure in the air, or hay, or grass, depending on the season. Lyxa smelled money in the air.

"I am working on a deal to set up a new star liner company for both freight and passengers to run between eighty systems. I have another deal in work to buy out media companies across a dozen worlds, covering ten billion souls. I am negotiating to buy herds of ungulabers on Vulti 5, and a...."

As she droned on, Jared nearly fell asleep. He sat up with a start. "So, Lyxa, what does this have to do with a guy in clean slacks and white shirt, hiding behind a holoscreen pretending to watch *xaelai* games but looking at me every two minutes…?"

"Maybe he is *shwulli* for you," she said acerbly, meaning gay.

"I don't think so. I wish you'd take me seriously."

"I am," she said with managerial detachment as if he were an employee. She tapped her fingernails on the armrest of his deck chair. "I already have that guy on your case, Jared. He's one of ours. He is protecting you and Stella."

"That's a relief, but from what?"

"I had enemies on Mercury FPC, and I have enemies here."

"Should I be scared?"

"No, just relax. Everything is handled."

"I like to know what's going on around me."

She nodded. "Fair enough. I didn't want to make you worry. You're my lover boy, the love of my life. I don't want anything to happen to you."

He rolled his eyes up. *I need to get a life of my own*, he thought. For this I worked so hard, carried that torch…

They'd had that conversation before, actually while yelling at each other. Her response had been that if he'd gone out on ordinary line duty with the star fleets, he'd be dead or maimed now, maybe buried or crippled in some remote hardship world that was little more than a zoo and he an exhibit. His answer had been that he felt like a zoo inmate with her and she'd replied that he had an obvious choice. Walk away… To what, he'd shouted back; you took all that from me.

Her eyes would bore into him with a calculating, passionate whirl of thoughts. One day, she implied without making any promises, I would give you a fortune of your own and set you up in luxury somewhere out of my reach, where you could be a big frog in a little pond. For now, just give me what I want.

Like you always get.

Yes, but you get so much in return.

End of discussion. They had not talked about that in months.

The more they argued, the more passionately they made love and clawed at each other unable to get enough. They thought about making it permanent, but both recoiled from the idea, knowing if they formalized their relationship, it would most likely atrophy into just another dull marriage of convenience. And he knew she'd be cheating on him with a passion, because her appetites were volcanic. She was a princess and a zillionaire, after all.

Moving on…

32. Cantamucho

One day, Jared sat at a beach cabana, having a small *cantamucho* (softened by plum nectar, which took some of the antifreeze fire out of the local drink). The weather was balmy as usual. Palms rustled in soft breezes, *Samba* tunes whispered and jostled in the undercurrents of air, and everyone around him was dressed for swimming or else to look at those who surfed and swam.

As he did every day, he communed with Stella for a bit, then left her to sun on the patio, holo with Lelli and other *djia*, and study plant science (which was a hobby of hers). He sauntered several blocks down the narrow streets full of mostly young men and women who were always in a festive mood. Many were students at a local college, while others were jugglers, singers, bartenders, street vendors, and the like.

He walked down to Beach Street, crossed the stone way, and crossed the crowded sand toward the sea. There, he put down his towel and shirt, and ran into the surf. Cooling off in the warm sun, enjoying the exercise and a good swim, he finally returned to lie on his towel and dry off. That done, he walked back across Beach Street to a café he liked (Starmate) and ordered a café *duro*. He flipped open his holobook and sipped coffee while reading the latest news. As always, the news about Mercury, the UGO, and the alien invasion was grim. There was also much trivial local news about smiling drunks having a cookout, pretty young women having a beach beauty contest, and *sambafazendes* giving a Samba concert near some pier at full moon and king tide.

Glancing up, Jared noticed his shadow sitting on a blanket with two young women across the street. Whoever he was—agent of Lyxa? — he appeared to be in an off-duty mode. Said shadow noticed Jared at the same time. Excusing himself, he crossed the street and approached Jared, who sat at a bench in a little cabana in Starmate. The cabana was thatched over with palm fronds and offered a bit of privacy.

"Can I join you for a few minutes?"

Jared shrugged. "You've made yourself part of my life for the past week or more."

He was a sunny enough individual, obviously educated and clean. He wore similar clothing to Jared's and that of most young men hanging around the beach town: light cotton shirt, blue denim shorts or pants, no socks, and sandals. "My name's Naxo Rees."

Jared shook his hand. "Jared Fallon."

Naxo (pronounced 'nacho') swung easily onto the stone bench across the table in the little cabana. There were about six similar cabanas behind the Starmate building, plus a yard with at least fifteen more tables. Lots of people sitting around idly talking, laughing, in a good mood. Naxo had long, glossy black hair that fell in waves. He had a caramel complexion in a ruggedly handsome face, whose strong jaw was plowed up by a mix of beard shadow and old acne scars. His nose was blunt, his eyes dark brown, and his forehead prematurely wrinkled under a large curl of black hair. "I thought I would introduce myself." Surreptitiously, he opened his hand, and as he did so, a digital card fell open, revealing an official looking police badge. "I'm not who you think."

Jared grew annoyed—not just at this stranger, but at Lyxa. "What do I think?"

Naxo sat forward with his arms crossed tightly over his chest, and brought his face close. "I'm a cop. And you're in the middle of an investigation."

Jared slapped his holobook shut. "Oh for god's sake. I'm not bothering you or anyone else."

Naxo nodded. "I know. We ran your file all the way back to not only Mercury FPC but through your Star Academy, all the way back to Lesht and Oudangad."

Jared felt himself blanch. "You're not just an ordinary local beach cop."

Naxo laughed. "Oh no. I'm not even an ordinary Arco detective, although my badge that I showed you suggests it. I'm on loan from the Federal Reporting Office or FRO. That's the investigative branch of the planetary government."

"Why are you telling me all this?"

"Because we need you on our side."

"We." It was a question.

"The legitimate government."

"Of?"

"Arcturus."

"This whole planet?"

"That's what planetary government means." Seeing Jared's shock, he added: "I hate to rain on your parade like this but your life is in danger."

"Again?" Jared was too annoyed to be scared. "Just when I thought I was high and dry."

"You're safe and secure all right, as long as we say you are."

"We?"

"FRO. I just explained. You're not slow. You're a highly intelligent guy."

"Are you crazy?"

"No, I'm working. I'm always working, Mr. Fallon. Can I call you Jared?"

Jared shrugged. "Naxo." He thought it over. "Can I just walk away? Mind my own business?"

Naxo kept shaking his head as Jared asked these questions. "You're in so deep you don't have any idea where the bottom is."

"What am I in so deep about?"

"A plot to overthrow our government, and your girlfriend is a ringleader."

“No.” Jared didn’t know whether to laugh or cry. “Lyxa?”

Naxo nodded. “The one.”

It was Jared’s turn to lean forward with folded arms, furtively looking to each side. “Where are you going with this?”

“It’s complicated. We’d prefer to have the princess quietly living here like all the other expats who bring a lot of money and connections. Our government makes a lot of tax revenue and they bring a lot of business. However, we happen to know that Lyxa was involved in a plot on Mercury FPC, which went wrong when the Ankh loonies and the Raskian bullies teamed up to bring the Starmeer down. That has opened the entire human galaxy up to alien invasion. You and your princess got out just in time. So now she is here with a thousand irons in the fire all at once.”

“I thought you were working for her, keeping an eye on me.”

Naxo’s dark eyes crinkled at the corners. He was one of those rugged types whose entire face crinkled when he made his glowing, cynical grin. “We’d like you to pretend you still believe that. We means FRO, and we’ve got a lot of people working on this case to prevent your princess from being named Queen of Arcturus. She’s got that House of Vega, House of Mercury background and all that. Nothing new for her.” He stared at Jared. “You are in love with her. We understand that. We don’t want any harm to come to her. There are a group of shadowy oligarchs and plutocrats from the old Mercury FPC league who have moved here with their money and their ambitions. She’s using them, and they are using her. She’s that sort of person—she manipulates people.” He added pointedly: “Like she’s manipulating you. And of course you are using her as well.” Seeing Jared’s anger rise, he raised a defensive hand. “Easy, Lieutenant. I can be on your side if you let me.”

“Your side.”

“Yes. Looking out for your interests. You want to keep your cozy arrangement. You want to keep your skin intact. I’m aware of your achievements and what she did to you, so you have my full admiration. I think you love her and don’t want her to be killed or hurt when this gets really ugly. Do you?”

Jared slowly nodded. “Yes.”

“Then let’s work together.”

“I see no other choice then.”

Naxo turned from cynical to passionate. “Dammit, Fallon, this is my nation, my planet, my world, and my life. Who the hell do you and your kind think you are, coming here and turning our lives upside down?”

“I’m just a survivor,” Jared said candidly. “My life was already turned upside down.”

Naxo calmed his fiery temper. “Right. I understand. Now you don’t want your life turned inside out as well.”

Jared shook his head. “I’m done with it.”

“Good.” Naxo extended a hand.

Jared shook it. “What am I supposed to do?”

“Nothing, really. Just be a lightning rod.”

“Explain.”

Naxo gave a furtive look to each side. “Let me explain a little about the game. You and I are just tiny cogs in a huge machinery. We can’t really do anything as such. We are conduits for events. We make it possible for things to happen.”

“Things? Such as?”

“The outcome we want.”

“Which is what?”

“Not what they want, the conspirators who want to overthrow the government and set up a new monarchy in all but name. An imperium with all sorts of pretty ribbons and banners, but basically nothing other than a tyranny. We have a democracy here, but too often people get stupid, listen to the demagogue who offers simple and brutal solutions, and next thing you know the demagogue is your new tyrant. It’s happened over and over again in the history of democracies. It’s how Mercury Free Port City went from a monarchy, shedding Lyxa’s ancestors, to a republic with a democratic constitution to a galactic empire and now to a huge smoking dustbin. They can’t help themselves, these zillionaires. It’s what they do. It’s all they know.”

“And Lyxa?”

“We’ve got a dossier on her that fills an entire room at FRO HQ in Ravane, our world capital. Garth, Lelli, you, Stella, you’re all documented and recorded down to your blood types, the brand of soap you prefer in your bath, and the amount of *sucro* you put in your *duro*.”

“Congratulations,” Jared said acidly.

“I’ll tell you something about spycraft.” Naxo leaned close again. “Nothing is what it seems. That’s how this business works. The side that fools the other best is the side that wins. Let me give you an example. This meeting we are having was planned a week ago.”

“Really?”

“Really. Look. You were made to think someone was watching you, and I was. You reported back to your girlfriend. We know, through ways you can only guess. We know what you said in your conversation by her pool over coffee and finger snacks. But get this, Jared. It’s all in the eye of the beholder. You think I’m watching you (check) and she thinks I am watching you (check) but she thinks I am working for her (wrong) and now you are a step ahead. Let me put it another way. Suppose you are a spy agency and you want to watch someone.”

“Yes?”

“You want to watch them, really really closely, and you don’t want them to know. So what do you do?”

Jared shook his head.

“You use a blind. I’m the blind. If I did not want to be noticed, you would not have noticed me. FRO has other people watching you, me, her, the whole caravelle. You see me, and you fail to notice the ones that are really watching.” He stared at Jared. “You still don’t get it. I don’t blame you. You’re in the game, you see? You're me now. Someone is noticing you, me, us. That someone is one of Lyxa's agents. Not hers directly. She won't know names. Those are agencies, free lance, no flag, just mercenary. Business. Corporations whose business it is to work like shadow governments."

"I'm lost."

"I know. Understand this. FRO and other agencies we won't name need to know who, what, when, where, how, and why. There is are key bits of information floating around among the overflow of data. It's raining data. It's a storm of data, day and night, that never stops. Data are not information but bits and bytes and points of dark. We need to connect the dots, pencil in the metaphors, and create the streaks of light that become information. We have to sort out the misleading information, purposeful or otherwise, known as disinformation, planted to mislead us, from the true, nail on the head information. Who, what, when, where, how, and why. We already have a good idea about what (a takeover), where (the capital, in the end), who (Lyxa and certain parties known to us, but we don't have all the names and faces), why (greed, ambition, ruthlessness), but we don't know how or when. How to fill in the missing lines?"

"You tell me."

"Fishing. We go fishing. We use you, me, even Lyxa as bait. We see who the sharks in the water are. They will send probes and surrogates and proxies and patsies and fall guys. They may send hit men or hit women. We have to keep our eyes open. We do that by watching you."

"And what do I do?"

"You enjoy yourself."

Jared tried to process all this.

Naxo rose. "We've had a good conversation. Are you in?"

Jared nodded. "On the condition that nothing happens to Lyxa or Lelli or Stella."

"We'll do our best. You understand that a whole world is at stake."

"I take that as a maybe."

"It's the best I can do. Either way, you're in and you can't get out."

"I see."

"Sorry. I didn't create this mess. Neither did you. So look…"

"Yes?"

"You can brush your effectiveness, your amperage, by circulating more. Walk over to the beach, get to know the regulars, have a party at your apartment and invite people. My cover is shot and my job is done for now, at least here. I'll be backup in case I'm needed. You can always come to me in an emergency."

"And so?"

"The watchers will track you, and we'll track the watchers while they think I'm watching you or the next person is watching you. That would be our agent named Vaeja. We pretend to be brother and sister. Give it a few minutes and then leisurely stroll across the street to meet her." He added: "Don't worry, plenty of eyes watching from all angles to see how and when." With a comradely rap of the knuckles on Jared's table, Naxo whirled and left.

33. Mala

Jared waited until his new acquaintance had blended away into the crowd of thousands thronging the beachside. He sat inside his isolated cabana, under dangling palm fronds, and reflected that he was not as surprised as he might have expected to be.

He'd been involved in Lyxa's affairs, and in those of Cyrus Mbe and the other players spiraling in the whirlpool of Mercury FPC's downfall. Here he was again, and Lyxa was an old player from an old game. *Nothing new.*

His thoughts actually turned to Stella and Lelli, two innocents who were more at risk than anyone. They were demi-human, programmed to utter loyalty above all, and ready to throw their lives away for their genesource.

His thoughts also turned to his escape valve, his dream, Lethe, on the periphery of the human galaxy, far from the sphere of anyone's interest. Surely it would take centuries before anyone noticed Lethe and came knocking—for what? A simple farming world, sparsely settled, full of innocent people living in mostly small towns. Largest cities, what few there were, boasted a few tens of thousands of souls. It was a revenant of millennia lost, ages ago. But if he left, he could not be sure that Stella would survive. Her purpose, to shadow him for Lyxa, would be gone. Lelli had taken her place as Lyxa's alt-safety.

He resolved to begin looking into passage out of here. But he also resolved to stay until he made sure Stella was safe and secure—in a home for wayward and lost *djia* if necessary.

Finishing his *duro*, Jared rose and sauntered across the sandy street to begin a new chapter in his life.

Hot beach sand engulfed his feet as he stepped into the blazing heat brilliance of the Arcturian sun. Sand poured into his sandals and between his toes. It was a comforting feeling.

He sorted his path among hundreds of beach goers until he spotted Naxo Rees's dark hair. He walked over. Naxo sat on a blanket with two attractive young women.

"There's Jared Fallon," Naxo said feigning casualness.

"How are you doing?" Jared said, in the game. He was intrigued by the women.

"Come sit down."

He dropped his rear onto the towel. One of the girls handed him a cool drink. The other one gave him a quizzical but friendly look.

Rees introduced the two girls. "My sister Vaeja, and her friend Mala."

They exchanged easy-going greetings.

"We're going to have a party this evening," Naxo said, giving Jared a wink. "Want to come?" He nodded quickly for Jared.

"Sure," Jared said.

Of the two women, Vaeja was slightly darker and bigger in a solid athletic manner. She had a head of frizzy black hair and very light coffee features, lighter than Naxo's, and more delicate. Knowing what he knew, Jared had to assume she was with FRO. He wondered about the other one. Mala, a blonde with a dangle of fine flaxen hair, was gray-eyed in contrast with Vaeja's dark eyes. Mala's features were narrower, while Vaeja's were broad but still delicate.

Jared sipped his ice *duro* and forced himself into the leisurely mood of the beach crowd. People talked, danced, played holo games, ran to the water, came back from swimming—an endless blend of ceaseless kaleidoscope activity. Jared actually began to relax for real. He'd missed the companionship of crowds for so long. Here was his opportunity to flow with a crowd of nice people. What had Naxo said? He didn't have to really do anything but be there. Spies would do the rest. That was a challenge he could easily take up. He smiled to himself.

Naxo produced a pack of old-fashioned playing cards to break the ice.

The one woman, Vaeja, readily agreed to play.

Mala, the pretty one who was starting to draw Jared's attention, rose suddenly without excusing herself and sauntered toward the water for a swim. Jared glanced after her, liking how smooth her skin looked, how lightly tanned she was, how her golden hair swung easily from side to side, cut to just below the ears. Had she given him a significant afterglance? Or was it a trick of light, of the blinding heat and sand, of water vapor in the relaxing air? There would be time to find out.

What a wonderful place this was—even better than Alda Meina III back in the home system. Here you did not have the crowding and the pressures so close to a besieged capital world.

Jared joined a game of tossing out cards, switching cards blindly with the deck, then with each other, and finally calling it to see who had the winning hand. The face cards were Arcturian, each showing an intriguing, mysterious face: sun goddess, moon god, smiling planet virgin, somber destroying comet. The rules were just complicated enough to keep things varied and interesting, and just simple enough to make a casual distraction while people watching—and boat watching, including colorful play-sails halfway to the horizon.

After a short while, Mala came walking back rubbing herself with a towel. She wore a skimpy two-piece in soft pastel colors. Something about her attracted Jared. It was a feeling he had not had since Lyxa barged into his life a few years ago. He was older and wiser, or less naïve now, by far, and this was different.

The key pivot came just about now. Jared still held the cards in his hand, waiting for Naxo and Vaeja to finish sorting out their hands. His own hand was forgettable, and he wasn't paying attention anymore, at least until the next round. So he looked up idly, admiring Mala's approaching form. The pivot came when he looked up, and found her staring at him—hard. She gave him a wounded, vulnerable, piercing, probing look. He could not think of enough terms to describe it. Her look shot through him the way the echoes of the report of a loud explosion slammed through the air. It lasted longer than a fraction of a second.

What was all the more remarkable was that, though he looked up expecting to just sort of modestly look over a pretty girl, an attractive woman—their eyes or their gazes interlocked and would not let go. The hard thing he saw in her gaze was fear. The softness was vulnerability. The sweet thing he saw was desire. Or maybe it was admiration. Or something.

Mala joined the card game, sitting next to Jared, between him and Vaeja. She pretended to be casual and seemed careful about her cards, but she was really being careful about how she revealed her heart to Jared.

He, in turn, melted inwardly. And each time they looked at each other, their eyes communicated in secrets. For all that it was worth, they were like *djia* who could communicate worlds by gazing into each others' scrambled faces. Mala seemed shy, but she also seemed sure of herself. She made no secret of her attraction to him, and he offered all the signals needed to continue cementing a new friendship.

Mala had a soft way of speaking, almost a lisp sometimes, and a deliberate way of chewing her words carefully while she spoke, to make sure she delivered them carefully and they were understood.

Naxo, no fool, sat beaming from ear to ear. Vaeja, obviously no fool either, favored Jared and Mala with calculating, approving looks. Then Vaeja and Naxo would exchange glances, devoid of any gestures, but their glances told Jared that FRO's plans were coming along far better than they might have dreamed.

Jared was prepared to think that Mala might be a plant or a fellow spy, but she evidently was a casual friend of Vaeja's from some ongoing relationship at a bookstore where Mala had a part-time job and Vaeja came to buy and download romantic stories. All three of them lived in Arco, which was a small town, and meant they probably had attended school together and grown up together.

It was too much to hope for, but in a flash, Jared had gained a new purpose and a new dimension in life. Naxo and Vaeja strolled off to look at swimsuits in the shops along Beach Avenue. The card game was long forgotten. Jared and Mala fell into conversation and sat close together with their foreheads almost touching.

As the afternoon deepened, the beach crowd thinned out. Time to go eat, and then party in taverns. Alas, Mala had her bookshop to work at this evening. He asked if she would be back at the beach the next day, and she said with a glow: "Of course. That's what we do in this little town. Will you be here, Jared?" She looked at him with intent hopefulness in her pretty features and light blue eyes.

Her golden hair hung limply around her wide forehead, over lightly tanned skin that was soft and flawless and invited touching, kissing, savoring…

"Of course." He leaned close, and she let him brush her lips with his.

She tore herself away. "I have to run." She brushed her fingers across his cheek. "Talk to you tomorrow." As she gathered a few possessions and folded them into her towel, she said "Watch the *cantamucho*. You'll have a hangover if you're not careful."

He gave her an intent look, a smile. "I want my wits about me when I sit here with you."

"Bye," she breathed, and fled into the growing dusk.

Jared ate a light dinner with Naxo and Vaeja in a beachfront cantina, followed by a beer and snacks.

"She likes you," Vaeja said. She was pretty in a different way from Mala's softness and girlishness. Both women were athletic and small-breasted, with strong arms and legs, and wonderfully muscular thighs. Vaeja was bigger and more robust. She wore a black wetsuit over her dark blue bathing suit, and looked more the wrestler, swimmer, skier versus Mala's girl next door softness.

"You're doing everything right," Naxo said. He seemed delighted at the interactions of people he brought together.

"It's happening naturally," he said.

"Whoo!" Vaeja said. "Love at first sight."

Naxo grinned form ear to ear. "Mala just sort of stumbled into our group today. We know here from school and the digital bookshop. Nice girl."

"She's a catch," Vaeja said with an admiring look at Jared. "You're not so bad yourself."

At home, Stella sat at the screen, reading about house plants.

Jared let himself in and turned on the interior lights. "Sorry I was gone so long."

"I kept busy," Stella said without looking up.

"What are you doing?"

"Figuring out the optimal chemistry for succulents in this region of Arcturus, given the salinity of sea air and other factors."

"You sound like a textbook."

The flickering on her face took on grin hints. Her dark eye pools swam with humor, even faux laugh wrinkles in the corners of her eye orbits. "I love being technical."

"I like when you talk to me that way."

"I want to please you, Jared."

He hugged her, and she clung to him.

"Were you happy here alone today?"

"I transponded with Lelli."

He let go, and sat on a couch near her.

"How are they doing in Imber?"

"Lyxa is fine. She says hello. She's been working on a secret project with some men."

"Oh?" Alarms jangled silently and metaphorically.

"Yes, in the library of her new house. Must be very important.

"Must be." He was going to ask: *Who are these men?*

Then he realized: FRO would already be on that. They'd be monitoring the ether talk between Stella and Lelli. If the Arcturians were worth their salt, they would know all this.

He changed the subject. "Are you getting enough exercise?"

Her voice sounded a bit startled. "I went for a walk."

"Did anyone bother you?" He was afraid for her; if nothing else, from jeering street urchins, or scheming gutter drunks.

"I ignored the comments."

"From—?"

"Sectarian fanatics, I think. Village idiots."

"I'm proud of you."

"I like to please you, Jared."

"Let me know next time you go for a walk, and I'll go along to protect you."

Stella turned toward him slowly. Her facial electronic clouds flickered in distracted and enigmatic patterns. She said "Thanks" in a small, dry, emotional tone. "You are different."

"How's that?" He felt like a child confronted about a naughty deed.

"There is a new woman in your life."

He felt dry-mouthed. "Stella—."

"I won't tell." She sat with her hands between her knees, turning a face full of tiny stars toward him.

"I like her very much."

"Very, very much," Stella said understandingly.

He nodded. "I have no idea what will happen next."

"Lelli already knows. I can't help it. You radiate since Lyxa had you altered."

He felt as though the ground had dropped from beneath his feet.

34. Star Mate

"You are one of us," Stella said. "You are fully a man, but Lyxa has augmented you. When you were drinking one night, not long ago, she drugged your wine and made you insensate. Then she had surgeons comb your neural kelp, implanting copper nanosnyps."

"How do you know all this?" he said with breaking heart.

"I comb you at night, my love as I lie beside you when you sleep. We make deep sea songs together."

"What?" It was beyond his grasp.

"My fingers strum you like a harp. I love you, Jared."

He sat down hard on a chair beside her. "Stella."

"You don't need to speak. I read your ambience."

"I love you too, Stella. You are a woman, and I love you for that. I am exploding like a nova star for this new girl I met."

"Mala."

"You read her name." It was a question.

"I read everything, Jared. I don't understand everything." As he stared at her, she added: "Love her, Jared. She will make you happy. Lyxa will only continue to hurt and destroy you."

Jared took her fingers in his. He saw his own tears fall like rain on his hands. "Won't you get in trouble for this?"

Stella was calm. She was pacific, like a great sea. "Our lives rise and fall with the tides, with the moons in the sky. I am ready for my fate." She squeezed his fingers with hers. "I hope you will find happiness with Mala."

"And you, Stella—can you be happy with me?"

She shook her nebular head under its gauzy veil. "Yes, my love. But I have to leave, because I cannot continue transponding for Lyxa through Lelli. I can't help it. It cannot be undone, either in me or in you. All people are really *djia* without knowing it, neural kelp encased in flesh and bone. Now you know you are diaphane like any *djia*, even though you are a man. You are a complete man, and I am a shadow of a woman. I cannot stay in your life. I have to go."

"Please don't leave me. I love you, Stella." He loved her not in the way that we wanted to love a natural human woman, Mala now above all, but he loved her in a special way: not quite a sister, not quite a woman lover, but as a woman who had taken part of his heart. "Don't go. You'll take part of my soul with you."

She sat looking at him as they held hands. Or what passed for looking. He looked into the electron storm in her face and it was like gazing far away into star clouds.

"Do you think Mala would mind having a *djia* always around?"

"You could comb her with your sea songs and your star songs."

Stella paused a moment, then said: "You don't even know if Mala will ever show up."

"That I need to find out."

"Let's rest then, and see what tomorrow brings."

With a final squeeze of their hands, they got ready and came to bed, where they lay in a pleasurable spooning under the covers while outside, far away, fog horns blared on the sea, and stars twinkled above night marine layers.

35. Samba

Mala came as she had promised.

Jared, sitting at a stool on the outdoor side of the Starmate café, saw her a block away. She was of average height, with that straight golden hair, and he could make her out above a hundred others. She raised her gaze, saw him, and burst into a dazzling smile.

He felt himself brightening inwardly, as if the sun shone from his neural tree or how had Stella expressed it?

From far away, through babbling and busy crowds, he could see that Mala lit up when she saw him. It was the human transmission: her smile was dazzling, and radiated the love and joy she felt. She hurried to be at his side.

She wore a loosely flowing white cotton summer gown, under which Jared could see (as intended) her shapely tan figure in a skimpy two-piece swimsuit of a wine-colored material that puffed slightly, looking tailored. She walked softly in even strides with a little bounce in them (happy to see him) while holding a towel over one arm and a decorative bag by its wooden handle in the other hand.

As always in the streets and on the beaches of Arco, there was that faint, insistent, driving Samba rhythm as a myriad transmissions from countless bands filled the airwaves around Arcturus. It was a lot like Alda Meina III, Jared thought, but far better.

When she arrived at his side, she set her bag down and prepared to say something.

He impulsively reached out and touched her shoulder with his fingertips. *Transmission...*

She paused for an instant, shocked. In that same moment, reorganizing her life, her wishes, her dreams, she reached up with both arms and embraced him around the neck.

This is the girl for me, Jared thought as he accepted her gift of love and faith.

He wrapped his arms around her, gently but firmly, and rocked her lightly from side to side. She swayed in his arms as if they were dancing.

Just for a moment. It was too early yet.

She pulled from his embrace, and he let her go.

She smiled at him, like a newly burst sun that warmed a planet that had been dark and alone for too long. "Glad you could make it."

"I wouldn't have done anything else. I had to see you."

She did have a little bit of a saucy edge. "Why am I not scared?"

He put his hands on her waist and held her at arms' length. She rested her hands on his forearms, accepting his possession of her, and taking possession of him in the same moment. He couldn't speak, though he wanted to tell her: *I am seeking a totally new life, and I think I have found it here with you...*

She gently disengaged, turning her side to him, and regarding him over one shoulder, though her eyes were slitted and secretive: "We do things slowly here, my friend. I feel so... so..."

"Yes?" He reached for his *duro*, which stood on the counter at his side, to finish it.

"So much like going for a swim!" With that, she bent in a swinging motion, gathered her bag, and ran away with a squeal of laughter.

Jared gulped the rest of his *duro*, left a tip, and walked toward the beach. He knew where to find her. And he did.

Already the beach was thronged. The air was hazy under a full sun with two small silver moons showing on the horizon. A dark curve, the distant shore, swung around pointing to the far ocean horizon. Colorful sails seemed almost frozen as the wind pushed them on distant courses.

All morning, Jared and Mala played in the thundering surf. She was Venus, walking in sea foam. He chased her, and she eluded him, laughing, until she was ready to be caught.

Somewhere in the throngs on the beach, he thought he glimpsed the faces of Naxo and Vaeja, watching in approval. Naxo had that wrinkled grin wreathed in frizzy dark hair. His eyes radiated raw pleasure as he wove nets with Vaeja.

Jared and Mala played, then had sea tea at a palm-thatched wooden stand overlooking the sand. They told each other all about their lives to date. Her full name was Mala Alameda, and he told her about his sister. He did not mention (yet) that she was a *djia*. So then they lay on the sand some more, and swam again. And again.

36. Apartment

In the afternoon, when they had lain on the sand together, side to side, belly to belly, back to back, butt to butt, and they were all talked out, and could no longer stand the hunger for each other, they walked hand in hand up the narrow, shady streets to Jared's apartment.

A vendor, passing by, said "Tourists" and waved balloons in their faces. Jared bought a red tea rose colored balloon for her, which she accepted with delight.

Oubrije, said the vendor in singsong Arcturian, *thanks*. He ran on to accost other tourists.

"We must look like foreigners," she said laughing as she waved the balloon happily in her free hand, on a pink silk ribbon, and let her other hand dangle all tangled with his between them.

"We are foreigners," he said laughing also, "in this new place."

She kept her next thought to herself, looking down at her feet brimming with joy, but he could read her mind with ancient instincts (no *djia* juice, no neural wireless needed). *Tourists but hopefully here to stay forever, yes?*

She gave him a sidelong glance, as if seeing him for the first time, and found him looking at her. He squeezed her hand encouragingly, and she squeezed back. *Done deal.*

Jared had an odd, empty feeling as they climbed the narrow stairway that had sand littered on its steps from many beach-going feet, and its air smelled faintly of onions and cinnamon amid distant sizzles of Samba rhythm.

Unlocking the door with a wave of his finger sworls, he stepped inside. Mala shadowed him behind, looking shy and ready to meet someone.

Jared stepped into the anteroom and knew instantly that he was alone. Stella was gone.

Light wood-grain floors gleamed. Everything was clean. Dishes neatly stacked. Window slightly open for fresh air. No Stella.

"What is it?" Mala asked, with a whiff of alarm.

"My sister," he said. "I need to explain a few things to you. Tea?"

She nodded. "Please." Setting the balloon aside in an honored place, she took possession of his space, in so far as it demanded a feminine half to complete it. She tied the silk ribbon of the balloon around an empty vase that stood glittering with cold, empty sunlight. Suddenly the glass glowed a tea rose red, warm and full. The tiniest gesture meant so much. She offered his heart the same glow.

Jared brought sea tea from the fridge and poured glasses for them. She sat beside him on the couch, with her knees pulled up, she held her ankles with one hand and the glass with the other, elbow resting close to his head. She listened attentively as he explained as best he could, without making an epic saga of it, that he'd fled from Mercury—who hadn't these days—she gave an accepting shrug—and he told her in rudimentary terms that he was a military attaché with the exiled princess, and that his sister was not his sister really but more of a sister of the princess, a *djia*, and Mala had heard about *djia* and was impressed if not a little scared.

That little bit of scared would remain in the air between them for a long time, for ever, but the deal they made was, as he expressed it: "I am separating myself from all that, from the past, and I want to start over here. I want to blend in, become a citizen, and see you for sea tea every morning."

I want to remain with you like this forever.

"I like that proposal," Mala said with a strong, humorous tone as she sipped her sea tea and demonstrated that she was an independent spirit of the beach and the sea, and would not be taken captive by foreign demons and their schemes. "I would like to meet this *djia* sometime. Is she pretty?"

"If you like electrons."

"I hear they don't have faces," Mala said a bit bitingly. *Jealous?* He loved it.

"They don't have a lot that humans do. They can be smart, can be your friend, above all they can be intensely loyal, but they cannot make love or even kiss. They have no holes and cannot make love."

"No holes?" Mala said with a throaty laugh, tossing her blonde fringe. Her mouth looked lush, her nose pert and slightly freckled or sunburned, her eyes blue as the sunny sea. "What fun is that?"

"We should become more comfortable," Jared said, making no body motions. Let her decide.

"I wish to lie down," Mala said, reaching up behind her neck with brownish-tanned fingers to undo her gown.

"I am suddenly exhausted."

"You should be," she said with a squeal of laughter. "You chased me around the water all morning." She reached out her hand.

He took her hand and rose. "And you ran from me the whole time."

"So very exhausting."

She led him to the bed, where she stripped off her small top and bottom. He did the same with his beach clothing.

They sank down naked beside each other for a long, delicious look.

"Kiss me."

He did.

And more...

...much more.

In the days that followed, Jared and Mala confirmed their love and spent every spare moment together. She was free, and moved into the apartment with him. He loved her more every hour. She was beautiful, as were so many of the Arcturian girls. Her physique was not exceptionally tall or slender, so much as it retained a hint of girlishness. Her skin asked to be touched: smooth and firm along the straightforward lines of her young and fertile body. She brought everything to Jared that he could ever ask, and she told him he was perfect for her.

He did not hear from Stella, and did not ask, but wished her well along the course of her stars. He did not hear from Lyxa or Lelli for that matter, and didn't want to know.

For the first time in years, he felt strong and in charge of his own life. With that in hand, he couldn't go backwards.

One day, when they returned from a morning at the beach, they found the locks had been changed and he was no longer welcome in the apartment that Lyxa kept for him.

Naxo stood out in the street, with his arms folded, and shrugged darkly.

Not a word needed to be said.

Accompanied by Vaeja, Naxo left in one direction.

Jared and Mala left in the opposite direction to walk to a distant beach, a smaller town named Onje or Onj, where she had a room with several other local girls who worked in the neighborhood—one girl in a shoe store on the beach street, another as data typist and bookkeeping clerk in a small warehouse for floss flippers, and other as barmaid in a wine bar, and then Mala as one of the shop girls in that bookstore full of glowing texts all around.

For a few weeks, they lived together and forgot all else.

One late evening, they even had a playful night-time ceremony in the surf, which was duly recorded in some local register as a legal marriage. Presiding was a drunken sea god from the local tavern, complete with messy beard and long hair and blurry eyes. His attendants were Mala's girlfriends wearing mermaid shells and wigs of glowing moon floss from underwater caverns. A few dozen swimmers and surfers and dancers surrounded them in a hemi-circle, a quarter moon of naked glistening forms, clapping and rocking in rhythm as the nuptials were sealed with sunshine and happiness. The darkness was illumined by a half-circle of bright smiles.

Jared reflected that he was now free of Imber, of Arco, of Naxo and Vaeja, of Lyxa and all, or so he hoped. It was a fresh start, and for the first time in a long time, Jared forgot about his vague dream of distant Lethe.

Mala gave him her love and her pledge, standing in the surf beside him, as the tide rolled in and the foam crashed around their knees and the super-moon, big daddy of Arcturian moons, glowed brightly in a blue-black heaven sprinkled with electronic dots.

Husband and wife...

37. Conspiracy Again

Just when he thought he had forgotten the past, Naxo showed up at the bookstore where he helped Mala out. Same frazzle of dark hair, same grizzle of beaming strength and dark purpose, but a new message from those dark and personable eyes.

They retired for *duros* at a nearby shop overlooking the half-moon of the little Onj beach, and its curling surf and dense forests shrouded in sea mist to the north and south.

"You've done well."

"I am happy. We are happy."

Naxo nodded. "We. What a wonderful word."

"Do you have 'we'?"

Naxo's youthful wrinkles shrank into a grin. "I do now. I have a thing going with Vaeja. She is incredible."

Jared nodded. "I was impressed from the day you introduced us."

"Funny how things work out." Naxo slurped noisily at his hot *duro* in its small glass cup. "I was attracted to Mala from the moment she wandered over to us at the beach. She swung in your orbit, and that left me with my fellow operative Vaeja. Who is recently divorced from her wife beater in Januarytown, and there was the perfect opportunity for me to offer assistance."

"I'm glad."

He said: "I came as a friend."

Jared was startled at the notion. "Yes, a friend. You brought me the finest gift of my life."

Naxo grinned. "The gift of love. You are a lucky man."

They toasted with their *duro* cups.

Naxo said: "I am here off the record."

"I can hardly wait to hear."

Naxo looked grim. "The other side will move at any moment. We are monitoring every move. They no longer care, because Lyxa and her allies have committed to a course of action that is foolhardy and dangerous beyond reason."

"Meaning?"

"Just to let you know—Lyxa and her allies are bringing a fleet of mercenary fighter ships into our system. The will try to take over the government here, turn it into a tyranny, and make her the queen. She already has a title."

"Oh no. What?"

"Mercuria. The lynch mob here, which is like anywhere else, loves drama and brutality and raw power. They don't understand that they're always the first victims. They have nothing, so they have nothing to lose."

"Can they be stopped?"

Naxo's face remained in that crinkle, but the smile was gone. His eyes were dark with passion and hurt. "We will stop them if it means we all die. We meaning all the military, the police, and normal decent citizens who understand what we would lose. It might mean civil war with the Stupid People and their demagogue leaders. I'm afraid the bad times have come here from Mercury Free Port City."

"I'm sorry."

"Not your fault." Naxo put a strong paw on Jared's forearm. "Just came to warn you. Take care of that beautiful golden girl."

"You take care of Vaeja."

Naxo nodded a final goodbye, turned, and left with hunched shoulders.

Jared did not immediately share the information with Mala. He didn't want to frighten her or cast a pall over their life together. Things were too good, for the first time ever, for ruthlessly greedy and ambitious, out of control oligarchs to destroy even this small joy in this little town.

Little town... Lethe...

He treasured what time remained, before something must be done.

Next day, they walked across the beach to a shady spot where they spread a sheet on the sand. After a swim, and a fanny-grabbing chase around the beach, they lay on the sheet.

Mala went off to get some sea tea and fruit ices.

Jared lay dozing on his belly, resting his chin on his fists. That old sadness gnawed at him, like the darkness of the Olympia House. He looked once again into the maw of horror, and pulled away. He started to rub his eyes hard with his knuckles to drive that vision away.

A foot was planted in his back and gently rotated there. He looked over his shoulder and smiled at Mala, no quite knowing what to say. She pulled him out of his reverie.

"What's the matter?" She dropped to her knees by his side and rubbed his shoulder roughly.

He made as if to bite here ankle. "I was afraid you ran away."

She laughed deep from a warm, tanned throat. Jared turned over and looked at her. He radiated him with a look of deepest devotion and sincerity. Her hair was burnished gold. Her eyes sparkled cloud-pale in a lovely tanned face. "I would never leave you, not ever."

He pressed his cheek to her warm, soft, tanned knees. When he felt their warmth against his face, he cupped the wondrous knees in both hands, and his head rose, first to look at her eyes, then to sink against a warm golden thigh, and he pressed his cheek against it. He kissed a slender golden hand. She held him to her, nurturing as if he were a small boy, and rubbed his hair comfortingly. She knew his past was filled with monsters, like those things rearing out of the fog and green biolume glow of the deep underworld.

He sweated, then relaxed, as she hummed a lullaby while holding him to her. He watched little waves roll in, turn up, bend in, gently dip down, and disappear—leaving just foam on the sand in a thin border like lace.

"Look what I brought, before they melt." Mala offered him a transparent gel cup of green and red fruit ice, glowing with the absorbed intensity of the sun.

They each took theirs, and enjoyed a few minutes of delicious sweetness, then put their cups on the sand to dissolve in sunlight and water.

"I'm sorry," he mumbled.

"It's all right." She hugged and kissed him, with her knees under his torso, and her arms wrapped around him from behind and above. She nuzzled his neck, and with her mouth made a loud farting noise in the soft skin under his ear. "You're mine, all mine, and I'm going to keep you."

He looked at her. She was smiling. "I'm keeping you too," he said.

She nodded. That was done. She was that sort of girl. Beautiful, in the moment, matter of fact, nothing to get excited about, *let's move on...*

They walked in silence to the edge of the sea and walked along the edge to the outer tip of a stone breakwaters. There Jared sat down on a sunken boulder and let seawater ebb and flow soothingly around his feet. She touched his cheek. Softness on stretched leather. "Who's in there?" she said speaking of his head.

He laughed. "I frighten myself sometimes." He added: "I frighten easily."

"Nothing ever changes here," she said. "You'll get used to it. So boring. So not terrifying, scary, deadly, or otherwise bad for your health."

"I believe you." They held hands. "I put all my faith in you, and in this beautiful little place. I don't want to be a warrior anymore. I don't want to be a champion, an athlete, a leader of warships. I just want to be a humble man living in a little town with the most beautiful young woman in the world."

"You realize that means having children?"

He grinned. "Is that what they do for excitement around here?"

"We have an annual seafood festival." She made a blank face. "Bring your own crabs."

They burst out laughing together.

He took her hand. She tugged, and he jumped to his feed. She ran ahead lithely, he watching delightedly as her supple golden body, with its small bones of porcelain and its firm fleshed limbs danced over the hazy water.

The bad memories went away. He felt happy again. The concept of Lyxa (Queen Mercuria) and an approaching fleet and dark war as he'd seen in Mercury FPC seemed distant again. Even if worst came to worst, they would hide hire until the fighting was over and peace restored. Life would go on, boring and happy, sunny with seafood, as it always had and always would.

They walked hand in hand on the beach. Same faint vapor, sound of crashing waves, smell of salt water, brooding sun like a lemon in crushed ice, same Samba sizzle in the way people walked and an occasional ground car passing on the ocean boulevard.

At the edge of the sea, where the sand was cool looked flat and hard, but mashed cool under the feet like wetted brown sugar. Mala stepped over the test the water with one toe. Jared lifted her and waded in. She kicked and yelled but he waded on. A cold band of water rose along his body and he gasped, and she jumped too. The water was lukewarm and filled with tiny particles. Mala was warm in his arms, her body heat mingling with his. Then Jared faltered in a great wave, was swept off his feet, and icy water only was where Mala had been.

Just like that. How things happen. She's gone.

Jared shivered, standing on the tips of his toes. The water began immediately to dry on his skin where it was exposed to the air. He poked about the water.

From behind, her soft, warm, long arms circled his neck, and he felt her body on his back, heavy with water. They went down together, spluttering. Jared dived forward as his head went under, but she clung while he twisted playfully. Stopping and letter her shoot on by momentum, he got her in front of him. He lifted her high up over his head. How light! He was chin-deep in water, his mouth gulping and spitting salty water, and he floundered blindly. While he tripped about, trying to get into position to throw her, she planted her feet on his shoulders and dived off with a back kick that sent him under.

They played for hours, until it was time to work in the bookstore. They walked along the beach toward the center of town, holding hands, while the first mellow little lanterns of evening winked on, and the sun became a dark-red splash of fruit ice over the hills beyond town.

38. Sun Flare

So the days passed.

The full summer sky started to deepen with Arcturian violet as the sun's savagely flaming hulk of incandescent gold plowed a vibrant furrow over the horizon. In the end, only ruddy brass was left, of neither air nor sea, soon resolving itself into flecks of dancing light and bits of fiery orange cloud.

Jared and Mala sat at the sidewalk café tables in front of the bookstore. Each had a sea tea and a *beandevanille* cookie.

She said: "They say it's a sun flare. We get those every once in a while. They usually make a longer summer, and a hotter one."

He chewed his cookie and made a cocky face. "You'll keep me cool."

She gave him a knee under the table. "You need cooling. Hot lover."

Despite the sun flare, at night in the town, the sky was a bare, unplowed field. A few stars winked, and a few air ships pushed slowly through the heavens. Streets were brightly lit with rows of lights that seemed soft and sleepy-eyed, because nothing bigger than people's little lives and concerns ever happened here.

By day, they woke when they felt like it, ate as they wished, and wandered hand in hand to the beach. If it became boring, they could swim, or they could read or watch screen shows broadcast from Imber or Arco. Jared enjoyed lying tangled with her as they watched boring news, silly game shows with babbling laughing men and women, dramas about family crises, crime shows, or horror that was more laughable than scary.

Jared would steal a glance at his wife. Mala's face, illumined so her faint skin hairs glowed honey and diaphanous like insect or fairie wings, was always so calm. Softly he liked to put his arm around her. She'd lean closer. A soft shadow deepened in the corner of her mouth as she smiled inwardly and mysteriously. Jared loved to study the glistening of her lips, to touch them with his own. Her lips were cool and delicate. He unfolded her love as a bee unfolds the sweet, honeyed flower…

Lethe only seldom passed dimly through his mind. *Lethe*...

…and he held Mala tighter.

One afternoon, while Mala was working in the bookshop, Jared sat alone on in their favorite little coffee shop. He was outside, in front, with the beach spread before him. Under his umbrella, he had his bare, tanned feet up and listened idly to Samba sizzle while reading a screen book about Arcturian plants. He and Mala were thinking of opening a flower shop. Oddly, wasn't it Stella who liked to read about plants and vegetables.

A man's voice cut him from behind like a gutting knife: "Starfleet Officer Jared Fallon."

The hard, paunchy man in his fifties slipped around and sat near him on the next bench. He looked totally out of place in this tiny town with its sea breezes and easy manner. "My name is Onatol Gorvy. I'm a, shall we say, friend of a friend of yours. You may remember Lyxa." He placed a tan, cloth-covered box on the table between them, with a leather grip on top. The box was about big enough to put a large melon inside.

The man continued, as Jared gaped. "Lieutenant Fallon...Late of the Mercurian Star Fleets, the United Galaxy Organization, and the Mercurian League..."

Shocked, Jared stared at the man. "You have the wrong guy."

"Oh no," said the man, rubbing fat hard fingers together as if they were worms. "No my friend. We know all about you."

"We." It was a question.

"Yeah, you ignorant fool. Friends of yours. Friends of Lyxa and her associates."

"Not interested."

"You remember Lyxa." He favored Jared with a sleazy look.

"I remember Lyxa. You shouldn't even speak her name, you turd."

"I like that. You respect your queen."

"My princess, last I heard. How is Lelli?"

"The *djia*? She is always by her majesty's side."

"And Stella?"

He shrugged. "Don't know any Stella. Never heard of her."

Jared looked out toward the enigmatic sea. Had his dearest friend walked out into the waters after all, ended it all? Had Stella's final act of loyalty been to kill herself so she could no longer transpond between Jared and Lelli and therefore Lyxa? He'd assumed Stella would go back to be with Lelli and Lyxa. He felt a fist of grief knotting in his gut.

Olympia House...

The beasts were coming loose again. All the joy of living quietly here with Mala was torn suddenly like a wound reopened, and pus and underground smoke issued. He remembered the mournful, enraged, and tragic bellowing of dying beasts echoing through the slimy corridors of the O-House.

"I am not interested in your schemes."

"Oh but you have to be. You see, right now there are important things happening in this world's capital."

"Not my concern."

"Wrong, Lieutenant. We need every hand on deck."

"I'm not an officer."

"You are commissioned, and you swore an oath. Your queen calls on you."

"My queen. Look, I'm going to walk away—."

The hard, fat, ruthless-looking man raised a hand. "One thing."

The tone in that voice told Jared what he was about to hear.

"Your little bitch here."

"My wife."

"A joke. A native girl. Son, we can help her to have an accident any moment. She could drown in a stray wave, or have a stack of book servers fall on her."

Jared felt frozen, enraged, helpless, even murderous.

"I love those eyes, son. You look like a bug stuck on a pin." He laughed and made motions with his thick yellowish fingers in front of his lips. "Now make gaping mouth." He laughed harshly, a sick, choking series of wheezes as if he were about to drop dead of a heart attack. Which, unfortunately, he didn't. As the stranger raised his arm to make motions, Jared noticed a gun holster under the man's coat. These people were armed, dangerous, and not fooling around.

As Jared stared, the man added: "You can keep the bitch. We don't care. We just need you in the capital now."

"Now?" Jared thought about sprinting away.

"Get up and walk quietly with me. Don't make any gestures, or I'll kill you. You've seen the gun."

"I've seen the gun," Jared agreed. "You're doing something very stupid. The Arcs are onto you."

"How would you know?"

"A bird whispered in my ear."

"Oh? Like this little birdie?" He lifted a flap in the side of the box.

Inside was a jar, with Naxo's head floating pickled in a urine-colored wine brine.

Jared's gut lurched. He nearly vomited.

Down went the flap, hiding the horrible vision.

Onatol Gorvy rose, a sleazy man in a rumpled dark suit. "Come along, Captain. Yes, we've promoted you to full command. We have work to do, and no time."

Jared walked automaton-like as the man walked behind him. "My air car is over there, Fallon. Keep going. Pick up the pace."

Jared processed a million thoughts a second. This was all happening so fast and so suddenly. For Stella it was probably too late. For Mala… that was unthinkable.

"Open the door."

Jared walked around the dark, glowing glassy-metallic ovoid with its black lift torpedoes on either side. It had a front cab, and a rear compartment. Two doors on each side. In the pilot's seat up front was a vaguely man-shaped robot pilot, visible only as a shadow from outside the lightly tinted port windows.

"In back."

Jared opened the door. He stepped up onto a lift vent, and put one foot into the passenger compartment. The inside glowed softly with yellowish courtesy lighting embedded like tiny scones in the plush dark-blue-gray carpeted walls. Same texture on the floor.

Jared had both feet up and stood in the compartment now.

To his left, the robot pilot looked frozen over his traveling, flickering controls

Telemetry is everything now...

Jared felt the pulsing flow of signals in his body. Stella had told him, and he now understood. He'd been partially *djia*'d by Lyxa, just enough for her to use Stella to track him. He was a transponder himself, without knowing it.

Onatol Gorvy made a groaning, coughing sound as he strained to heft his ungainly body in its dark clothing up onto the vent. It would take him another minute of concentrated, red-faced fumbling to get a grip and pull himself up in to the compartment.

Jared took one look at the signal relay in the cockpit, surrounding the pilot with a subvisible energy net, so that a transmitter atop the thing's so-called head sent a signal to the broadcast transponder, which was a dark donut atop the flying machine.

His second look, as Onatol Gorvy's fat hands grasped the door frame to pull him up, was at the gun wavering in the man's hand. "Excuse me," Jared said, "you need a hand. Let me help you." In that same instant, he tore the gun from Onatol Gorvy's hand. In one whirling move, he lifted the glast window, a narrow strip that separated cockpit from passenger compartment, and shot the transponder cube off the robot's head. The second depleted uranium slug took the robot's head off. The third slug went into Onatol Gorvy's wheezing, shocked face, sending a large blob of brains and bone and hair out into the night air.

The agent crumpled over the broad surface of the vent grill on the lift torpedo slung to the side, one on each side. Working fast, Jared pulled the heavy blob of dead meat and fat into the compartment. Swinging out onto the vent, he kicked the door shut.

He pulled open the cockpit door and hauled himself into the quietly blinking control unit of the air car. By shooting the transmitter, he'd severed the connection to the nearest flight cell, meaning there was no connection with the sending air field. They'd start looking for their missing air car any minute now.

By shooting the robot, he'd disabled any chance for the thing to mechanically alert its handlers there was a problem.

The robot was a squarish tangle of boxes, now dead and frozen with its insect-like mandibles stuck in mid-air and mid-something, whatever it had been about to do.

Jared used his foot to shove the man-sized robot, now a ruin, along a dual seat-track so it rolled to the passenger side and stopped dead cold against the door.

The remote handlers could start searching any second now. Their first action, after loss of telemetry, would be to activate the remote viewing lenses. Jared spent another bullet blowing away the telemetric glass eye staring at him. He noticed its status light was orange. Active would be green. So he'd gotten to that before any human miles away thought to take a look through it.

There was no time left. He overrode the remote and the robotic controls, and spent a sweaty several minutes figuring out how to reprogram the vehicle to drift slowly out to sea and sink itself about ten kilometers out, where the ocean was at its deepest.

Feeling the vehicle start to move, he spent the rest of the bullets shooting holes in the black boxes that were a search party's last resort. With all the telemetry gone, searchers would assume that Onatol Gorvy's air car had crashed. They would then begin a search for the black boxes.

Jared jumped just as the air car began seriously moving.

He landed two meters below on soft sand, and rolled to soften his landing. It was jarring nonetheless. He caught one last glimpse of a dark, lifeless shadow fleeting across the beach road, over the sand at about three meters up and rising, and dwindling rapidly into a dot and then nothing. In a few minutes it would stop, ask for instructions from the robot, and not getting any, it would set down. Only instead of parking to await further instructions, it would sink a kilometer or more into the lightless mulmy sea bottom, never to be heard from again. And Onatol Gorvy with it. *Good riddance…*

39. Hurried

Not much time…

Jared burst into the apartment, where Mala was just starting to relax after working at the bookshop.

Golden girl…

She looked thin and frightened as she sat stiffly on the couch and he knelt before her, confessing that he'd just killed a man who had threatened her life.

Mala sat frozen in terror and shock, holding one hand with splayed fingers over her heart.

Her corn silk hair trembled as it hung around her head.

Her eyes were wide, and darkening as if their pale gray were storming up.

"We've got to leave here now." He knelt before her, holding her arms in his.

"Jared… this is our home…"

"It is, and it will be. As I explained, the people I've told you about want me back. They've threatened to kill you if I don't obey."

She didn't cry, but regarded him with stone-cold, horrified icy reason. Maybe Stella had been like that too, walking into the sea if that's how she'd disappeared. Where could a *djia* hide on a planet where she was such an anomaly?

Jared took her hands and kissed them, left and right, over and over.

"What if we go to the police?"

"He had the police's head in a jar. These people are very powerful."

Mala considered. "I know there is rioting in the big cities. Mobs are turning on the government and smashing windows. We don't understand it here in the provinces, but I heard in the bookshop that it's spreading."

"We need to get out of here."

"Where too, Jarry, and with what?"

"We have a car, and a little savings."

"That's true." She considered all this with cavern-like eyes and pale, narrow features. Her bones seemed to glow. "I may be pregnant, too. I don't know yet. I was going to tell you if it's true. I've been so excited." At that, she lost it, and dissolved into tears. She crumpled into his arms, and fell on the floor beside him. He held her while she silently quavered, until her crying became loud. It hurt his heart more than his ears, this sound like glass cutting into the delicate flesh of his love for her.

She composed herself and crawled into his embrace. Just the two of them, alone in their cozy little apartment across the street from the sea. It was so nice…

She sniffled, and wiped her nose with the bottom of her wrist. "Tell me what you want me to do."

"Well, I love you with all my heart, and if I could save you just by leaving, it would break my heart but I would do so."

"I'm prepared to leave here if it means being with you."

"The other problem is that Lyxa neuro-wirelessed me so I'm a transmitter. I think Stella is gone…"

"Gone?"

"Dead. Probably. She never contacted me, and I have no idea. I'm a walking buoy in the sea, Mala. I send out a signal, and a *djia* like Lelli could find me in an instant. Would Lelli turn me in? I don't know. She is loyal, and she was a friend of Stella. Where her loyalty would go first, I don't know. What I can't afford is to have you here, being killed by Lyxa's goons just out of spite or whatever."

"Oh my god."

"Yeah. The other part is that wherever I go, I can be tracked. If you're with me, you are in as much danger as I am."

"So we have to split up?"

"Just for a while. I want you to leave here right now. Do you have someplace to hide, in one of the cities?"

She nodded. "I know of a woman who owns a bookshop in Cordulee. That's a town on the other side of the world. I think she'll take me in for a little while."

"Meanwhile," he said, "I'll get to the ferry port, and out into space."

She gave him a long, resigned look. "Lethe?"

He'd told her all about himself, his origins in the simple farming world of Lesht to which there was no going back, his triumphs at the Academy, the great promise of his athletic career whose pinnacle was that run over the Arch of Victory, and then the unthinkable—his seizure by Princess Lyxa, and the end of his dreams. Mala understood about Lethe, his last-ditch refuge.

"I'm sorry I came into your life."

She shook her head. "No, my love, I married you for best or worst. No matter what happens, I will be as loyal as your *djia*. I would die for you."

He squeezed her hands. "I would die for you as well."

After a moment of staring into each other's eyes, a distant explosion startled them.

"What was that?" he asked, jumping up.

"Probably just fishermen, shooting harpoons out in the deep sea. We hear it every summer."

"Close call then, and lucky for us if that's all it is. Let's go."

They packed lightly, leaving only a note saying they were going on vacation, and drove away down the coastal road.

At the edge of the capital city, not far from the orbital shuttle port, they had a long, clinging goodbye. Then he watched as their small ground car puttered away into the night. In a few days she'd arrive in Cordulee and visit with her friend, where she'd be safe until he called her.

He turned and walked toward the ferry port, where blazing ferries rose and fell in the night sky. He had enough money with him for a hop to one of the orbital satellite cities. From there, he must use his ingenuity to cage rides across the Temporale interstice between times and spaces, until his landing on the remote system that contained the frontier world of Lethe.

40. Flight

What hurt the most was not only being separated from Mala, and losing their wonderful little existence by the beach—but the question of how long they would be apart, or even if they would ever find each other again.

His journey to Lethe involved a bit of serendipity, luck, and for once fate and fortune were with him. He wandered about the orbital star port until he happened to meet a guy who knew a guy who told him of a guy who worked in a bar where a guy from some remote place often came when he brought huge cargos of logs, furs, and other goods from the frontier worlds. Yes, one of those frontier worlds was Lethe. And yes, they needed a trained ship's officer to manage the cargo section and its forty humans and twenty androids as well as all the paperwork and so forth.

So, in a journey lasting a little over ninety standard UGO days, which translated into about 2200 standard hours (as set by UGO for all humankind based on ancient records from Old Earth) Jared at last found himself alone and broke, but on Lethe.

Part III: Lethe

A frozen swirl of hazy light glowed in one sector of sprinkled stars above the horizons of Larth Atuuinl and Ramtha Aprui's world.

That was the Great Silver Shell Galaxy, to which the sun Rama belonged. According to the Old Ones, the fore-parents of Larth and Ramtha and their kind, this shell contained a great black snail weaving an endless blanket of stars with many splendorous fabrics: Gold thread, silver thread, jewel-crusted electrum thread. The solar system of Rama, with its sixteen planets, had been born from that glistening stream of beauty, including the planet Vellallo and its two silvery moons.

Larth thought it must be cold up there. A sudden chill touched him as he saw what looked like movement. Tiny wavering stars in that region seemed to be saying something from afar as they communicated in a code of twinkling.

Ramtha sighed in her slumber beside him, unaware of his unease. She must be dreaming, Larth thought.

Ramtha Apatrui.

She was his—a golden one, a love, the woman who made his life complete. He was jubilant with fire as he looked at her and saw her beauty. With greatest concern he brushed a glowing bug off the soft skin of her face. Her face was pale and liquescent, deeply glowing like a pearl in the soft light that bathes the night; a small face nestled amid ample hair that had all the subtle tinges of dark, polished wood. Larth smiled when she wrinkled her nose as his finger brushed against it.

Clumsy…!

To his relief, she slept on, which kept his vision intact, so delicate in lunar light.

He rose. Something disturbing was in the air. The launch complex was just half a horizon away, nestled among the grassy hills. Lights glowed softly in the city there, where thousands of souls slept now but tomorrow the first orbital rocket launch would be ready, and Larth must be in the cockpit.

Back soon, he thought, as if speaking to her.

Back always, her dreams said woman-like. Her eyes remained closed, but her smile glowed in moonlight.

Larth strained his eyes to look into the darkness some distance across the meadows. The world's first cosmos ship, a pioneer needle, lay there lost in its own shadows. The wooden rack, a wedge spun of dark strands, with its complex arrangement of tremendous girders, lay out there, pointing upward in the night.

On it, also pointing upward, lay the needle-nosed bulk that was to take Larth to the edge of space and back.

Will it work? he wondered, feeling some fear. *Will I survive and return to Ramtha, or will I burn up and become a brief twinkling of stars?*

He pushed such thoughts aside. What ever happened, it would be quick and painless.

He thought that it was strange that he, of all the inhabitants of Vellallo, should have been chosen for the first step to the stars that had since antiquity presented such a puzzle to his people. But he thought of the world to come, and shivered in his determination.

Magic was in the night. Larth could almost see fairy Nannamae and Lillallai playing with the strange, carefree nudity of their kind among grass blades and toadstools, one of which was the fabled throne of their ruler; or so the Old Ones said.

The Old Ones...

Larth looked across the meadows stirring softly in the night, over the forests in their angled gloominess, at a small wan glow. Apatruila...their village...from which he would go and...

He felt impatient. Ramtha Apatrui slept. Soon, if all went well on his space flight, he would be back with her. He leaned close over her, almost touching her, but did not waken her. He leaned over and breathed in the warm sweetness of her breath.

Then he felt again the fearful impatience, afraid that anything might be changed. Rising, he scrutinized the velvety dusk and soft lights.

There. That odd, gnawing feeling, his fears, became real. Or unreal. But true...

A strange thing happened. A crackling and rustling came from the woods nearby, as though a great wind were rustling among the trees. Larth was rigid with fear that one of the ancient gods might be coming to stop him, to slay him, voice of the wind, vision of shadow, impression vague and without knowledge.

A small gale embraced Larth, and he fell to his knees—hard on the good ground of Vellallo.

As he held his head and coiled up in a mixture of marvel and terror, a singing wind enveloped him. He was inside a spacecraft of some time, a flying thing that had come from the stars and slingshot around the sun and now sizzled with cold energy cross-tangent the surface of Vellallo.

Two beings laughed and chatted in the cockpit of that starship with its myriad rolling control lights and dull brassy shimmering interior glow. They were a male and female, ghosts of long-ago living beings, somehow very much like the inhabitants of Vellallo or a billion other worlds across the galaxy. For a moment, he felt their freedom, their exhilaration, their love, their self-assurance. He glimpsed laughing faces, happy eyes, behind heavy rippling cabin pressure suits. Their helmets were round, shadowy, with shining spots around their dark upturned eye shades.

A moment later, that ephemeral pressure relented.

Already they were past, gone, flown over the horizon, invisible, at great speed.

The singing wind seemed to pass, for it abated momentarily.

41. Lethe

Jared listened in the silence for a moment. The ferry's engines were still rustling as they settled and cooled. The monotonous droning had ended. The engines were stilled.

The flight down had been routine. Nothing dramatic. Decompression at 5,000 meters, then the last bit as an ordinary air flight.

The realization was overwhelming: at last, he was on Lethe.

"It's raining out," the pilot said. "But you can feel the warmth of the summer air."

Jared smelled it—like flowers, like perfume.

Jared brought his carrypack to the hatch. He could hear the rain. It beat on the hull as on tin. Jared waited for the pilot to open the hatch, the last thin layer between himself and Lethe.

He felt like a man who had died and wished he could stay there. Being without Mala was worse than death. Not knowing… that was even worse. But now, if anything, he must make a new life for both of them. They would stay here in this idyllic place away from civilization until things resolved themselves back on Arcturus. With luck, the conspirators would be killed or imprisoned. He had no love left for Lyxa, not even the shred of an illusion. The fat guy, Grover Overshoe or whatever, had been the final straw. Lyxa had to have known what his threats would mean to Jared. He wished the best for Lelli, and a loving memory for Stella… and now he must get on with the future, what was left of it. Mala was everything. Without here, there was nothing. With her, anything was possible.

The pilot, a trim little man in a flight suit, with short sandy hair and an easy-going expression, finished flicking his switches. The pilot then came to the door, slipping on a thin raincoat and, sticking his flight log between his knees, turned the heavy wheel that controlled the mechanisms of the door. "It's raining out, I'm told."

Jared smiled. There was no hiss of decompression equalization; no jangle of bells, no slashing of signal lights, merely a nondescript bang as the door sprang open.

Lethe: Lethe entered with a gust of rain, aseptic wind, and the smell of wet fields and soaked grass. This was no gloomy coffin of the night, lit up by the billion candles of the Mercurian night sky; no churning, chilly fog and drizzle. It was the rain, clean and fresh with a long, tail wind that dashed the water in all directions. A cold, wet leaf plastered itself in Jared's face. He brushed it off, blinking as the icy spray found his eyes. He spouted a fine spray of water from his lips. The air was almost too, too fresh; it filled his lungs with exhilaration.

The pilot ran down the steps into the rain, his feet resounding on the metal gangway. Jared, immediately immersed in cool water, followed him over the rim of the bus berth, which was overgrown with wild grassed. They ran across a primitive sort of asphalt field, long crumbling and puddle-riddled.

A high wall loomed overhead, and they pushed blindly through ha gate in this wall. Jared's feet met old wood. The door slammed shut behind. Here it was dry.

They were in an old general store. "Anyone there?" the pilot shouted. A high, clear old voice answered form the depths of the store: "So you finally made it, eh? I've been waiting three hours past closing time, that's how late you are!" The voice belonged to a paunchy, bald man with long, stiff arms, dressed in coveralls and a brown leather apron. The man noticed Jared. "Oh, one passenger? Here's sit down and make yourselves at home, before I throw you back into the rain."

The pilot put a hand on Jared's arm. "Why don't you take off your coat. You can hang it on the door there." Jared hung up his coat, feeling a tingle of excitement at their friendliness, and stepped back beside the pilot.

"Chairs," the storekeeper said, and brought three. "Hot chocolate," he said, and hesitated—"I'll have to reheat it. Damn your soul, Efraim Bondy, that ferry cart of yours gets more and more sluggish as the days go by!"

When the old man went away, Bondy told Jared: "Do you want to take a room here? They run about one *shel*, if I remember right."

Jared shrugged. "Sure." Tomorrow, he would go exploring , searching for a place in this new world. Now that he was faced with the real immediacy of doing that, his initial excitement changed into a more subdued determination.

It struck him that there was something very familiar at this store. That big hunting trophy there...all done up in beads and tickets of cloth. Hadn't he once sat here and wondered for long hours what culture of people might have hunted and decorated that exotic three-horned beast? The words stumbled over his tongue: "Bel...Beryl...Bar...BARIN!"

The old man turned and held out two mugs of hot chocolate, spilling some on the floor. "That's my name," he answered, surprise.

"Kodi Barin! Don't you remember me? Years ago, I came here with the Mercurian Space Navy!"

Barin guffawed. "Oh, yes. The crazy Mercurians!" Casually, he bent down and mopped up the drops of chocolate with a rag.

Jared bit his lip. "I heard one of your boys was killed." Indeed the Mercurians hadn't been too well liked. He'd have to make it clear that he wasn't with the Mercurians anymore.

Barin nodded, tossing the rag aside and settling in one of his chairs. "Yup. Almer's boy. Tried to stow away in one of those infernal space ships that came and crushed our ferry port and blew out a thousand acres of good land."

He was...burned, wasn't he?"

Barin nodded somberly.

"I'm here to settle. I want to become a Lethean," Jared pleaded.

Barin looked at him suspiciously. "Why?"

"I fled Mercury City before the big war."

"What big war? Where are all the big space ships?"

Jared blanched. "They're all gone."

Barin brightened, shedding some of his suspicion. "You know, come to think of it, someone was saying that there was a big war. Is Lethe in any danger?"

Jared winked. "Not a bit."

Barin thrust his chin out. "Are you a deserter?"

"No," Jared smiled grimly, "a single, fragile human being who wants to be free of dictatorships and assassinations and madness.

"Well, you have to live with your mind," Barin said. "As long as you feel you're right to the moment you die, that's what counts."

"I may be the last survivor," Jared said to Barin.

"Really bad place, huh?" Barin said, staring at the floor between his elbows.

The pilot put his empty cup aside and wiped his mouth with his sleeve. "Tell us about the war."

Jared shrugged. "We'll know after a long time, when it doesn't matter anymore."

Barin nodded. "We have heard stories about seven-story monster robots that can fly like space ships, and planets suddenly breaking apart without warning, and so on."

Jared lowered his head. "Probably all true."

"Drink your hot chocolate," Barin said, picking up his rag and tossing it from one hand into the other.

Jared looked into the cracked top of a barrel on which his steaming chocolate stood. A dark green mass floated in liquid in the barrel. When he took his first sip, Jared thought he detected a hint of tuma, but that was probably an illusion. Cocoa was rare in the Galaxy, and few people had accurate sense memories of its true taste. On the other hand, tuma did create illusions; that was its function; a fascinating dilemma.

Barin's was a cluttered little store, not filled with the glaring colors of a large store on the more advanced planets, but plain packets and wrapperless tools.

There was a feeling of wear about the place. Many feet walking had blackened the floor so that the wood resembled swarthy ham, and headless nails in the floorboards gleamed. A draft regulator banged tiresomely somewhere, and a soggy rain rattled on the wooden roof with its tin covering. Smells of fish, sawdust, floury cereals and strong coffee permeated the interior, and it was a good aroma.

Barin ventured: "Have any plans about staying?"

Jared nodded. “I’m going to stay. Maybe get a small farm.” Somehow he had the feeling that his aspirations were a little big, even considering that he’d once been a simple farm boy far away. His tone was close to asking.

Barin rubbed the gray fuzz on his cheek, which made a rasping noise. “Have any money?”

Jared shook his head. “The war took it.”

Barin proffered his hand. “Well, you’ll need money to buy a farm. Probably several hundred shel. Would you be willing to work for me until you earn that much?”

Jared bit his lip. “I would want to make as much money in as little time possible.”

Barin shook his head, smiling darkly. “On this planet you’ll never work in the city and be able to save for a farm. Even if you save for a farm, there are plenty of regulations that would keep your money tied down to the city.”

“Why is that?”

“Why, you remember the big landowners don’t you? They own most of the farmland, so they control the rural assemblies. They don’t want any new farmers coming in from the cities, so there are laws and taxes against it.”

Jared thought hard. “That doesn’t sound too good for what I had in mind. All I want is a small farm.”

Barin nodded. “You can get your small farm, but by law you’ll have to raise the money for it in the country. Not in the city. When you do get your farm, you’ll have to pay a tremendous land tax on it. So, on that score, you’d be better off being a tenant farmer and paying part of the Free Farmer’s tax, which means you’ll be paying less than half as much. Tell me, why do you want to be a farmer?”

“To be close to the land, that sort of thing.”

Barin grimaced. “Bullshit. Farming is hard. It’s a bare existence. I don’t think you’ll ever make a farmer.”

“Well? What would you have me be?”

“Why not get a job with a Free Farmer, where you can take a walk whenever you want, but still not have to break your back tilling a field. Can you write?”

“I graduated on the Commandant’s Roll of Honor at the Mercurian Academy of the Stars—finest school in the universe.”

Barin whistled. “You could get any job in the world with a record like that. Look, why don’t you get in touch with the Free Farmer’s Council in Vladis. They’ll place you in a good position.”

The pilot, who by now had risen and was putting on his coat, interjected: “Isn’t that Farmer Vardis looking for a diploma-type individual?”

Barin snapped his finger excitedly. “That’s right!”

Jared said: “What type of work is that?”

“Oh, you know—someone who works with figures…maybe even a school teacher.”

Jared's mind began to play with new and frightening, but interesting possibilities. School teacher…revolutionize the world…

"For a tenth-shel an hour," Baron interrupted Jared's thoughts, "I'll give you work until you get a better job."

"Have a good time," the pilot said, leaving.

"What sort of work?" Jared asked Barin, his mental machinery turning amid a daze of tiredness.

"Oh—deliveries, keeping shop, that sort of stuff. Easy work, but low pay. I'll give you plenty of time off to see Lethe, and get established."

"Fine. I'll take it. Where will I live?"

"Give you a good room with a mountain view for eight shel a week. You can buy your food and necessities here at half-price, since you're working for me."

Jared agreed. "Do you own this place?"

"Nope. The Farmers own it. I'm an *urbani* myself—from the city, but pretty much of a free-thinker. I don't see anything wrong with liking the countryside."

Jared shook his head. "I came here to get away from the bad. I only hope, for the sake of my sanity, that this planet gives me the peace I need."

Barin put his hand on Jared's shoulder. "It will. It will. It's a good planet, with lots of open country. If you love the country, you'll be happy here. Just realize that people here are people like everywhere else—which is, after all, good. You have to live with the bad."

Jared brightened: "As long as the bad things can be lived with, I guess you're right."

"Sure. Now tell me. What do you know about Lethe?"

"Not much, I suppose."

Barin slapped his knee and laughed. That's what I thought. I couldn't believe it at first. I couldn't believe that someone would come to a totally strange world just on the basis of its greenness."

Jared shook his head gravely. "You don't know what that means to a spaceman."

"I supposed not."

"What are the city people called?—*urbani*?"

"That's right. The urbani in the city; the *volgai*—those are the country folk; and the *domraiga*, who are totally worthless, live in trailer camps, and steal to stay alive."

"Oh." There was a moment's silence. Jared got the feeling that no matter where humans lived, the same sorts of animosities and class differences existed. It was disappointing.

Barin had rattled off the three categories with a vehemence that perhaps showed something of an uglier side in his thoughts. He appeared to have an innate hatred for the last category of people, and Jared wasn't sure if there weren't more types of people than 'city' and 'country' who could be useful. "Oh," he said, and said nothing more.

Rain continued to whisper about, like a spider as it wove a snug nest. They talked about the country store and rainy season and uses of robots—not well known here; and Jared, sitting in his wicker chair, fell asleep. He did not dream.

42. Rain Looking

A crush in the distance awakened Jared Fallon. He sat forward in the hard wicker chair, arms sore from the arm rests.

His first thought was Mala. In the confusion of his sudden wakening, he wondered why he was not sleeping on his side, and why she was not in bed beside him.

As though all during his sleep he had been tightening and tightening like a coiled spring with the knowledge of his being on Lethe, the realization surged through his marrow, leaving him in a majestic wash like that of great organ: Lethe!

It was a hot summer morning, promising more of the same throughout the day. It was a Guaranteed Day. Plenty to do, plenty to see. He saw Barin outside the window, lip-mouthing with a man in farm clothes and in heat and brightness.

Jared touched the barrel of floating greens at his side. Yes, yesterday had happened, because the cocoa cup still stood there. It was morning, yes, because that was what the air said. He rubbed his eyes. A beam of sunlight, bar of fiery gold, slanted in through the window, silent and from beyond the far, far mountains. The sun ringed the window with notes of light and probed into a shadowy corner of the store, illumining the coarse, ragged material of a flour sack cast in dust.

"So you're awake at last!" Barin tramped in and made the door crash. "Why, I must be a farmer! Time was, when I could sleep past sunup." He carefully lowered a small bag of seed against the wall. "Now…"

Jared remembered what had been said in the store the night before. "Kodi, you wanted me to do some work?"

Barin grimaced, looking at his hands. They were big, rough hands. "Naw—eat some breakfast first. I haven't eaten either. Let's go to the kitchen."

"I have a government inspector coming," Barin said in the kitchen, reaching into a cupboard while Jared sat down behind a small wooden table overlooking a window on the road leading to the star field. "Just do a little cleaning-up for me while I run a few errands, and then you can take the day off."

"Fine," Jared said gratefully.

Barin mixed a batter in a glazed earthenware bowl. "Where would you like to go? To the city?"

Jared shook his head. "Just walking, I guess. I want to see if I can find my way around here still. I want to see if it really seems like a long time ago that I was here." In the long run, there really wasn't ever much to do. What work there was, involved simple tasks that left much time for contemplation. It was a hard thing to get used to, so Jared did more than was expected of him, though still leaving time each day to go out walking. He worked fast, which made Barin satisfied. So Barin and he became quite intimate on the island of the little trading post. As time wore on, as the days rolled by, Lethe seemed to expand. Jared sank into the routine and his world became increasingly more peaceful. He loved Lethe.

"Whatever you do, keep on the good side of the old men," Barin advised him once. "I'm a city man myself, by birth. I look at things a little more broadly. But many of these people have never been to the city. Some are really afraid of the city and its people. Act religion, talk weather." Jared shrugged: "That's fine with me." Then he thought: I've been here seven days now. What's happening to me? He dismissed a little qualm of self-doubt. Lethe was fine. He loved it.

Life on Lethe was slow and routine. Now was the season when city people moved to their country escapes. Jared saw many city families when delivering things from the store. They were small-town people, and whispered behind one's back. None ever said much to Jared. They told him where to leave the packages. Usually, with the cook or the gardener. He didn't like them. Anyway, they were the wealthier city people. The women wore long white dresses. City women seemed perpetually dressed in a mendicant sort of white. They moved about in lofty innocence. Usually one saw them only at a distance. Often they sauntered in brilliant white troupes over the field paths. The men wore drab clothes, but summery porkpie hats of bleached, rough-woven straw ragged at the brim. Their shoes were dusty and their bearing proud, and Jared didn't like them. They, too, moved in troupes. But his life rarely touched on theirs, and their presence did little to sour his existence.

Often, when Barin left the store, assigning Jared to guard the counter, Jared would sit for hours waiting for customers, sinking deeper and deeper into a restful half-dreaming air of satisfaction. His happiness, though, seemed vaguely anchored in some unspecified brighter future. He couldn't shake that feeling.

The sun would come in the morning, moving around the sky from window to window until evening, when it cast its last Auber puddles on the floor before the counter.

This peace was like sleep. The silence of Lethe was sweet and precious…once could listen, and savor the vagueness of sound as it came through the high, waving-grassed meadows. Sound was not close and loud as it had been in years past: It was as the aroma is to the steak: Tantalizing, distant, promising, shadowy; it was the same with the other senses. One could not be a glutton about the satisfactions of Lethe, except on certain sunny mornings, or before certain little streams on whose surface diamonds gave birth to themselves in microcosmic solar lifetimes, or things. One could never tire of this listening, of these deep inhalations, of those bright yet unimposing colors. And when Jared closed his eyes, everything would merge into a happy admixture.

The people of Lethe, too, fitted into this pattern. In a way, Jared felt as though he were much younger and knew much less, though actually it was more of a process of forgetting. When he inadvertently found something to remember him of Oudangad, it forced all sorts of other memories out. He found ways, though, and was very happy with Lethe and his reading. Often he thought of Mala. He devised a way of counting days and miles in one. Sometimes he tried to trace mental paths through the whirling dust motes of the window sunlight, but he couldn't bear it for long.

Jared got to know Letheans. They seemed farmer, citizen, gypsy, or whatever, by nature. It was more than profession. It was a way of life. They were all a proud people, Jared thought.

Early in the mornings, even before the sun showed itself, troops of farmers could be seen tramping to their fields with a tangle of ancient machinery.

All the day then they would work in their fields—the men half-naked and bronzed, the women scarved against the rays of the sun. After they straggled home in the fading light and faint church bells, a good supper would warm them back to life.

The men would gather outside with wine and madly wailing instruments and dance. Soon their women, flushed and squealing, would join the festival amid large metal canisters and earthenware jugs, which had accompanied them to the fields with beer and cold coffee, and which now lay wine-heavy in the shadows with generous spigots.

Only fairs and religious processions broke this pattern. As yet, Jared was still more of a watcher than participator. Gradually, more and more Lethe flowed through his veins like a languid oil, calming, soothing, slowing.

Over the period of the first three weeks or so, however, an occasional crashing note would present itself suddenly, jarring his memories, of perhaps Lyxa, or Mbe, or a dice-rattling Jardin. Just as quickly, waters of forgetfulness drowned the intruding picture. The sun shone on Lethe as it had and would for twelve billion years.

One day, Barin took him to a grassy hill behind the store. They were two tiny shapes lost in the lush green ever-ever. Barin pointed to the sky. There, on the horizon, roiled a massive mountain of cloud. Jared nodded. The day was hot and sullen. Nothing moved. The air pressure was very high.

"That big cloud," said Barin. "That's what I was telling you about. Every year it comes in mid-summer. It means the end of hot-summer and the beginning of good-summer. It'll be stifling for about a week, maybe only a day. Then it'll rain without warning, maybe for a minute, maybe for an hour—no longer. It'll cool everything off, turn the hot dust to running mud, drain the sun itself. Then we'll have clear skies and a month or so of perfect weather. Jared nodded uncertainly, wiping the sweat off his neck. His neck was sun-burned and was peeling hotly.

For days, the cloud built on the horizon, like a massive timberline that had sprung up overnight and was daily growing, black and threatening. The people saw it, too, and they shook their heads and groaned and fanned themselves as they passed each other on the country roads. Jared sweated and cursed the bloated thing.

"That cloud," Barin sighed once, and slammed the door shut. It was early morning. Barin came to the counter and showed Jared a smudgy slip of paper.

"Stuck in the window still last night," Barin said. "It's from Farmer Vardis. I wrote to him about you, and he's interested in seeing you. According to this, you're hired outright on the basis of your education and traveling experience."

Farmer Vardis. Was that not the name spoken with the reverence due a god by those in the fields?

"I'd jump after it," Barin advised. "The man owns just about everything in the province. Here's your big chance."

Jared nodded, slightly reluctantly. It wasn't—"You're right, of course. I'll be glad to see him. What does he offer, and for what?"

"Two hundred shel a week, to start. Maybe you'll have that farm in a few years. That's more than you could ever have hoped to hope for."

Jared nodded. "I'll do it," he breathed, afraid to let the mountains and the earth know that he was turning his back; afraid to let his bones feel any pleasure, lest they gather him into the city and never let him truly be with Lethe.

43. Bel Air

The road to the farm was a long one, winding through the incredible countryside of Lethe. He was going to the farm of Arnen, a major tenant of Farmer Vardis. One of Arnen's hands had come in an old rig to pick Jared up, along with the mail and some seed. The farm cart was hitched to a single, wide-backed, bushy-heeled, stub-tailed plow horse, which plodded along through deep dry ruts in the road. Every time they reached a crossroads, where one set of ruts turned to run in the direction of a farm house or loading silo, the cart would swerve and jump sharply in order to regain the ruts on the main road. Jared's stomach began to simmer, what with the heat and the stench of the horse and cart, and the severe jogging. From time to time, the nag would snort wetly and emit a train of hot, strawy buns from under a stubby tail.

At times they passed over roads between the timbered banks of some forest echoing the clatter of wagon wheels. At other times, they would rumble along a tangled microcosm in the flat, rich farm lands miles and miles around.

Jared's travelling companion was an elderly man with bright blue eyes set at odd angles looking around the circumference of a carbuncular nose. His bluish lips were puckered in what seemed to be a good-natured, perennial grin that made his lump features glow bright red. There was a hint of some rough-hewn peasant brew about the man's breath, and a strong suggestion of the barnyard in his home-knit sweater, his stone-colored trousers, his calf-high boots. Jared's nose stayed balanced in a half-rumple; he couldn't decide whether the assortment of odors was making him sick, or if he was sick and the odors were keeping him revived.

This was a time of dry hay. Barin had said there would be another crop, of wet hay, in the early fall. Barin; Jared had said he would be back. He hadn't said all the things he would want to be back for. He wanted sometime to see the sunlight puddle its last drowsy dregs before the counter.

The air was heavily pungent with the volumes of hay being moved for miles and miles in all directions. People were working hard before the rains. In many places, Jared saw, a primitive sort of combustion-mower was being used, and the machines' whining set the rhythm for bits of cut hay flashing through the air.

It was a wide-open and rambling world like the wave-swept ocean, but solid, peopled and peaceful.

The old man coughed.

Jared looked at him quickly. "I'm sorry?"

"I say, do you like Bel-Air?"

Jared smiled. "That's a pretty, feminine name. It's from the Middle French. It means "beautiful air."

"Oh?" the man drawled.

Mala, Jared thought. Mala, and beautiful air.

"Have you ever met Farmer Vardis?" Barrimer asked.

Jared groaned as they hit a bump. The bump was almost like a personal blow. Nasty old coot! "No—!"

"You'll have to wait," Barrimer said, adjusting the rains and pulling a beautiful crystal bottle from his pocket. Jared stared at the bottle while Barrimer drank deeply, wiped his mouth, put the bottle away again.

"That's some bottle," Jared ventured.

Barrimer looked away. "Yup."

Jared bit his lip and made a fist. "Where'd you buy it?"

Barrimer looked at him deeply. "Bought it."

Jared, not sure if that was a question or an answer, said nothing.

Barrimer brought the bottle back out and drank again. "This," he said, putting the cork back on, "It's a gypsy bottle."

"Oh."

"They're nice if they're really old. The domraiga aren't making bottles like that anymore. Actually, it was only one family, and they haven't been around in a long time."

At that moment, they rounded a bend of trees. There was the farm house. The house was surrounded by a jagged wall of slate slabs set in very old cement and covered with moss. Crisp little roses grew all along the top of the wall, and in a coronet over the wide gate into the farmyard.

The wagon turned neatly on its two wheels like a compass. The horse clattered into the cobbled yard.

Jared's first impression was one of the great age and a sort of gloom; but he reasoned that the feeling was due to the sudden change form bright countryside to old, sedate farmyard.

On the right, was a long low dung hill. A macadam road led straight ahead, where a barn stood. A narrow strip branched from the road and led to the door of what appeared to be the farm house. Barrimer led horse and cart to the left, stopping against the inside of the wall.

Jared hopped down. The farmhouse sprawled ahead. A weathered cube, in grays and gray-greens, of a building, it had more windows than one could count in a single glance. That, by Lethean standards, was a big building.

"Why don't you go into the kitchen?" Barrimer grunted, busy at unhitching the horse.

The mud to one side of the walkway to the door was crowded with cackling, dirty chickens. A dark-brown rooster, his comb chewed up in many fights, stood on a slime-draped iron hoop, the outer rim of a long-rotted wooden sheet, and he was arguing frenziedly with a gimpy cur whose vulpine features were split into two rows of fangs. Jared hurried past the resounding gunfire of staccato barking and rooster-whoops.

When he stood in the kitchen, he was alone. Sweat rolled into his eyes. Blinded, he rubbed his eyes.

"Yes?" a woman said sharply.

Jared looked through a diminishing red haze. He smelt strew, tobacco, coffee, and cat. The kitchen was very spacious, so the great china-laden cupboards and sinks and coffee urns and the wood-burning stove seemed pleasantly lose against the freshly whitewashed walls.

She was middle aged, gray haired, and tanned. Her face was severely set and lined from windburns.

"I'm Jared Fallon."

Her eyes softened in back, but on surface there remained a cold blue that made Jared feel a certain indefinite need for caution. "Mr. Jared. How do you do? Won't you have a seat?"

Jared, still uncomfortable, pulled out a chair to sit on at the big central table.

"Would you like something to eat?" Jared quickly nodded yes. She as civil. That was all. He looked out the window, where he could look into the rising slope of a thick-bosomed orchard.

"Alvea!"

Both Jared and the woman turned. The man who had called out her name stood in the doorway. The perfect match for her, he thought: Tall, deeply tanned, with kindly blue eyes.

"Mr. Jared?" the newcomer said smiling. Jared rose, relieved at this geniality. "Welcome to my farm." They shook hands. "Do you have any idea how long you're going to be staying with us?"

Jared shook his head. "I'm afraid I'm imposing on you. But I have no idea. I haven't talked to Farmer Vardis yet."

Arnen nodded thoughtfully. "Well, he's supposed to be driving through in a few days on regular business. I imagine he'll want to talk to you then. As I said, I don't know how long you're supposed to wait. I have no idea for what job he wants you."

Jared became annoyed. "Does he always act in such an offhand manner about people he's hiring?"

Arnen smiled. "We'll find you the best room available. We'll see to everything you need."

Jared stuck his hands in his pockets. "He must be an awful busy, important man."

Arnen still smiled. "That's right."

"Still, he could let me know what he wants me for, and if I want the job…"

"Let's not talk about it," Arnen said, turning to his wife.

"No, wait a moment. This is a bad spot for me to be in. If I can't take his job for some reason, I've lost a week of important time. I've got a wife coming on the next starship around Scholion, and I'd like to have some sort of a secure household ready for her."

"We understand," Alvea said. Jared looked at her in surprise. She suddenly seemed full of good will. "The way Farmer Vardis works is this. He gives his clients a place to stay and free board if they're in the position you're in. There are all sorts of other considerations given. Obviously, for him to ask you to live here, means that it's pretty important for him to hire you. He's almost certain to hire you. He's a very wealthy, important, wonderful man, and he'll give you a good job no matter what."

Jared shrugged. "I'm sorry." He sat down. "I guess I'm tired and tense." Still, he resented her talk about the position he was in. He was no common drifter , after all. Also, her talk about the virtues of Farmer Vardis struck him as somehow a little off-key.

"Alvea, is noon-meal ready?"

She nodded, raking a large pot off the stove. "Potato soup. I've also got some ham and salad."

Arnen grunted, pulling up a chair close to Jared. "I hope Barrimer hasn't said anything untoward. He's sort of a black sheep, if you know what I mean."

Jared looked at Arnen's rough, dirt-stained hands, and couldn't think of anything Barrimer had said. "I guess he is a little odd."

Arnen's grin was suddenly oafish "How do you like Lethe? I hear you're a stranger here."

Jared kept his yes fixed on the food Alvea was setting out on the table. "It's a very nice place."

Fresh fruit, potato soup, lots of milk. These things were rarer on the civilized worlds than one ever thought to realize.

44. Gypsy Jug

Silvery machines occupied his afternoon. They were the first thing he saw when he took a walk after noon-meal. He spent the afternoon talking to some broad-shouldered, loud farm hands about their silvery machines. Apparently, on Lethe had been developed a paint that was the color of quicksilver and prevented metal from rusting.

After dark, Jared entered the gate with the roses over it. Supper stood on the table, and about fifteen farmhands dug in amid raucous laughter and loud talk.

Later, the men played cards, while the women retreated to a nearby parlor. A shaded lamp suspended from the ceiling lit only the table top, leaving the rest of the room immersed in gloom.

Barrimer put his arm over Jared's shoulder and invited him to sit in for cards. Jared accepted a glass of wine, and learned to play a game called Kreg. He wasn't in the mood for much talk, but the fellows were friendly, even respectful, and they drew him out with questions about other worlds.

"I was talking to Gernin this afternoon," Jared said at one point. "I really like your machines. They're amazingly shiny." That seemed to please them. "Also," he added, "this wine is good."

Everyone laughed. A hand of Kreg was won by a dark-haired boy named Pol, who couldn't have been eighteen, but wore work clothes just the same.

"This wine," Barrimer said, holding his cup high, "is bled from the finest grapes this side of Dumaville. Arnen is the only farmer around here who can afford to buy it."

The men gave loud assent, and someone briefly argued with someone else about a two-point Kreg.

"I also like your gypsy jugs," Jared said, half remembering Barrimer's crystal flask.

When he looked up, the dark-haired boy had run from the room. A general silence hung over the table. Jared, in the act of putting some cards on the table, froze. People looked closely at sleeves, insides of wine glasses, cracks in the table top, anything to avoid eye contact. Barrimer looked at Arnen, who glared back with balled fists. Jared could think of nothing to say, nor could he even begin to guess what he'd said wrong.

Jared sensed that Lethe had deep secrets, dark truths, and life here would not be as perfect as he'd hoped. Still, it was all he had left, and Mala was on her way to join him. He had no choice: he must build a new life for both of them here.

45. Pol

Crews were already at work in the fields when Jared rose next morning. Arnen's wife was cooking when Jared drifted into the kitchen. For a moment, he studied her: A robust woman, handsome in a particular way with her large breasts, long legs, trim torso, pretty rear, long hair, and her attractive, stern face with a strong nose.

Jared coughed so she'd notice him.

"Well, well! The sleeper," she called out.

Jared said good morning. "You folks don't believe in getting up too early, do you?" he kidded. "Smells great in here."

"Have a seat. Fresh fry-eggs this morning." She rummaged on the windowsill, where piles of paper were stacked with many protruding, ripped pages. "Farmer Vardis is coming the day after tomorrow. At night."

"Look at this," she said, handing him a digital news sheet. "There's a story about the war in it. It's the first thing the paper's said about it." Jared rubbed sleep from his eyes. He glanced at the article briefly on its grainy, flickering page. He absorbed mixed text and holovix: No UGO any longer, no League existed anymore. On Arcturus, a Vegan princess had thrown herself from a high window after attempting to intimidate the President of that world. An uprising of Mercurian refugees had been radically annihilated there. Arcturus was under attack from a league of alien cities.

"Farmer Vardis is definitely coming?" Jared said, putting the article aside.

She put his breakfast before him. "That's what he said. He called Lador this morning."

"Mrs. Arnen—"

"Call me Alvea."

"Alvea, still no word about what he wants me to do?"

"Boy, Jared, are you impatient. I know you're anxious, but I'm sure you can wait two more days."

"It's just that I feel bad, freeloading around here. If only I have some work to do…"

"No, no no! Don't worry about that. Farmer Vardis pays for that. But tell me about the women at—on Mercury City. Are they really the most beautiful, as they say?"

"Some, yes. But there are many beautiful women elsewhere." Charred, blackened dolls strewn about among the ruins of Mercury City: sediment at the bottom of the great seas of fiery hell, staring with gutted eyes into the nothingness above.

"You look so sad."

"I was half-asleep."

"At this hour? How do you like your room?"

"Beautiful view. I looked into the orchard for a while."

"Did you hear the trees outside last night?"

"They lulled me to sleep. I was exhausted anyway."

"No, I mean, did you hear them talk? They speak among themselves every night. Ever since I was a little girl I've opened my window every night and listened to them."

"What do the trees say?"

"I must sound rather foolish."

"Not at all."

"Well, it's not a language, really. They tell you the weather, for instance, by the sound the wind makes in their branches."

"How much do you charge for forecasts?"

"I do believe we're in for the storm soon. Probably in a matter of a day or two. The branches are uneasy, and sometimes a gust of wind knocks a fruit down, and the fruit hits the wall of the house, or it'll hit the back door as though someone were knocking."

"I'll be afraid to close an eye tonight!" Jared protested.

She sat down, wrapped melancholy around her coffee. "I wish sometimes there was a law against old houses. I wish this were a small, bright little cottage."

"How long have you lived here?"

"How long have I lived here? Or the Arnens?"

"Both?"

"The Arnens have owned this house for two hundred years. I've only lived her the last thirty or so."

"Oh."

She smiled. "Are you confused? We marry early on Lethe. I was ten. Lador was eleven. I am fortunate. We were like brother and sister even as infants."

"Where was your house?"

"Barrimer is my father." She sniffed: "That's the only reason he's managed to stay here, the old drunkard. He was one of the foremen for Lador's grandfather."

"And your mother?"

"She died when I was young." Alvea looked at a tiny birth mark on the inside of her wrist. "Sometimes, the wind comes in through the cracks. The wind brings back the old days into the room, when I was a little girl, and the whole world was faultless. The wind skims the smells of old age and many deaths off the old walls, and brings them to my brain like…like a very wet smoke of tuma *hashif* in cold weather."

Jared pushed his empty plate aside. He stirred his coffee silently. She spoke of magics.

The sun shone in through the open doorway. Bright flowers outside shone among puddles, while a pair of bright bees nuzzled their blossoms. Water twinkled mesmerically among stalks.

"Jared, are you sleeping again?"

"I'm sorry. What did you say?" Another person had come to stand silently by the table. Jared recognized him as the boy who had run from the table the night before. Immediately, he remembered the tensions of that incident.

"Jared, I've got to get out to pick up the milk. This is Pol. Pol, meet Mr. Jared. Jared, Pol will show you around." She put her coffee cup in the sink, picked up two empty canisters, and left in a flurry.

Jared looked at Pol. The boy glowered suspiciously. Dark skin, raven hair bleached dark mahogany by the sun.

"I'm pleased to meet you," Jared attempted.

"all right."

Jared gulped his coffee, put the cup on top of Alvea's in the sink, and walked out of the kitchen. Pol followed a few steps behind, scuffing his sandals into the macadam.

"What do you want to see?" Pol grumbled.

"Nothing. I've seen the whole place already." If that curt statement did nothing, and if this creature suddenly decided to become more aggressive, Jared thought he might always revert to fine Olympic form and run as fast as his legs would carry him.

Pol seemed unnerved. "Then—why did Alvea tell me—?" He snapped his mouth shut and stared sullenly at the ground.

Jared said breezily: "So, unless there is any point to all this, I'll just…"

"No, no!" Pol reacted horrified. "I wonder if you could tell something about Mercury City."

"Sure. Why not?" Let's sit down over there." They passed through the gate, crossed the road, and saw on some boulders strewn among a grove of trees. "What did you want to know?"

"Where…" Pol began hesitantly, "…would you rather be? There, or here?"

"Here."

"Why?"

"It's beautiful here," Jared said, wiping sweat off his neck.

"Isn't it beautiful on Mercury?"

"No, not for a long time now."

"But how can that be? We always say *like Mercury* when we mean something good, or beautiful."

"Don't you like it here?"

"No."

"Why?"

Pol cast a hateful glance over his shoulder. "It's like dying."

"How so?"

Pol shook his head. "I don't care if you tell them I said so."

"I won't tell."

"I said I don't care." The boy removed a sandal and scratched his heel.

Jared leaned back against a tree. "Tell me about Lethe."

Pol made a grimace. "Lethe. Sounds like a vegetable of some kind. Something you eat when you have a fever."

"It's a very beautiful name. It—"

"Hah! And what isn't beautiful to you?"

"Some things."

"Like what? Mercury, maybe?"

"Right."

Pol became exasperated. "But why?"

Jared told him of Mercury City, of the War of Suns. He barely mentioned Mala. But he was thinking of her.

Pol gesticulated. "At least, though, you've traveled through the galaxy. I've never been more than forty miles from this farm house. Once, when I tried to run away. They brought me back in an air skimmer." He seemed slightly proud of the last statement.

"Don't talk about leaving, Pol. Lethe is a great place. Anyway, where would you go? This is where you've lived all your life. This is what you're made for. There are all the wonderful things in life that you should prepare for. There is no more Mercury City. No more Arcturus, or Raskia, or anyplace. Everywhere, people are starving, and there are soldiers."

"Soldiers?" His eyes lit up.

"Yes, war."

Pol sighed. "But if you are in a place you believe is bad, and you want to get away, should you give up hope? I just want to leave here and find a new life."

"Pol, the starships themselves probably don't exist anymore. Where would they take you, even if they existed?"

Pol shook his head condescendingly. "This place is rotten. You will wait too long yourself before finding out, and by then there won't be a single starship left to take you away."

"I'm staying, Pol." *I have nowhere else left to run.*

"You don't understand."

"What don't I understand?"

"Look," Pol exclaimed. "The big Farmers, like Vardis, run everything. The urbani, in the cities, are equal to them, but there aren't too many urbani. There are millions of farmers, like Arnen, and their farm hands, to help the Farmers keep the cities small. Then there are the domraiga; that's me."

"What does that all mean? Maybe you'd be good with lots of political rabble rousers."

Pol looked at the sky briefly. "It's not political. It's real. I'm a domraiga, and I'm on the shit list. For example, one word from Vardis, and I can be thrown in jail, or even killed. It's legal."

"Where are the whips? Where are the torture chambers?"

"They don't need those, Mr. Jared. It's the way people think. And the domraiga suffers the most. We're too spread. Every year, we lost more people. They're killing us off slowly!"

"But how?"

"Let me tell you about Alvea. When I was small, I hurt myself. I ran into the house crying. Alvea, now, she's afraid to touch me. She's very superstitious. I grabbed her skirt and wanted to bury my head in it. She beat me. She hit me right and left, and she was so damn scared that her whole head glowed. Her eyes bugged out and was all teeth, like a skull, like death itself.

Jared shrugged. "I'm not much older than you. One of the things you learn, if you haven't yet, is that some people are your enemies, others your friends. To you, everyone's your enemy. To you, the whole world's bad. I feel sorry for you."

Pol continued doggedly. "Let me tell you about my family. I was a little kid. I was a domraiga. Domraiga skin is darker. I had parents then." He choked. "We camped near here. We came just before a big drought started. Some really superstitious farmers swooped down on us. I got away." He swallowed hard. "They burned them alive in the wagons. But first they stole all they could get their hands on."

A light dawned on Jared. "Barrimer's jug!" *No wonder they all looked so darkly guilty when I mentioned domraiga crystal.*

Pol ignored the remark. "Arnen didn't hate. He took me in. He didn't know that Barrimer and Alvea were at the burning. He didn't find out until years later, when he got it out of Cree."

"Cree?" Jared asked, while thinking: *Lethe is quickly revealing its very dark and ugly side—the Human Condition that never changes from time to time, place to place, eon to eon.*

"An old witch. At least, that's what they say she was. She used to come here selling herbs. She was as old as the hills. She lived in a cave in the woods somewhere. They said she was a witch, and they wouldn't let her near. She was the last survivor of an ancient clan of domraiga who used to make beautiful carpets for the agrarchs, hundreds of years ago. That was what they called the Farmers then, when Lethe was cut off from the rest of the galaxy during some wars and chaos. One day, she came, and Alvea was yelling at her. She saw me standing there—the old woman, I mean—and called me over. I tell you, I was scared out of my mind. But when I went, she told me she knew my story. She told me that most of the ones who killed my people were either dead or diseased. She put curses on them!"

Jared was listening closely. "Was she a domraiga?"

"Yes, and very old. After a while, I began to understand her. She gave me a tea and three spells, and I understood her. I was little, and she told me stories about my people, and oh, how my heart would ache! You see, before the agrarchs, my people were the musicians and artists and poets of the cities. We're dark, because we know many secrets. People fear us.

"One day Cree didn't come anymore. I was on my own. She always told me to be proud, and after she didn't come anymore, I had to see that myself."

"I see. What stories did she tell you?" *Stories.* What food they were for a child. Jared remembered legends of the Bread Ships.

Pol's face brightened for the first time. "All about domraiga heroes. She'd hold me to her knees. Not hug me, of course, because I had to be a man. When she talked, she'd wave her crinkly old hands a lot, or point with her chin, and her voice would sound like a bird's. It didn't sound much like singing though, because she was very old, and her voice was cracked like a dish."

Jared felt the bitterness and futility. He thought carefully that he maybe understood. He wondered if any of the stories were about the stars. He wanted Pol to tell him about the domraiga heroes who conquered a thousand suns, who moved majestically in the magic signals of the zodiac. "Tell me one of the stories."

"I couldn't! Not the way she could!"

"That's all right."

"I haven't ever told them, and…"

"Tell me your favorite," Jared urged closely.

"Promise not to tell anyone."

"Starman's honor."

"It is a dark and terrible story, but so are our lives here."

"Then listen…" Satisfied, the young man spread his hands and this is the story he told:

46. The Legend Of Valdo Rey

—*And* (as all such stories among the domraiga will start, because those are the ends and beginnings of an unending chain of incidents in their timeless saga of terror, courage, suffering, loss, and redemption)…

—After we lost the beautiful ages, long ago, there lived a handsome young domraiga, with two beautiful, raven-haired wives, and seven strong, tall male children.

One day, while hunting in a deep, deep forest belonging to the Agrarch Hater of Scimitane, this domraiga Valdo Rey came upon a lovely sylvan spring, the like of liquid diamond. Surrounded my massive shelves of stone, covered with thick, velvety moss, it tempted the thirsty hunter.

So, he dropped his crossbow and his quiver. He dropped his pouch with a forest animal dead inside, and lay on his belly to drink.

No sooner had he done this, however, than he heard a thump and much rustling behind him. He whirled, on his feet, drew his knife—and faced a squire of the Agrarch, who dropped out of a tree where he'd been hiding.

"Ho, mighty hunter," laughed the squire. "Hast thou thy wits lost in yon waters, and seekst them on thy belly thus?"

But Valdo Rey, who would strike a man dead for less, could only look on helplessly, for the squire held a crossbow, bolt aimed square at Valdo Rey's heart.

"Ho, ho, ho, Master Woodlark, why so grim? Render merely this favored squire that which these woods have given thee wrongly: The best part, say, of yon bleeding gast, which thou hast so villainously spirited in forbidden field, and thou mayest consider thy cincts for this wicked deed completed, without use of hand or blistered foot."

Now Valdo Rey knew that the forest and all that was in it was free to the world, but he also knew to keep the rogue's favor. He therefore smiled and hid his anger. "Don. Yes, Master, I would gladly give thee breast and liver of the gast, and have thee speak well, or even better, not at all, of me at the great lord's table."

So they supped that evening at the house of Valdo Rey, with his two beautiful, raven-haired wives and seven tall, strong male children. The house of Valdo Rey was but a domraiga tent, but very old and very large, the craft of his father's father's father, who had made precious rug in the east before being driven out by a wicked agrarch whose name was Iron Sword…though that is another story.

Now when the fires had died, and the embers glowed faintly, the domraiga and the evil squire bedded down to sleep. But during the night, while all slept, the evil squire rose in all stealth and padded to the women's sleep place. One woman slept therein alone, for the other was with Valdo Rey. This lone woman the evil one grasped and bound and violated, all in that one fearsome night.

Come morning, the squire was asleep in his appointed place. Innocence was on his face, where he had told stories of Scimitane the night before.

But Valdo Rey, upon finding the woman stilled in death, no brooking knew his misery . He hastened to the squire. To him he said: "A favor at the manor, my dear squire. A favor at the manor."

"Yes," the squire said. "I suppose it's worth it now."

Blood of domraiga, and noble womanhood, had been violated, and Valdo Rey saw his greater course open to him, and no other course would do. "Yes," he smiled falsely, "She was but a lesser wife, a good price to pay for favor with the powerful!"

But in all guile he builded himself an explosive, and did set it, and told no one, and kept it under his tunic. "They who are innocent, shall know their time too."

The squire called for his cape.

The youngest child brought the cape. The domraiga family gathered close around him, because Valdo Rey had so ordered.

"My cape!" The squire called out. "And now my sword!" It was done as he said, by Valdo Rey.

"What, Valdo Rey," quoth the squire, "*gras*! Would you also be my little page? Why, at the court of the great—"

But ere he could finish his word the explosive detonated, destroying the remaining beautiful, raven-haired wife—o bereaved sisters, o wailing brothers—and his seven tall, strong male children, and the house that his father's father's father had builded...and with them died the squire of Hater, Agrarch of Scimitane, Lord Agrarch of Duma, Lord of the Sword. To the maker's justice, and honor be preserved.

For vengeance, O Children of the Earth, despised domraiga, comes true in the next life: Forever burning, forever despairing, forever, forever, while the dead sing their lovely chorus in voices of women and children, runs that evil squire in the heavens before the celestial crossbow of the mighty Valdo Rey!"

47. Vardis

Somewhere, a day or two after Jared heard this story, a bird rustled among leaves. Somewhere, a woodpecker clattered at a tree trunk. Occasionally, a sickle would flash far away in the fields in the sun light. Roads flowed as if golden, as evening drew near. In a patch of woods by a clear stream, Jared, who had been lying on his back watching the towering trees and the sky, rose and began his walk back to the farm.

Alvea brought news when Jared walked in the front door. "Farmer Vardis is coming! Farmer Vardis is coming!" She barely glanced at Jared, who stood motionless in the doorway. "Farmer Vardis is coming. Quick, Jared, take a shower, get ready for the evening meal. He's coming tonight!"

Arnen ran past just then. "Hello, Jared. Getting ready for the big event?"

Jared extended his hands in a helpless gesture. "He's coming tonight? Why?"

Arnen threw up his hands. "Who knows? Who wants to ask? The thing is, he's coming. About nine, his office said."

Alvea grabbed Arnen by the sleeve before he could run off. "Get the men showered and shaved. Dressed in their best. And make sure…" (her voiced dropped to a whisper)…"that Pol and Barrimer are kept apart from each other, and at least one of them out of sight. Pol, preferably."

Arnen whispered back in a nervous laugh: "I doubt if Farmer Vardis even knows Pol exists—at least this late date."

Alvea nodded emphatically. "So much the better. Send the boy off to town with some pocket money. Anything. But get him out of here."

Arnen, on his way out, called back: "I'll see what I can do."

Pol wasn't at supper. Jared thought of Mala. He ate sparingly, wondering what would turn up in his meeting with Vardis. The great Farmer! He snorted to himself mentally.

Showers were already running and bright lights burning when Jared came to the shower cubicles. Night threatened to throttle the bare, dim light bulb in Jared's shower. He stood and let the hot night air dry him quickly.

A crowd had gathered in the kitchen. In an air of mixed excitement and a feeling of imminent doom, the hands and quite a few women he hadn't seen around before bustled around the big table. Everyone was dressed stiff and formal and black, and no cards and no wine were evident. There was little talk. It was a sort of game. The men never seemed to speak the word "Vardis." Barrimer was the only one who tried, once, in asking for some pie, and frowns descended on him. Farm wives ran the roost, while men looked apprehensive The women served up plate after plate of food, of which the men ate little, and the women spoke in high voices about the great man's coming. Jared was sleepy. He tried to make himself disappear into the back of his chair, but Barrimer, who sat next to him and kept talking, and some woman with buck teeth and a foolish laugh who kept putting food and drinks in front of him, annoyed him continually.

Late in the evening, Barrimer exclaimed: "Well, they can take it and! All right boys, let's bring out the cards. Game of Mitre, come, come!" Arnen tried to object, but the cards appeared too suddenly, and even he sat in grudgingly for a hand. "Money in the Bishop's Mitre!" the old man bellowed lustily: "I've got a complete castle!" The game lasted for hours, and money travelled around the table at the whim of Fate's breeze. From time to time the men would cheer and hoist a round of drinks, but the least sound from outside would send them scrambling for the sink. Alvea stood by, wringing her hands in despair.

Time crawled slowly on the white-enameled kitchen clock. Jared watched the clock until his eyes burned and he could no longer distinguish one of the time piece's hands from the other...lost in the multiplicity of shadows thrown by the wan light on the white background. One by one, the men drew away from the table and left with apologies to Arnen. Only Jared, Alvea, and Lador remained in the end, Lador shuffling the cards idly by himself.

With most of the light off, they settled into a semidarkness, floating between the sleepy reality of a hard chair, stiff collar, smarting, tired eyes, and a strong desire to float off to bed.

At last, a knock—the door! Arnen leapt like a frog to open it. Jared sighed: At last, he was going to be able to write away this sub-chapter in his life. At last, he was going to be able to make the vital decision about the job, and get on with the process of living, of doing things, of enjoying life.

Mumbling outside the door: "What? What?"

Arnen yelled into the room: "Jared, come on! I'm getting the jeep out."

Alvea frowned. "What's the matter, Lador?"

"Farmer Vardis has been shot. He's dead on the road not far from the store!"

48. Vengeance

The wind whipped in their faces, and the jeep's single-engine whine in the night on the empty roads cut into their ears. It was a flat, dark world, and their echoes rolled up under the starry heavens as in an empty room.

"Who did it?" Arnen yelled over the din. "That dark son of a bitch," the man who had brought the message yelled back.

Pol. Jared put his hand on his cheek. *Not Pol, bitter, wistful Pol...*

Arnen cursed, cutting into Jared's reverie. Jared remembered the cruel tale of Valdo Rey, and felt death's rattling bones.

"Come along, let's claim the body and see justice done," Arnen growled while seizing Jared's wrist in a hard, painful grip.

The jeep ground to a halt under the searchlight of a parked police air cruiser. There, at the side of the road, on a bald spot on top of a low hill that rose up out of a sea of silent waving wheat, lay a dead man under a bloody sheet. A sparse crowd of farmers and uniformed police stood around.

Jared shivered, cold and sleepy. "We're going to Dumaville," Arnen, who had just conferred briefly with the police chief, told Jared. "Get in the air bus."

The body rested on a pallet in the middle of the floor. Around the circumference of the bubble-top skimmer were leather seats. The pilot seat was raised, facing forward, with his hands in reach of banked instruments.

Blood pooled on the floor. Pol sat in a seat facing the body on one side, with his arms strapped to the armrests. He said nothing. In the light inside the ship, he glowed in outline sharply against the darkness behind him.

Jared sat opposite him. Jared tried not to look at the body, only at Pol, or elsewhere. Soon the pilot came to his seat and touched the engines to life. Gravity flickered off as some sour-looking men in expensive clothes took their seats, and the ship rose toward Dumaville.

The ride was a long one, and the dim orange flying lights outside the craft were hypnotic. As the craft approached Dumaville, travelling over a corridor of trees, a strong magic began to make itself known.

Tall landing beacons flashed past.

Their lights played many colors over Pol's face.

Pol's skin seemed to become near transparent. His skin seemed no longer to exist. *Or is it the horror I am feeling,* Jared asked himself numbly. *Is this how they do things here?*

The boy sat well-behaved: Shocked, at most. Certainly not heartbroken. Pol looked relaxed, if anything. His face was slightly averted, not looking in any definite direction. His eyes seemed fixed on something far, far away somewhere through the floor of the air bus, something in the forests and fields.

His black eyes glittered warm and wet in the night.

A trace of a smile played about his lips.

As one particularly bright, passing light briefly cast a glare over the cabin, Jared saw a slight flush on Pol's dark cheeks.

Then the skin was no longer there, and the eyes yawned like those of a skull. As successive lights passed, those eyes would light up. They were the first to light up. Last, after light had reconquered the entire Pol, brightening his features with a ruddy phosphorescence, Jared could see the mouth literally shining. So delicately balanced between a smile and a blank frown…When the light passed, everything darkened at once.

The vehicle touched down into its berth. Jared let himself be swept along, first to the police station, then to the house of an urbani friend of Arnen's where they were to spend the night.

"Pol." Jared went to see the boy. No one else would come Pol looked at Jared.

"Why did you do it?"

No answer.

"Somehow," Jared said, "we're a little older than Valdo Rey. But it's Cree we still hold in awe."

The boy looked at him gratefully—an island of understanding in a sea of hate and doom.

So they brought Pol to a prison of concrete and steel, in the middle of nowhere—an Olympia House or was it Lethe House—where life entered and death was to walk out the doors.

Jared must flee because there was yet Mala for him…

Pol held him back a moment and said through the bars: "They're going to kill me. But would you do something for me?" Jared nodded. Pol's face broke into a tearful grimace. He could hardly talk. "There aren't too many of me left. There will never be another Cree. But if anyone asks you, sometime, a long time from now, when there are still stars shining on the country roads at night, and the farmers are comfortably asleep, if anyone stops you on a dark road and asks…you can tell him why."

Jared reached through the bars and touched his roughly clad shoulder, feeling Pol's trembling body hidden there. He thought of the things he'd seen on his path to this place, and nodded. Words did not come, but he nodded. Their eyes met briefly, and they communicated understanding.

Jared whirled and rushed out, remembering, strangely, the blood cry of the *Ankh, Ankh, Ankh* surging in a million corpuscles against the gates of his sanity.

Am I there again, though I came so far, and had such hope?

49. She Came In A Blaze Of Stars

Within a handful of days, news came that her ship was due to arrive from the stars. Mala would land on the green grasses of Lethe, amid sweet night winds and chirruping crickets. Jared rode in an air skimmer with Arnen to meet her, under a starry sky, alone in a field. Nearby stretched a barren landing strip, marked by twin rows of blue and white lights. Nearby was a small store, shuttered and dim for the night. Arnen left him alone, and went to the store to knock and share a beer with the owner, an old card-playing crony.

Arnen left his skimmer, which held a communications dash. Jared clutched the dash as he and Mala spoke to each other while she was still far away.

Golden Girl... love of my life and hope...

"Jarry!" Mala, new and old, and golden, her voice came from the stars. Jared closed his eyes and loved her and the music of her words, filled with love from him, for her, for both in the unity that transcends aloneness.

Her voice is like crystal water, like fine red wine.

Mala was far away, in a silver ship suspended among the stars and falling down the star paths toward Lethe.

Jared touched Arnen's radio, which was by the magics of interstellar civilization tied into the circuits of the breathing massive spaceship that careened in orbit around Scholion.

"Jarry, I love you! I'll see you within the hour."

"I love you. I can almost see you, like a shining star."

"We're turning, Jared. We'll be out of touch for a little while. I have to talk fast, and I can't talk long. Where shall I meet you?"

He smiled happily. "By a little country store in the woods, all green and beautiful, on the last landing strip either of us will ever need."

"Oh, Love, I've got to go. I love you. Until soon..."

Jared stared up into a comb of thin night cirrus clouds. The next moment would wipe out the past, and begin a new life. Fate was going to change everything.

Mala...Minutes, seconds, passed dreamily.

Mala, oh Mala, golden and happy in the sun, framed by the tirelessly, slowly, timelessly heaving oceans.

He spoke with her again when her landing craft entered the atmosphere like a distant comet. He was alone in the skimmer.

"Jarry...how long can we talk?"

Forever, now. We'll talk forever. We are free now.

She was in the ferry, which began to drop from eternal space.
"I've been so lonely."
"Me, too."
"I hear a bell. Oh, that means we're in the atmosphere."
"Just think, Mala, soon you'll be in my arms."
"I can't wait. Oh—that feels strange."
"What does? Stop chattering. It's the braking vector."
"I see it! I see Lethe! It's night, but it's beautiful! I can't wait! I can't wait!"
"Lie down!" In his memory, he carried her golden body to the beach near Arco, amid a gentle summer rain on Arcturus. He remembered how she felt in his hands, her arms around him, her warmth close to him. Closing his eyes, he felt his throat choke with a sob of passion. His abdomen thrilled, and his blood ran hot: *Her tanned, warm, soft skin filled with love for him, panting for him amid a tangle of wild golden hair as her eyes and lips and fingertips sought to touch him...*
"Jarry, I see a bright light. Is that a town? Now it's gone."
"Probably just a—."
"No! There's another! And another! A whole lot of them! What are they?"
Static boiled.
"They seem so clo—." More static boiled.
Jared jumped to his feet. "Mala!" he cried out. Something was terribly wrong. He knew it.
"It's hot in here! Jarry, I'm afraid!"
Static.
Jared stood staring helplessly at a bloody streak in the sky.
"Jarry, the window's turning gray!"
That would be thick glass starting to melt.
Static.
"Are we supposed to be going slower now?"
YES THE UNIVERSE MUST SLOW DOWN.
"Jarry, it's so hot. It's—burning...!" Her voice broke down into a wail, and static cut her short.
Jared circled himself with his empty arms.
JARRYY
As her terrified voice filled his head, he fell to his knees. He stared up to heaven, praying and the stars were—
JARRYYYY
—many and they all glittered silently, watchful eyes, but Jared was—
"Jarry..." (her last word)—
—rocking back and forth, cursing the stars until it seemed as though his head and throat must become choked with blood...
Mala, no, no.
Her ferry's tiny comet sailed across the black sky, bulky with flame. It trailed flaming metal like a river of molten gold as it roared past the empty landing field.

Jared gasped as the fatal drama lit up the entire sky, but he could not be certain because the stars were so bright, and he was blinded by the fireflies that bumbled before his swimming eyes.

A glow arose form the nearby woods. A glow rose up, and met the falling ball of flame that crashed to ground with a deafening explosion. On a nearby lake, the glow doubled with its reflection as silence followed noise. A rumble cargoed through the hills and then grew deadly still. A pyre of light rose up up… and then darkness settled down with silent jaws of finality.

50. Star Bath

Slowly, Jared finally brought his aching head, his gaze, up. Then he looked down at his hands now stiff and cold.

Arnen came running from the store, with another man trailing. They were tiny running shapes. Jared was alone with his fate. He ignored their distant shouts.

Slowly he turned his disbelief up toward the sky.

A long tatter of cooling fire lay across the stars, dissipating in high, icy night winds.

Bits of residue, on fire, slowly drifted down.

Tatters of flame chose their way carefully downward.

On his knees, raising his firsts, Jared drew a shuddering deep breath and uttered a cry that rose like a rocket, shooting up from the stifling field, before he collapsed in a heap, sobbing softly in despair under the red glow.

At last, when he stirred, his movements were those of an old man. Pain flamed, and the cold snapped at his battered bones like wolves with their white teeth in the forests in the light of the stars…

He moved first one hand, then the other, or were there more?

—And,

Pain…

He moaned through parched, crushed lips. One leg…the pain threatened to tear him apart…Slowly he stretched out the other leg. The dead weight of his legs pulled him down as he struggled to rise. His dimmed eyes were raw, the eyes of a blind man.

In the sky now—nothing. Black and full of stars.

Nothing left. All gone. Silent.

The grass in the darkness…

Eternity.

…The grass around his feet in the night was cold.

Was there a place somewhere? A silent street lined with trees? He remembered the place. Trees danced in the street, crying out to the stars. But he was a bush, close to the earth, tucked sedately away. He knew what the trees at the edge of the road were doing before he ever even opened his eyes. *Don't do it* he mumbled, straining to catch sight of them in the darkness. In a mist, stems of alien grass slipped around him like furry fingers. It was his ancient dream, to leave the clodded loam and search for fire among the stars. And now the stars had brought their cruel fire to him.

He shivered, letting the dark night air probe about him as he lay alone at the bottom of the great, mysterious sea. He stretched and stirred on the ground. He became a part of the earth, rooted in its silt and sand. His feet bent and turned inward and entered the ground and his toes grew in and took root, so that he could not move them. Likewise, his arms went in to his shoulders, his hands touching deep clay where sixty million years had built a net for spider and snake; likewise, his phallus entered and took root and ceased to be; only his head rolled from cheek to cheek.

Not yet, he told Olympia House.

Whirling convulsively, tearing these bonds, he rose. The stars of Lethe were different from those of Arcturus or Mercury or probably even the *Ankh Ankh* stars near Raskia.

But their flame-light had not changed. To them he had prayed, and they had given and take as they saw fit. Surely this was the face of the divine.

Among the motionless stars darted the night life of Lethe in its summer before the rains…glowing, fluttering, darting, brushing against his face. The night was filled with myriad bodies. The night was dense with life.

Jared stood wrapt in dreams. He brushed off the tangled web of emotions and ageless hunger, and the dry bled-out remnants of his lifeless anguish.

He felt oddly scorched, purified, new. The universe, it too was new. He stood under new stars, and he longed for them. He longed for the stars as he had not done in ages. He was a boy again. He was a boy again on Mercury Cosmopolis, and this alien grass was the grass of Mercury City. He had come out to look at the many stars and star stations moving—you could only see them move if you looked closely for a long time—in orbit.

The eternal stars let it be fulfilled that a small boy walked through a meadow on Lethe at night, grabbing bright insects and filling his pockets with them as he went.

51. New Stars

Mala was gone. *Lost. Dead.*

Jared took Arnen's skimmer, ignoring the man's hollering, and roared off into the night.

Everything is finished.

The engine whined in the night. Grit flew in all directions as the skimmer plowed through moist and fragrant air.

Mala is dead. How was it possible?

Forever gone. A dream, a phantom, someone as if she never happened. Just a dream.

Jared roared past Barin's place. If anyone was there, the noise of the engine drowned everything out. Where the old road crossed the new highway to Dumaville, he navigated over the dimly visible gray strips of road, turning toward his destination.

He pressed on faster and faster, until the windshield became dangerously hazy with heat and grit…

Long ago vision: Halim Bar, Admiral and aged teacher at the Academy of Stars, leaned fuzzily over a glowing panel and said: "Strive to reach speed Li!3 speed at all costs. It's the one and only way to save your necks in this sort of jam."

Mala is gone. Golden Girl.

Endless, thick black forest land passed on both sides without so much as a break.

Jarry, are we supposed to be going slow?

Something cried out in the airstream, a radio voice, but he barely took notice.

Jarry, I'm burning!

Dumaville light ahead. Something was smoking.

A whiff of—oh god! The engine was burning out. He left the skimmer in a ditch, and barely escaped staggering up a hill and throwing himself over the top, while the vehicle blew up seconds later.

He began to run and stagger. Sirens wailed, while he ran through the back yards of town homes.

He relieved himself against the wall outside the police station. Night cold snipped at the newly exposed flesh like pain at a wound.

Entering, he found only one old guard. The night men had gone to see about an accident. He told the guard that…he must see the prisoner…the domraiga, yes…yes, it was very important…yes, here was his identification card…

blah blah blah

beefy mouth

Mala is lost

The night sky of Mercury City glowed hazy with festive floats, and he was running lightly over the Arch; but what cold!

Jared manhandled the old man, the guard, to Pol's cell door. In a sickly greenish radiation of biolumes, Jared strained to see across the cement and steel cavern. At first all the cells looked alike, all empty but one. Pol was on his feet, pacing. Pol stared at Jared and the terrified guard.

The old man took a swing, but Jared decked him. The guard lay barely moving on the ground—semiconscious.

"Jared!" Pol cried. "What are you doing?"

"I'm setting you free," said Jared. "We're going to conquer the universe!" Jared said, smiling confidently.

Pol stepped out of his cage, looking dark and puzzled.

Jared, patting the boy's back, said encouragingly: "We'll conquer the universe, won't we?"

Pol gritted his teeth manfully.

"There may not be many of our kind left, but we'll escape from here. We'll find something better. Many bright worlds left to explore in the galaxy."

Out on the street, Pol asked: "You must have come with a skimmer. Where is it?"

"My…what?"

"Skimmer."

"Skimmer?" Jared mouthed the words numbly. "My boy, we'll get on a space ferry! Don't worry, the important thing right now is that we're free."

Pol stumbled, said nothing.

A drop of water hit Jared's forehead. Broad, hot, greasy. It splashed on his nose. "Rain!"

Pol stuck out his arm. "Yes! It's raining. It'll be storming soon."

Wet grains of the rain, second reaping of which the farmers spoke. It was here—the Blood harvest.

Sounds of wailing sirens rose from a far outpost, and from approaching police vehicles.

"Pol! Quick! Into the woods!" The boy whirled and leapt over a humped drain pipe in a ditch at the edge of the forest leading to Barin's store, and Jared followed head-over-heels.

At the same moment, dark, wild shapes with flashing lights and howling sirens streaked over the highway surface toward Dumaville.

"Police," the youth groaned. "We're done. They'll be on to us soon." Pol turned without a word and ran.

Jared followed. The woods were dense, and progress was slow, and scratches multiplied on their bodies as they crashed about in the almost opaque dimness.

"Pol—have you noticed?"

"What?"

"There's not an animal sound anywhere. Not a bird, or a rat, nothing. It's too calm."

"Because of the storm. The rains are starting." Pol slowed, gasping for breath.

Jared grabbed his sleeve and they stopped. "It's near dawn. We'd better get some rest; otherwise, we'll never be able to outrun them." They staggered more slowly, then dropped.

Slumped against separate trees, they rested.

Jared was exhausted, but his eyes took some minutes before closing. He saw again the burning, her screams, the golden fires in the sky. Gold became blood-red, then black. Nothing stirred.

52. Hunters

Jared awakened—filled with terror. Surely this was hell, or some unbelievable planet like the Aldeb gas world!

In the twilight of the ruby sun ball that hung low over the horizon, the dense growths of bushes and trees had assumed the color of blood, darkening steadily. What little light there was glowed though mostly blotted out by black, flying clouds racing over the hazy face of the sun. Harvest time storms were here.

Savage wind blew, and stirred the forest like a stick a clogged cistern. Trees heaved and bent, and branches snapped off and shuttled like birds into the shaken crowns of other trees. Twigs, dirt and pebbles hailed, adding to the din of dancing trees, falling logs, snapping wood, leaves torn by things flying bullet-like.

In a rumble of thunder and lightning, like a vast army, came leaden rains. Falling straight and heavy like a million treading boots, they marched over everything and through everything at quickstep. The wall of water crossed a clearing, overran Jared and Pol with a bath of hard water, and ran on endlessly toward Dumaville. Water cascaded around Jared and he grabbed for Pol in a terror of drowning.

Pol was on his feet, mouth moving inaudibly. He motioned for Jared to follow him. Getting to his feet, Jared thought he heard a cry. Glancing over his shoulder as he prepared to run, Jared espied a dim, poorly defined figure, a phantom or a domraiga; possibly, some Agrarch, dead now these long centuries, taking careful aim. Shots cracked out—real rifle shots, from an old style chemical gun.

A bullet struck Pol in the back. Jared collided with Pol, who fell forward onto his hands and knees, with his head hanging down and hair in sheets as rain beat down on his broken body.

"Pol! Pol!"

Slowly the youth in darkness raised his face toward Jared. He looked dazed, with a stare of finality in open-mouthed features.

More shots rang out, and the figure again stood there, just within range, and barely visible, gun at cheek.

Damn single lucky shot! Jared thought. He wanted to help Pol on through the thick underbrush and around huge trees.

The youth was unable to move. Jared tried to lift him. Pol's responses were unthinking, sluggish. Jared tried to lift him, to carry him on, but got only as far as a shelf of stone, overlooking a great green valley filled with a gray haze.

Pol's mouth moved, trying to form painfully slow, unintelligible words, as Jared crouched over his slack form. Water beat down in savage gusts that took Jared's breath away and made him sightless and unhearing.

Jared got up. The wind nearly doubled his legs over, pressing into the backs of his knees. A twig lashed him about the eyes like a whip. He fought the twig away with a sudden, overwhelming fury. Shielding his bloodied face from slashing twigs and knives of flying water, he staggered back the way the winds had brought him. His clothing tore like tissue paper. He dived behind a boulder to wait, clinging to the coarse, wet surface with raw hands.

No phantom, no domraiga, no agrarch from ghostly halls of Duma or Scimitane, but a policeman, rushed past. The stranger was a Dumaville policeman, clad in a bulky rubber suit that shed water right left. The policeman carried a homing-rifle. No wonder they have been found so quickly, Jared thought bitterly; no wonder their aim had been so perfect. Water streamed from the gun barrel as from a gardening nose.

Jared lifted a rock and threw it, but it fell short. The man's shadowy figure ducked away.

A shot cracked farther away.

Even as the shot's echo rippled among wet trees, Jared felt flying mountain hit his back. All breath knocked out, he fell forward under the impact. Numbly, he felt a tremendous weight and pain in his left shoulder. His left arm was limp. He moaned and rose unsteadily to his feet. Vaguely, he heard police whistles in the din of the storm as he stumbled back to Pol.

It was as he had feared. The body lay on the rock shelf, legs outstretched, arms raised slightly with limp hands dangling. Already the dark wax of the body was in complete possession of swirling waters. Wetness encased Pol like a fine glue. Water welled out of his eyes, and out of his mouth like springs, and the body danced like a small sticky reed. The poor, lifeless eyes were looking far away into nothingness, into the direction his arms were reaching, at some vision, perhaps of a world of happiness only domraiga could see.

Another bullet crashed dangerously close.

Sharpshooter.

Jared wanted to run, but the next bullet kicked him in the back. He felt fire, felt his spine melt, and with it all pain, and his legs and the lower half of his torso were devoid of sensation.

Jared fell onto his belly on the stone shelf and waited for the tormentor to come.

The storm beat upon his numbed senses. Time stopped. Through burning eyes he could make out a pair of rain-washed rubber boots that glinted in the yellow glare of a hand light. A rifle barrel cautiously scanned him, hosing him with more water.

"Don't waste any more ammo. He's done." So said a man's quiet, disgusted voice.

"We'll pick them both up at morning time," said another.

After the glare was gone, and he was alone, Jared could still smell the freshness on the water-scoured rubber boots.

This can't be. All of this is too crazy to be real.

He drifted into a sweet semi-sleep as though he were sleeping on a fresh pillow in the bachelor officers' quarters at the Fleet base on Pyropus K.

53. Ministering Stars

The rain had stopped. Jared was alone. All was quiet in the great, dripping wetness all around him. The storm had passed. The forest was full of a million drippings on hard bark and slippery stone. There was no wind, only the cold.

High up were the stars, the ministering stars.

He lay at the bottom of the sea once more, alone but for the stars, the eternal stars whose heartbeats were measurable in eons. He lay naked and exposed on the frigid stone, unable to move, and he watched the stars preparing to come down to him. He waited a long time, and his breath began to come short, and he was very frightened. He felt himself slipping. He felt the forces under him move, as though the bowels of the earth were getting ready to receive him.

Blood rose to his head crying *Ankh Ankh Ankh!* He had to get to the stars he thought wildly he must march with the Starmen from end to end of the Universe. He had to become one of the stars somehow, peaceful and immobile and undying. He must—

At last he saw the stars, descending in great numbers to minister unto him, but the earth was beginning to yawn open. He was beginning to slip, into the darkness, and he could not help himself.

He could only manage a strangled gasp as his mind began to swirl the liquid of forgetfulness, though his mind still struggled toward the stars, which were slowly descending dressed in flaming chlamyses, bearing jars of ointment and incense and ambrosia, and he wanted to be taken up to hunt with them. He felt the nepenthe of the cold, and the earth's body was a yawning canyon, and the stars were descending slowly, so slowly, and he cried out to them, and all the while his head was filling with the rush of the milky waters…

54. Three Angels

He'd been shot, and he lay dying while someone went to get a bag to put his body in.

"Jared."

He opened his eyes.

"Jared, sweetheart, my love."

Not Mala.

"What? Who?"

"Stella. It's me, your loyal diaphane, your *djia*, who loves you more than her own life."

He crawled forward with effort, even as blood ebbed from his body, and his flesh grew cold.

He reached out with one hand, which was all the energy he could muster.

Stella's form was familiar, and a taste of home.

"Jared…" Who was that now? *Another voice…a woman…*

"Mala?"

"Your ancient dream, Star Man."

That warm laughing voice was Stella talking. "Flying free with nothing but star wind in your sails. Now it is reality."

He didn't want to go without Mala. "Let me die."

"Jarry," Mala said. *Star Mate.*

He looked up in the rain, and saw that Stella's spectral form had Mala's face, complete with straight blonde hair hanging in fine gold threads, a page boy cut framing her young features. Her eyes were Mala's—same pale blue, full of Arcturian dawn and summer by the sea, eternal sails on the ocean, breezes fine as a brisk morning *duro*…

"Love," Jared said as invisible hands helped him up. He staggered toward the rainy apparition.

"Nobody can hurt us now," said Stella-Mala.

Stella explained: "When I left your apartment to give you life, so you and this woman could be happy, I returned to the palace and communed with Lelli. That was nice until Lyxa ordered me to go back to Arco and find you."

"But you didn't betray us," Jared said weakly. He held his bloody side, from which blood still runneled amid rain streaks.

"I was going to end it all," Stella said. "Instead, I dined on coal and air, hiding in the hills above the city. Some people saw me and thought I was a ghost. But I was clever and evaded them. All the while, I blocked your neural transponding, with Lelli's help, so nobody could find you and spoil your love with Mala. When you went to hide in Mala's little town, Lelli and I thought you had escaped for good." She paused, as if swallowing with difficulty, but it was an illusion of Jared's fading consciousness. "I protected you from the hills there as long as I could. When the fat man tried to kill you, and you killed him, the game was over. Lyxa and her council began the assault on the capital that night, and a great battle broke out. You made it offworld just in time. You never knew of the great war that happened."

"What became of Lyxa?"

"She wanted to become queen," Stella said, "but she is ashes now, along with all the conspirators. You'll never see her again."

"And Lelli?"

Stella said: "Lelli is with me."

Jared became conscious of yet another phantom, a *djia* he knew all too well. "Hello, Jared," said the lost djia of a lost princess. "I am here to be with you. Lyxa is gone forever."

Mala said: "Arcturus is free again, at least until alien fleets arrive and make everyone dead or slaves. That will take centuries. In the meantime, people will continue to Samba and have fun and live their happy lives in all those coastal towns."

"But Mala and I," Jared said with deep regret. "I lost her."

"No," Stella said, "we are together now. The three of us."

Mala said: "When I was on the ferry ship, and it burst into flame, most of the other people were already dead. When I spoke with you as we came down from Komorov orbit, fire was already in the cabin where I tried to hide. And then Stella walked in."

Stella said: "I meant to shadow you both, and bring you happy life. I thought maybe I would have a purpose again.

"I," Lelli corrected her. "We."

"Of course," Stella said. "Lelli transpondered into me across the distance even as Lyxa and her soldiers died in a chatter of guns and the sputter of deadly rockets."

Stella said: "I thought I had lost you. Then I had new hope."

"We," Lelli chided gently. "We are now one body but two girls, and we love you as only *djia* can.

Stella said: "We found new purpose—to be your *djia*; make you happy."

Lelli echoed: "As Lyxa loved you, so I love you. But it is my love, not hers. She is dead and gone, and I am free."

"We," Stella chided humorously.

"We," Lelli agreed.

Jared stared at the spectral, golden-glowing phantom before him in the rain-beaten forest. The storm raged without touching them.

A new voice came from the same figure: “We three,” Mala said. “As the room on the ship burst into flame, Stella opened her arms and said I should come to her.”

Jared remembered how Lyxa had coldly entered Lelli, thus nullifying Lelli and becoming Lyxa reincarnate, while old Lyxa lay dead on the ground. It had only been a sort of joke, a cruel one, and Lelli had loyally opened her arms to accept her fate, until Lyxa laughed and reversed their exercise. Lelli had come back to be Lelli, and Lyxa climbed back into her old body.

Now, he could picture how, in the burning ferry ship, Stella had opened her arms, and Mala had stepped into Stella’s neural kelp. But Mala wasn’t Stella’s template—Lyxa had been—so evidently now they formed an imperfect but functional union.

“Our neural jellyfish tails are fused,” all three females said in one voice. “We are stronger for you, together.”

She spread her arms apart, and the gauzy veil came apart. They welcomed Jared into their loving embrace.

Jared, with his last energy, staggered toward them, and threw himself into the arms.

The arms of Mala-Stella-Lelli.

And now they were Stella-Mala-Lelli-Jared.

He left his corpse behind, for the unknowing locals to find and bag and burn or bury along with that of Pol, maybe a domraiga cemetery somewhere. Jared left it all behind, forgetting Lethe, the river of forgetfulness, and its many souls.

Jared left his earthly shell behind without regret, because already he was filled with the combined love of Stella and Mala and Lelli, and what a Samba it was.

His three angels wrapped their neural nets, all those fine tendrils of kelp trailing, their neural roots, around his so they all spoon in that warm, dry bed near the sea. Which bed, which town, which beach, no longer mattered.

They were going to sail out among the stars, into eternity and infinity. Maybe they would one day find and samba with Naxo, or sail past the galaxy where Valdo Rey and Pol hunted agrarchs.

Jared’s lifelong dream—at last it could begin, for all eternity.

55. Star Mate

Nothing could hurt them now, and they were happy together.

Lights flickered in their neural starship. Control buttons glowed. Light moved up and down in flickering sequences. A gentle radio music filled the air inside the ship. Faster and faster they went, lighter than ions, propelled by the solar wind of a trillion stars. They crossed over hills of galaxies, mountains of nebulae, and oceans of dark matter that was nothing but platelets of pure gravitation without substance or energy. They sailed in utter happiness, relieved from the surly bonds of gravitation and earthly circumstance, and crossed through one universe after another. It became clear that dark energy was nothing more than a universe being pulled apart (falling faster and faster in all directions) to become the raw material (dark matter) for the next universe, the next bang, the next attenuation past its cosmopause and into nothing… but not nothing; rather, something because in its amorphous platelets lay the template for entire universes, and its inhabitants like Jared and Mala and Stella and Lelli… Faster and faster they flew, and yet the laws of science being the same everywhere, they encountered nothing new but more of the same wild and overpowering beauty. Sometimes their phantom ship, their diaphanous cockpit, would streak through a solar system, and brush past a planet, and there, for just a second, they might blend with the neural tendrils of some sentient being, maybe a Larth or a Ramtha, who were still lost in the myths of sleepy ages, before they ever shot their first little slingshot stone rocket into orbit… and leave a memory of love and longing and wonder before streaking away into the measureless cathedrals of the motherverse…

Epilog: Vellallo

Larth Atuuinl lowered his protective arms that had shielded his love, Ramtha Apatrui, and raised his eyes to the sky.

He watched in amazement as something rolled onward in a straight course toward the open plains of Ish with the speed of a comet. The thing was a ghost, insubstantial, alien yet familiar, cold yet glad…

Larth looked at his hands dumbly. His head echoed with strange sensations. Those echoes reminded him of the time he had gone on a tour of the Cave of Ghosts at Thonn, where one's head was filled with whispers and strange truths, and a song so vague it was both audible and inaudible.

The wind had filled him with a new knowledge. The wind had been like a dark cave, an empty place, filled with vague reminders of electronic clack and electric sputter, and two voices laughing in tones of metal…like the quietly humming, night-lit interior of some great vessel sweeping along its path of transit among the stars.

In that instant, that instant of transformation, Larth had felt someone else's jubilant laughter at the base of his throat. Whoever or whatever they were, ghosts, their joy and laughter seemed to rise from Larth's throat.

After the single, gloomy glimpse, Larth watched the wind packet as it streaked along, lightly fluffing the dense grasses, on its way into oblivion on the open plains—back into the vast fields of space.

There! Larth saw something. A small light near the shadowy space ship. Larth looked hard, but no other signal came. Perhaps he hadn't seen right? Was that the awaited signal that all was ready and he should come…or was it merely a memory of the quiet blink of a glowing night transit lamp in the dim, hushed apparition?

Dazed, Larth looked toward the complex, into the shadows, and then down at his beloved, who stirred, smiling, and reached for him signaling time for another whirl of passion…

Entity without form, free as wind, as pollen suddenly released—whether after a moment or after a millennium, that was not clear, that did not matter—the spirit that had been Jared Fallon of Mercury Cosmopolis rose unseen and climbed into the night sky with the gentle motion of a blade of grass uplifted by a breath of wind, only it was not rooted in the earth, so its flight was ready and free and soaring.

At last free, he drifted far out across the star fields of space in the cockpit of a ghostly cruiser.

There, stars were dust, and each microcosm of dust in that measureless expanse was a fire by itself.

There, galaxies were revolving mill wheels overflowing with their oceanic loads of stars, each ocean containing more oceans, which in turn contained more oceans overturning.

The entity that had been (strange names: Jared and Mala and Lelli and Stella) drifted endlessly, out of the narrow, measured trickle of their human time stream, deeper and deeper amid convolving oceans where time was lost like tenuous valley flume…drifted, a feather high and tiny over mountain clouds.

At some moment in time, and some place near a random sun, there materialized a dark sphere, without the fire or radiance of the stars, directly in the being's flight path, and his spirit recognized the nature of the sphere abstractly and thought little more of it than dust imprisoned by cobwebs in the darkest corner of a chilly cellar.

However, since the spirit was headed directly toward the darker, the night, edge of the sphere, and it would brush against the sphere for perhaps one tiny subjective moment in an inconsequential time stream before moving back out into the vast night, it thought nothing of that either.

It touched against the surface of the sphere at a point tangent to the circumference of the arc of atmosphere and drifted slowly along. Barely brushing against the gloomy, tangled organisms of this nether region, the spirit in his ghostly cockpit full of blinking lights and whispering electronics descended, then moved along a the direction of whatever saturnine countenance compelled the motions of the air here.

The spirit came to an outcropping of mountains that rose high up out of the Plutonian wilderness; drifted through a pass in the cliffs; and began a free and easy journey across the open surface on the other side.

While rolling across night-dark plains of wind-blown grass and fragrant flowers, the cockpit momentarily intersected with the thoughts and emotions of two sentient beings of another world. For a few moments, breezing across the night fields, the spirit left a faint, rustling memory with puzzled Larth Atuuinl.

This was moments before the ghostly apparition would begin to lift off again into eternal and infinite space…

About Clocktower Books

Clocktower Books (CTB), a pioneering Internet, e-book, and San Diego small press publisher, launched in April 1996 by publishing the world's first entire (not partial) proprietary (not public domain) novels (long works, industry standard) for reading online in HTML format (not for reading on portable media like CD-ROM, floppies, or other intermediary media). Some reviewers are confused and think Project Gutenberg did this first, but Gutenberg specializes in public domain material. We were the first (John Argo: *Neon Blue*, *This Shoal of Space*, *Pioneers*; John T. Cullen: *The Generals of October*) to publish proprietary novels within the noted parameters. We were brand-new, pioneers treading on freshly fallen snow (so to speak), and had excited readers around the world on all continents except Antarctica. Then came the money, the e-commerce, cybercrime, and all the rest, and we vanished into the haze of the lost Genesis world of the fading World Wide Web. As the CTB Museum site below indicates, we have had lingering recognition at the Encyclopedia of Science Fiction. Our long ago efforts are mentioned on a few Wikipedia pages. We remain hopeful that our place in history will eventually be recognized by fair, competent, truth-seeking scholars.

www.clocktowerbooks.com

Clocktower Books Museum Site

You will find at the Museum Pages on our website a detailed history of our pioneering publishing house starting in early 1996—including references and documentation (ever a work in progress).

www.museum.fyi

From 1998 to 2007, Clocktower Books also published what was, during its decade-long run, the world's first professional Web-only (online) magazine of speculative and dark fiction (or SFFH). We published new authors as well as officers and top names of the Science Fiction Writers of America (SFWA); more on our pioneering work at the Science Fiction Encyclopedia online (look under Far Sector).

Our magazine's major names over the years included Deep Outside SFFH (1998-2001) and Far Sector SFFH (2001-2007). We published many nominees or later awardees of the Hugo, Nebula, Sturgeon, and virtually all other major global SFFH awards including British, Canadian, and Australian. The leading SF magazine historian, author, and anthologist Mike Ashley (Liverpool University Press) has stated he will recognize our pioneering magazine in the final volume of his authoritative SF magazine histories. Mr. Ashley ensured that we are mentioned in the SF Encyclopedia (see: Far Sector SFFH).

Author's Special Note

BRY-2019

I began writing this novel as a boy of 15 in the summer of 1965 at my aunt's house in Meriden, Connecticut, USA. After numerous drafts, I completed the novel at age 19 at the University of Connecticut, as a sophomore English major with Relateds in History, Languages, and Classics.

Since childhood, I have been an avid reader, especially of science fiction, historical fiction, and mysteries. I counted among my favorite authors Andre Norton and Ray Bradbury. I remember sending each a fan mail, and receiving a very nice letter back in reply, filled with encouragement. I had later complimentary contacts with each (during the World Wide Web phase of our world).

My favorite movie of all time is Ridley Scott's 1982 *Blade Runner,* and I am writing this in the final weeks of BRY-2019 (Blade Runner Year).

I have been a story teller since toddlerdom, and started writing poetry at age 7. I wrote my first little novel at age 11, which became lost by age 13 (but I treasure the memory, and plan to write a sequel, now that I'm in my 70s; story for another day).

Years later, as a pioneering Internet and digital and Web author, editor, and publisher, I had the opportunity to revisit my deep admiration and affection for both Andre Norton and Ray Bradbury. Ms Norton accepted my SF novel *Pioneers* for her library and research facility High Hallack, which was sadly lost after her passing. Ray in January 2008 sent me a personal rave review (I like to call it fan mail from a master) after he read my dark holiday fantasy novel *The Christmas Clock*, an homage to Charles Dickens' *A Christmas Carol* with (I wrote to Ray) "a lot of you in it as well."

I wrote at least five full drafts of my teenage SF novel ages 15-19 (final draft as a sophomore in Room 310, McMahon Hall, Univerity of Connecticut). I wrote several more novels in my twenties... in fact, I made myself a vow that I would write at least one novel per year for the rest of my life, and I've kept that bargain with nearly 40 in print and another ten or so floating around (some of which will never see daylight, and others may eventually be typed up by a trusty friend from dusty old manuscripts and we'll see where it goes from there). I also wrote a huge body of poetry that I am quite proud of, over 425 poems, during my teens and twenties. You can find that in several collections (see my poetry website at www.poetryjournal.net).

An odd note about my aunt's house was that it was (and still is, I assume, although she is long gone) on a dead-end cul-de-sac. During my occasional visits over the years, I would stay in my late grandmother's empty bedroom, which had a desk facing a window that looked out over a vast graveyard full of Gothic statuary and somehow always had a full, custard-yellow moon lurking among the mossy crosses and lichen-pocked angels. I think I was okay with that, as long as I kept the window tightly locked at night.

My teenage novel, typed through hundreds of hours by day and night at dorms on the UConn campus, evolved into much the form you'll find it in today. It was of course ignored for half a century by the investor-driven fast food book industry—as they say in New York City: *what-evvah!*—and finally typed for me in the 2010s from one surviving, faded 1960s copier machine copy surviving in a Yale University thesis binder (I did grow up in New Haven, after all).

In today's renaissance, when authors can enjoy their First Amendment freedoms to publish and reach readers after all, I have left the story unchanged except for one or two details. For one thing, the diaphanes (*djia*) or translucent people (virtual companions of a cruel world advanced in technology but not in human values) were there to some extent, but I fleshed them out with the experience and artful skills learned over half a century of professional writing. I might add that, aside from three college degrees, every job I ever had involved writing—even my six years in the U.S. Army, serving in Cold War Germany (FRG) in the 1970s (where I wrote several novels, various short stories, and my last poetry inbetween duties and when not traveling in my orange VW bus to Paris or Brussels or Heidelberg and many other points of lovely interest (girls, beer, wine, archeology, museums, what more could a young man desire?).

The only other thing I did was polish a few rough spots (not many) that I missed or didn't know how to handle so well as a teenager; most notably, in the section where Jared falls in love with Mala, his golden surfer girl, on the summer planet of Arcturus... before evil Queen Lyxa shows up to ruin everything.

Yes, there is a melancholy tinge to the whole confection, but I remain quite proud of it. I hope you enjoy it, and tell your friends about it. As I like to say, a lot of investment is poured into the YA (Young Adult) industry by the fast food publishers in New York City. Very few of those novels are actually written by teenagers—so you have one before you now. Happy reading!

Oh, and this led to a series I've developed over decades, which I call Empire of Time. Read all about that at my webplex (www.johntcullen.com, www.empireoftime.com, etc.)

For example, when I wrote *Star Clans of Corduwaine* in 2017 or so, I referenced the ruins of Mercury Free Port City (destroyed by both enemy human and alien war fleets in this Summer Planets novel). Aside from Ray Bradbury, Andre Norton, H. G. Wells, and so many other wonderful SFFH authors, my all-time favorite SF author is the late Cordwainer Smith. *Star Clans of Corduwaine* is an homage to Cordwainer Smith (hence the name of that remote fictional star system). Having lived for years in both North America and across Europe, I consider myself a citizen of the world. I speak several languages, and hold dual U.S.-Luxembourg-E.U. citizenships. My main reason for mentioning this is to illustrate the deep currents and tidal energies that influence a writer on moonlit seashores. *Corduwaine* is both a tribute to Cordwainer Smith and to the profoundly emotional experience I have had with the Turkish folksong *Telgrafin Tellerine* (which sort of translates into "What the birds on the telegraph wires are saying"), specifically as performed by two wonderful Turkish singers: Zara (Neşe Yılmaz); and separately by the late Ahmet Kaya (1957-2000) of blessed memory. You can explore those wonders and many more online at Wikipedia, YouTube, and other gifts of our perilous yet wondrous age.

When it became possible for ignored writers (to use Agent Jeff Herman's phrase) to break through and reach readers at last, by virtue of the Internet and new digital publishing technologies, I was an early adapter in 1996. I believe I published the first several HTML novels (as I call them) online, by standards including (a) proprietary, not public domain, which eliminates most other novel-length publishing of my type online before 1996, to be sure; (b) to be read entirely online in HTML format, not carried on portable media like CD or floppy as a few adventurers were doing; (c) entire novels, not teasers; and more that you can read about at the Clocktower Books Museum site (www.museum.fyi). The first suspense novel was my suspense thriller *Neon Blue*, while the first SF novel was my novel *Heartbreaker*, later titled *This Shoal of Space*, then

Woman in the Sea, and finally as of 2019 *Starlight Deep Within a Gothic Sea.* Clocktower Books (originally C&C) published others as well, but those were the first.

In honor of the new world of wonder (WWW), I adopted the pseudonym John Argo, which refers to the ancient ship of wonder (the Argo) on which Jason and the Argonauts (literally, 'Argo-sailors') ventured out into the Outer Space Cosmos of their time, the Aegean and Pontic Seas. My Classical education lent itself to honoring those mythologies of the Bronze Age during our own millennial age with all of its wonders and horrors.

Oh yes, and BTW, I tried publishing my teenage novel under the pseudonym A. T. Nager when I finally got my typed and digitized copy done in the mid-2010s, but nobody got it. It's A. T. Nager, or A Teenager. I remember asking a bookstore clerk to look it up, to see if if was in their catalog, and she chimed brightly: "I found it. Ay Tee Nogger..."

Oh well. Live and learn. I'm explaining about the John Argo (naut) name in case you wonder why most of my SFFH output is under John Argo, while I am republishing my teenage novel under my adopted US name John T. Cullen.

Okay, another explanation needed. My real name is Jean Thomas Cullen. I was born in West Germany after World War Two. I was born a U.S. citizen, an Army brat, with special U.S. State Dept documents and a baby U.S. passport (still in my possession). I am one of nearly two million U.S. citizens born overseas to families serving the U.S. in military, State Department, CIA, and other capacities beginning in the 20th Century. My a father was a much-decorated war hero from Connecticut, who fought in the Pacific Campaigns (with our U.S. forces), and was stationed in the Federal Republic of Germany and other European locations after the war. My mother was a Luxembourg citizen. That's not Germany; in fact, my family in Luxembourg tragically lost family members to the Germans in both world wars.

During my twenties, I was stationed for five years with the U.S. Army as a young enlisted soldier in West Germany, and (among many ups and downs) ultimately came away loving Germany very deeply almost like a second home. Which is odd, because I am a U.S. & Luxembourg citizen, and feel certain peculiar tidal pulls toward Germany, France, and Belgium, as do many Luxemburgers. *What-evvah!*

Please read this novel, read all my novels and my nonfiction, enjoy yourself, be good, have happy thoughts, and follow the Golden Rule: treat your fellow humans and all living things as you wish them to treat you, as Jesus tells us in at last two Gospel stories, based on teachings from Jewish and other ancient scriptures; common sense, when you think about it. That means letting go of hate and ignorance. I'm a Progressive social thinker... but that's philosophy, and for another time and place.

Being a story teller, here's one more little story for the road. I like to pop this quiz on my friends. "If you're in Luxembourg, which is not much bigger than certain large cities like New York or London, you can be in a total of five countries within one hour all at once. What are they?"

Most people get the first four right away. You're in Luxembourg, so that's number one. You can be in Germany, France, and Belgium within one hour's drive, mostly on the A13 highway, through southern Luxembourg. So what's country number five?

Answer: The United States of America. Right outside the capital, Luxembourg City, is a U.S. military cemetery, officially called the Luxembourg American Cemetery and Memorial. The cemetery holds 5,073 U.S. military war dead in 50.5 acres of beautiful land, andwas dedicated in 1960. It is administered by the American Battle Monuments Commission; residents include Gen. George S. Patton. The people of Luxembourg, grateful for their liberation after both world wars, dedicated this land for perpetual U.S. government use, exempt from taxation, so it's a tiny overseas bit of U.S.A. territory.

The people of Germany and Luxembourg and their neighbors are great friends again today, given the longer-term historical and cultural realities. Remember the famous photo of a French and a West German leader holding hands in the massive memorial of senseless carnage (1914-1918) at Verdun as one example. If you drive a quarter mile or so from the U.S. cemetery at Hamm (near Findel International Airport in Luxembourg) you will also find a beautiful cemetery dedicated to fallen German soldiers. In a United States still torn by memories of senseless carnage 1861-1865, and everlasting hate with no basis in logic or faith, those and other examples might serve as an inspiration to let old times go. We have enough terrifying crises looming ahead to keep us busy (climate, political chaos, corruption, and I believe genetic engineering horrors yet to come).

John T. Cullen
San Diego, CA
17 November BRY-2019
Rev. 22 Jan 2020 (Vision Year, we hope). Come visit me at:

www.johntcullen.com

www.ingramcontent.com/pod-product-compliance
Lightning Source LLC
LaVergne TN
LVHW090939080826
845145LV00003B/812

* 9 7 8 0 7 4 3 3 2 3 5 4 3 *